Published by Bookouture

An imprint of StoryFire Ltd.

23 Sussex Road, Ickenham, UB10 8PN

United Kingdom

www.bookouture.com

ISBN: 978-1-78681-286-5

eBook ISBN: 978-1-78681-285-8

Christ
at
Mistletoe
Cove

D1589955

Christmas at Mistletoe Cove

HOLLY MARTIN

To the lovely, gorgeous, supportive and fabulous Kim Nash. Thank you for everything that you do and for always being there at all hours of the day. You are amazing.

CHAPTER 1

Eden looked over at the door of Pots and Paints, her pottery painting café, for what felt like the hundredth time. Wanting something to distract herself, she rearranged the mini Christmas cakes in the glass cabinet. It was ridiculous to be this nervous but no matter how many times she told herself that, she couldn't stop the butterflies from swirling and dancing in her stomach.

Her childhood best friend and the only man she had ever loved was coming home.

Only this time Dougie Harrison wasn't just here for a few weeks, staying at her house and tormenting her by walking around half naked, torturing her with daily hugs and kisses on the cheek and then heading back to America again, leaving her with her heart in tatters and impossibly more in love with him than she was before.

This time he was moving back to Hope Island for good.

Although he'd still be staying with her for a few weeks. The house he'd bought wouldn't be ready for him until after Christmas. The house he'd bought *right* next door to hers. If she didn't know better she'd think he was doing this deliberately to wind her up. Except Dougie had no idea about her feelings for him. They had been best friends as far back as she could remember, they were incredibly close, always hugging and holding hands, but it had never been more than that and she had never been brave enough to share her feelings or to try to change their relationship into something more. And what would be the point? He had been living in America for the past twelve years; it was hardly going to work when he was so far away, even if by some remote chance he returned her feelings – which of course he didn't.

The door opened and she jumped as she looked up, desperate and afraid to see him in equal measures. She sighed when she saw Barbara Copperthwaite coming in for her daily cup of coffee and cake, stamping her feet and clapping her hands against the cold. The pottery painting café was busy today which was a good thing; it meant she could try to keep herself occupied while she waited for Dougie to get here. She served Barbara her gingerbread coffee and a slice of Clare's delicious mulled wine cake and then looked back towards the door.

Would things change between her and Dougie now he was living here for good? She didn't dare hope for anything romantic to happen between them. She had given up dreaming and wishing for a happy ending for herself many years before. Twelve years before to be exact, when Dougie and his family had emigrated to the bright lights of New York.

'Will you stop staring at the door like a puppy waiting for her owner to come home,' Clare said. 'And leave my cakes alone, no one is going to buy them with your fingerprints all over them.'

Eden smiled at her assistant. Clare Crissell had worked part time for her in Pots and Paints for years but recently had gone full time, which Eden was glad for. Although Eden could make cakes and pastries well enough, they were nothing like Clare's creations and, with her taking care of the baking side of her pottery café, it left Eden to be creative and help the customers to paint their pottery pieces. It also meant that she could take days off whenever she wanted and, although Eden didn't do that very often, she planned to take a few days or afternoons off in the lead-up to Christmas. The shop was busy today with lots of the island's residents painting mugs, plates and other pottery items to give to their loved ones as festive gifts. As it was only a week until Christmas, today was the last day they could guarantee that the painted mugs and other gifts would be glazed and put in the kilns in time for the big day.

'I'm not staring at the door like a puppy,' Eden laughed, knowing she'd been doing just that.

'You jump a mile every time the door opens. Dougie will be here soon. I don't think the flight from Exeter arrives into St Mary's until two.'

Eden nodded. Hope Island was the most westerly island of the Scilly Isles in Cornwall, and she knew that it would take Dougie a long time to get here. Suddenly she realised what Clare had just said. Eden opened her mouth to deny that she was waiting for Dougie but there was no point. She'd never discussed her feelings for Dougie with Clare, but it wasn't hard to work out. Embarrassingly enough, everyone on the island seemed to know. The only person who didn't seem to have any clue was Dougie himself.

'I just can't believe he is really coming home for good this time. When he first spoke about this at Easter, I never thought it would happen. And then he came over in the summer to house hunt and it just didn't seem real and when he came over for Rome and Freya's wedding, he was so excited about moving back here for good and now he's here, to stay, and I don't know why. He always wanted to live in America when he was little, he had posters of New York in his room and he kept saying that one day he would have a big office at the top of the Empire State Building. And although he never made it to the Empire State Building, he did have a big office at the top of one of the other big skyscrapers, plus a beautiful luxury penthouse apartment that takes up the entire floor of one of the tall buildings, with amazing panoramic views of the city. His own video gaming company is a huge success. He was living his dream and now he's coming home to tiny Hope

Island. He's sold everything, his car, his luxury home, almost all of his things, and for what? The tallest building we have here is a six-storey hotel. We have two pubs, three restaurants, no theatres or cinemas, no McDonald's or Starbucks. He's bought a tiny cottage when in reality he could easily afford one of those huge houses on the far side of the island. There's nothing here for him. I can honestly see him staying here for a few months before he gets bored out of his brain and decides to sell up and go back to New York again. What has Hope Island got that could possibly keep him interested?'

'The one thing that New York doesn't have?' Clare said, as she loaded some iced ginger cupcakes into the cabinet to nestle alongside the fresh mince pies she'd made earlier that morning.

Eden looked outside onto the street, wondering what Hope Island could possibly offer him. The cobbled streets, the cute little unique shops with their beautiful Christmas decorations hanging in the windows and the old Victorian-style lamps all added a vintage charm to the island. The cottages and houses were all unique, many of them painted in bright colours. The friendliness of the locals and that lovely community spirit was another attractive feature. The beautiful beaches and little hidden coves were something the tourists flocked to see. She loved it here and never wanted to leave but, like Dougie, many of the younger generation couldn't wait to get off the island. She supposed the coastal aspect was something New York didn't have.

'The beaches? He has always loved the beaches here,' Eden said.

'You, you idiot. He's coming back for you.'

Eden sighed. Clare wasn't the first person to say this to her and she was sure she wouldn't be the last.

'He's not coming back for me. It's not like that with us. We're best friends and it will never be more than that.'

It had *never* been more than that for them. Nothing had ever happened between them. Apart from one kiss. One incredible kiss when she was seventeen years old, standing on the shores of Mistletoe Cove. The kiss had been so wonderful that Eden had immediately gone home and dreamed of her wedding to him, imagined the house they would buy together and the little red-headed babies they would have. The next day, Dougie had announced that he was moving to New York with his parents and she'd had to smile and pretend she was happy for him. The kiss was never mentioned again and she had never told anyone about it, keeping that moment in her heart just for her. Nothing had happened between them since. He'd come over and visit, they'd laugh and talk just like they always had, but he had never shown any inkling of having feelings for her. And though she always hoped she would one day get over him, it had been twelve years since he'd left and she loved him now as much as she did then.

'Honey, I promise you, he isn't coming back here for the beaches,' Clare said.

Eden sighed. There was no point in arguing. The islanders had made their own minds up about the reason for Dougie's return, and most of them thought it was to marry her and have lots of babies.

She decided to change the subject. 'Do you know when the pottery wheel is supposed to be delivered?'

'Well, if it's arrived on St Mary's we might get it this afternoon, but you know how these things go. Nothing moves quickly here. I hope it doesn't come tomorrow; the shop will be closed in the afternoon for the Christmas festival. Are you taking Dougie to the opening?' Clare asked, switching the Christmas music on the iPod from Bing Crosby crooning about a White Christmas to Michael Bublé's Christmas album.

Eden wasn't sure if she would be 'taking' Dougie anywhere. Yes, he was staying with her and they were best friends but she was sure he would be doing his own thing, whatever that was. He wouldn't want to be hanging around with her the whole time. But the Christmas festival was a big deal for the island, they'd never had anything like it before. The whole place had been buzzing about it for weeks and when the lorries arrived off the landing crafts a few days before, some of the locals had lined the streets and clapped as if the lorries were responsible for bringing Christmas itself to the island. Eden had been looking forward to the festival herself, there was a Christmas market, ice skating, sledging – on fake snow of course – and lots of Christmassy events happening throughout the week leading up to the holiday.

Bella, Eden's adopted sister, well technically her cousin, was the brains behind it, having spent months creating a week-long Christmas event in order to raise money for the homeless charity that she worked for. Most of the events that Bella organised were held in the bigger cities, especially in London, but Bella had wanted something for the island this Christmas and especially something that would bring the tourists to the island at a time when they never really came.

Eden adored Bella. She'd not had an easy start in life and came to live with Eden's family when she was a child, and Eden felt very protective of her because of it. So it was important that she go along and support her. As Dougie was also Bella's cousin, as well as one of Bella's closest friends, Eden knew that Dougie would want to go to the festival and support her too.

'We'll probably pop over tomorrow for the opening,' Eden said vaguely, hoping that Clare wouldn't pick up on how much she was looking forward to going to the festival with Dougie.

'There's the couples' snowman-making competition tomorrow. Maybe you two could enter,' Clare said, clearly deciding that she wasn't going to leave this alone.

'Well, we're not a couple so…'

'That doesn't matter, I don't think there's any hard and fast rules about what qualifies as a couple.'

Eden was fairly sure a couple had to be in some kind of relationship to count as one, not just two friends who had kissed once many years before.

'Rome and Freya are entering, and Bella and Isaac too,' Clare went on. 'It'll be fun to compete against your brother and sister.'

Eden smiled; that *would* be fun. It surprised her that her brother Rome had agreed to be a part of such a thing. Normally he preferred to keep to himself, but since marrying Freya he had mellowed so much, walking around the island with a permanent smile on his face. She liked that he seemed to be having more fun now.

There was no more time to argue as the door opened again. Her head snapped up to look without her permission and standing in the doorway, silhouetted against the weak winter sunlight, was Dougie.

She wanted to run and leap into his arms, though she knew that wasn't appropriate. He dropped the bag he was holding, watching her with that beautiful smile lighting up his face. And though her feet remained frozen to the ground, he didn't seem to have any such reservations, walking quickly across the pottery café towards her. Her legs carried her forward the last few steps and suddenly she was in his arms as he lifted her off her feet, hugging her so tight.

'I'm home, honey,' he whispered against her ear.

She closed her eyes, resting her cheek on his shoulder so he couldn't see the myriad of emotions that were no doubt racing across her face at having him here. She had no idea how she should be feeling about his homecoming. There was a huge part of her that was delighted but she knew she was desperately sad too. He would never be hers and now he was back here for good, she wouldn't even get a reprieve from these feelings like she normally did when he went back to America.

'I can't believe you're really here,' Eden said. 'I always wondered if you'd ever come home. I hoped you would but you seemed so happy in America.'

'You make me happy,' he said, holding her tighter.

He always said things like this to her, he was always this affectionate with her too. Hugging her, holding her hand, kissing her on the head or cheek. They'd even slept together in the same bed several times while growing up, and although it hadn't happened that often since they were adults, it had happened once or twice, normally after one too many drinks. It wasn't a normal level of intimacy for two people who had only ever been friends, she knew that, but they'd always been overly affectionate with each other, as far back as she could remember. It was one of the reasons she had started to believe that he'd had feelings for her too when they were teenagers, but as nothing had ever happened beyond that one and only kiss she had just put it down to Dougie's flirty personality. He was such a natural flirt anyway; he could charm the birds from the trees. Every woman he spoke to walked away feeling a million dollars. He kissed and hugged every girl he was friends with and always had a big smile on his face.

'And thanks for putting me up, it'll only be for a few weeks. My house will be ready after Christmas.'

'Couldn't leave you homeless now, could I?' Eden said.

'Hasn't stopped you trying to kick me out of your house before,' Dougie said, letting her feet down on the floor and holding her at arm's length so he could look at her. She drank him in too, his red curly hair that curled at the back of his neck, clover green eyes, the smattering of freckles on his nose and cheeks. He was so beautiful. Her eyes cast down. And so big. She was sure he had filled out even more since the last time she had seen him. His shoulders were so broad, even his forearms seemed muscular.

She realised he was waiting for a response from her.

'That's because you walk around half naked most of the time.'

His mouth quirked up into a sexy smile. 'And you don't like seeing me naked, honey?'

Behind her Clare barely contained her laughter, turning it into a cough a fraction too late. Eden realised that most of the café was listening in to this conversation too.

What on earth did she say to that?

She swallowed down her embarrassment. 'How would you like it if I walked around naked all the time?'

His eyes widened to comic proportions, a big grin spreading on his face. 'I'd like that very much.'

'You're such a pervert.'

'Is that what's going to happen when I stay with you this time: twenty-four-hour nudey parties? If I'd known that, I'd have flown over earlier.'

'We are not having nudey parties,' Eden laughed but Dougie was clearly not to be deterred.

'In fact, Clare honey, can you take over here for a few hours? Eden and I are going to have a nudey party right now.' Dougie took her hand and led her to the door and to her total mortification all the island's residents suddenly cheered their approval.

'Sure,' Clare laughed. 'Knock yourselves out.'

Eden pulled back and Dougie reluctantly let her go.

'Will you behave? We are not having any nudey parties.'

'OK, maybe now is not the best time. But promise me we'll do it later.'

'No, Rome and Bella are supposed to be coming round to see you and I'm not getting naked in front of my brother and sister.'

He pulled her closer to him again. 'So we'll wait until they leave.'

She batted him away, her heart pounding at the thought of the two of them naked together.

She dug into her pocket and passed him her spare house key. 'Go get yourself settled and unpacked and I'll be home soon.'

He flashed her a devastating smile and then bent to kiss her cheek. 'Don't be late.'

He winked at her, grabbed his bag and left her alone. She brushed her fingers absently down her apron before she turned back to face the islanders who were all grinning at her inanely. She pointedly ignored them and walked back behind the counter. Having him here was going to be trouble but she couldn't wipe the smile off her face if she tried.

CHAPTER 2

Eden smiled as she watched Dougie snoring softly, his face lit up under the soft glow of the twinkling fairy lights as he rested his head on the arm of the sofa, his big, strong body stretching out the entire length of it. How could she love him so much? It was ridiculous to feel this way after twelve years but no matter how many times she told herself that, she didn't seem to be listening.

'Eden, are you listening?'

Eden looked round and could see that Bella and Freya were watching her expectantly. Oh god, they had been mid-conversation when she had glanced over to look at Dougie and she had zoned out completely after that. Was that how it was going to be now he was home: her staring at him inappropriately every time he came anywhere near her, being unable to carry out a simple conversation or function at work? She was in serious trouble if that was the case.

'Sorry, I was miles away,' Eden said, ignoring the smirks from Bella and Freya.

Everyone had come to welcome Dougie back home. Her brother Rome and his wife Freya had cooked for Dougie in Eden's kitchen, looking every inch the happily married couple as they flirted and touched each other constantly. It filled Eden's heart to see that Rome was happy again after so many years alone. Freya was showing the first signs of her four-month pregnancy hidden beneath her baggy jumper and, although no one was supposed to know yet, naturally that meant that everyone on the island was aware of it. Freya had been given more knitted jumpers, hats and booties than she knew what to do with over the last few weeks.

Eden's sister, Bella, and her fiancé, Isaac, had spent the evening talking about the plans for their forthcoming wedding that was taking place at the end of January. It sounded like it was turning into a huge event. Bella seemed to be getting a bit stressed out about all the arrangements, but as an events manager for a local charity, this was the sort of thing she excelled at. Eden was quite sure it would be a beautiful day but she was worried that Bella wasn't getting the kind of wedding she wanted. She seemed so desperate to impress all of Isaac's business colleagues that she was putting aside her own dreams. Eden hadn't said anything to them, and she didn't know Isaac as well as she knew Bella, but it seemed he was getting a wedding he didn't want either.

They'd all had dinner together, laughing and chatting as if Dougie had always been part of their family. And in many ways he had. Living in America for twelve years hadn't changed that. Growing up, Dougie had been best friends with Rome, and with Eden and Bella they had been an inseparable foursome. He had also known Isaac as they'd both been in the computer club at school. When Isaac moved away from the island as a child, Dougie had stayed in touch with him, their mutual love for computer games cementing their friendship for life, and now they were going into business together in Dougie's own computer gaming company.

It was testament to his friendship with everyone that no one cared that they'd all come round to see him and he was snoring softly in the corner. They all knew he had been travelling for many hours to get there. Everyone was just carrying on as normal regardless that Dougie was no longer part of the conversation.

Rome and Isaac were in the kitchen at that moment discussing an app that Rome wanted for his stained glass shop. They were getting more commissions than they could handle and, as far as Rome was concerned, he and Freya were spending too much time dealing with enquiries on the phone than actually working on the commissions. What they needed was an assistant but Isaac was trying to persuade him that an app that people could use to enquire online would take away a lot of the hassle for them.

Eden, Freya and Bella had been chatting in the lounge. She tried to remember what she had been talking about with them but she had no idea.

Bella took pity on her. 'We were talking about what love means to us. There was an article in one of those wedding magazines I seem to have collected in abundance over the last few months about what different women expected from a loving relationship or marriage. So, what are you looking for in love, what would your ideal relationship look like?'

'That the man I love loved me back would be a good start,' Eden said, unable to stop her eyes drifting over to Dougie again. Bella and Freya remained unfazed; they both knew about her feelings for him.

'That's a given – in this hypothetical conversation, you're married to the man of your dreams,' Freya said, stroking her belly unconsciously.

'Would you get married?' Bella asked. 'Is that important to you? Some people don't believe in marriage.'

Bella knew as well as Eden did that Dougie wasn't exactly a fan of marriage after his own parents' relationship ended so badly. But that was quite important to her.

'In an ideal world, yes, I want to get married. There's something special about standing up in front of your family and friends and declaring your love for each other and promising to love each other for the rest of your life. It's not essential though. As long as we were together I'd be happy with that. But yes, if we are talking a perfect relationship, then marriage would feature in that.'

'So what does your perfect happy marriage look like?'

Eden thought about this for a moment. She had spent almost her whole life in love with Dougie, and a good too many years to count hoping and wishing on every birthday cake, shooting star, or lucky penny that he would someday be hers before she'd finally given up on that dream, but she'd never really stopped to think what a perfect marriage to Dougie would look like.

'Amazing sex,' Eden giggled.

'Of course,' Bella agreed. 'Every day, twenty times a day.'

Eden laughed. 'I want to talk with my husband, come home from work and we'll talk about our days and the other person will genuinely listen and care even if it is mundane. I want to laugh a lot, make silly jokes, tease one another; I don't want that to change just because I'm married.' Her eyes fell on the small bunch of white roses that Dougie had given her when she had got home from work that night and how ridiculously touched she had been by such a small gesture. 'I think romantic gestures are important, or romantic moments. Little Post-it notes of love left around the house, flowers – not for my birthday or Valentine's Day, but just because my husband had thought of me on his way home from work. Romantic dinners at home, sitting at the kitchen table with candles on the table, taking baths together… I just want to lie in a bath with my husband, cuddled against his chest. Watching movies, the cheesy romantic ones that I love and the big action films that he'll love, and neither of us will complain because we just like watching films together, going for walks along the beach, holding hands while we walk, holding hands when we watch TV. Cooking for each other, massages…' Eden was getting into her stride now. 'I'd love to do a couple's massage, I think that would be sexy as hell. I want to make love in front of the fire in a room lit only with candles. Picnics, flying a kite, playing board games, watching a sunset together, watching a sunrise together. A horse carriage ride. Spooning, I've never done that and I've always thought it would be nice to fall asleep wrapped in my man's arms. He'd let me sit on his lap and at the end of the night he'd carry me to bed. I want to dance, a lot. We'd get a puppy and it would be our baby. I'd dress it up in ridiculous costumes and my husband wouldn't care. Then later we'd fill the house with real babies of our own.'

Bella smiled at her, fondly. 'You don't want much then?'

'I want the fairy tale,' Eden said dreamily and then the smile slid off her face. 'But fairy tales don't exist.'

'Of course they do, me and Isaac are proof of that,' Bella said.

'I never thought anything would happen with me and Rome, but it did. Your fairy tale is waiting for you, it's just not your time yet,' Freya said. 'And maybe it won't happen in the way that you hope it will,' she eyed Dougie who was still fast asleep. 'But true love and happiness might come along when you least expect it with someone that you never expected, if you open your heart to possibilities.'

Eden knew that this was Freya's attempt to persuade Eden to move on and fall out of love with Dougie. If only it was that easy. She had even wished for that once too. The one time her wish had deviated from the usual one was when she'd wished that she was no longer in love with Dougie – and that hadn't worked either. She glanced across at him. She would always love him.

🌲🌲🌲

Dougie knew he needed to get off the sofa and go upstairs to bed – he would ache tomorrow if he slept on the sofa all night – but the bedroom was too far, his whole body felt too heavy and he was unable to open his eyes.

By his calculations he had been awake for over thirty-six hours, though his brain was such a fog of exhaustion he wasn't sure if those calculations were right. He had dozed on and off for the last hour or two, aware of his friends there, but not really aware of what they were talking about, or of anything beyond the comfort of their voices. Though silence had descended on the house a while ago so he guessed they'd gone home at some point.

Nearby the crack of the log fire told him it was still burning merrily and he could hear Eden softly moving around tidying things up. He needed to get up and help her but his body wasn't responding to any commands at the moment.

He was suddenly acutely aware of her leaning over him, her wonderful sweet scent that reminded him of toasted marshmallows drifting around him.

'Dougie, you need to go to bed,' she whispered, gently.

'I'm sleeping,' Dougie muttered, still unable to open his eyes.

The glow of the fairy lights was suddenly turned off, plunging the world beyond his eyelids into darkness.

He felt her lean over him again and tug on the blanket on the back of the sofa. He forced his eyes open. The blanket was clearly stuck, probably because he was lying on top of it, and as she frowned as she tried to release it, he couldn't resist running his fingers across that spot he knew was really ticklish right above her hip bone. She squealed in protest, bringing her arm down to protect herself, and fell on top of him, hard.

He quickly wrapped his arms around her so she couldn't escape. 'This is the only thing I need to keep me warm.'

'Get off me,' she laughed, trying to get up.

'Stop wriggling, I'm trying to sleep,' Dougie said, closing his eyes again.

'With me on top of you?'

'Can't think of a nicer way to go to sleep.'

She sighed and rested her head on his chest, curling her fingers gently into his shirt. 'You know this isn't normal, right?'

He opened his eyes to look at her. She was looking up at him, her blue eyes inky in the darkness.

'It's normal for us, we've slept in the same bed together before.'

She rested her chin on her hands to look at him more easily. 'Do you have this relationship with any of your other friends? Have you ever cuddled in bed with Rome?'

He laughed. 'That's different.'

'Why is it different?'

He stroked a hair off her forehead. 'We have something special.'

'But that something special is just friendship right? You said this is normal for us, so… are you saying it doesn't mean anything?'

He swallowed, not entirely sure what the right answer was and too tired to think it through clearly. Of course it wasn't normal; he was closer to her than any of his previous girlfriends. He had been flirting with her for years with little or no reaction.

'Of course it means something,' Dougie said, his eyes drifting closed without his permission. There was silence from Eden and he replayed what he'd just said in his head. That wasn't good. He definitely needed to be more awake to have this conversation. He was in dangerous territory here. 'You're my best friend and you have no idea how much you mean to me.' That wasn't much safer either.

Eden didn't answer for a while, then she rested her cheek right over his heart. 'I have some idea.'

He pulled the blanket off the back of the sofa and covered it over Eden, making sure the blanket was tucked round her shoulders, then he wrapped both arms around her in case she tried to escape and let his head fall back on the arm of the chair and closed his eyes. Her tiny, warm body against his was the best feeling in the world. Well, it would be even better if neither of them had any clothes on but he'd take any victory he could. The conversation about their relationship seemed to have passed but he knew it was only temporary. Now he was back on Hope Island for good, things would have to come to a head at one point and he wasn't sure how that would turn out. But for now he needed to go to sleep.

'I've travelled thousands of miles, three plane journeys and a boat ride and right now it was all worth it. Falling asleep with my girl in my arms, nothing beats that.'

He forced open one eye to see what her reaction would be to that – she was resting her head on his chest with a big smile on her face. He closed his eyes again and shifted her tighter against him. Sleep was taking him now and he knew it would be several hours before he'd wake back up. A sense of complete and utter contentment washed over him. He was home.

CHAPTER 3

Eden woke the next day to find she was lying side by side with Dougie, her arms wrapped round his neck, one leg hooked over his hips, the other tangled between his own legs. His arms were around her, one hand on her waist, and the other had slid up the back of her t-shirt and was warm against the lower part of her back. It looked like they had spent the night making love when nothing could be further from the truth. The best thing was their mouths were mere millimetres from touching – she could feel his soft breath on her face and it felt incredible. If she just leaned forward she could press her lips to his and then they'd be kissing. Well sort of. He was still fast asleep.

'Thinking about kissing me?'

Her eyes snapped up to see his were filled with amusement as he watched her fondly. She tried to shift back a bit, embarrassed at being caught out in her fantasies even if he couldn't read her mind to see what she had been thinking, but his arms were locked around her and she was unable to move.

'You can kiss me if you want to, I wouldn't mind,' Dougie grinned at her.

'I bet you wouldn't.'

He laughed. 'What does that mean?'

'You're such a flirt. You flirt with anything that moves.'

'That's true, but I don't give my kisses away to just anyone, they have to be special.'

'And I'm special enough?'

'Oh definitely.' His eyes still sparkled with amusement; he wasn't taking this remotely seriously. But that was Dougie all over, everything was a joke or a game to him, he had no idea how much this conversation actually hurt. How badly Eden wanted to kiss him, how her heart ached for him. And whereas before when he used to visit she'd managed to put up with this pain, knowing it was only for a few weeks, now this was what it would be like for the rest of her life.

'What's the frown for?' Dougie said, his eyes filling with concern as he gently rubbed away the frown between her eyes with his thumb.

'Just thinking how much my life is going to change now you're home,' Eden said, honestly, though she'd never reveal the reason why.

'Change for the better?' Dougie asked, the grin back on his face.

'The jury is still out.'

'It's going to be amazing, we'll get to hang out all day every day.'

'I have a pottery painting café to run, you have your big gaming empire, so I don't see that we're going to be in each other's pockets all day.'

'I can run my *gaming empire* from anywhere as long as I have my laptop. I could sit in your café every day and you can bring me cups of coffee and Clare's delicious cake while I work.'

Her heart sank a little. 'Is that really what you plan to do? Won't the noise of the café disturb you?'

He shook his head. 'Not really, I can zone it out. But don't you think it'll be fun to work alongside each other?'

He was winding her up, she could tell by the little smirk on his lips. 'Oh sure, I can come over every five minutes and ask you what you're doing, spill coffee over your laptop, get cake crumbs over your papers. It'll be a blast.'

He laughed. 'OK, maybe me encroaching on your space every day at work might not be the best way to maintain our friendship but we can hang out at night or on your days off.'

'You'll be too busy *hanging out* with all the other women of the island. There has been much excitement amongst the single women about you coming home. I'm sure you'll be off sleeping with a different woman every night.'

She frowned again. He had never done that when he had visited in the past, preferring to spend his time with her, Rome and Bella, but now he was back for good of course that would change. That thought had never really occurred to her before. But what did she expect – that he'd stay single and never date or have sex with anyone ever again? She knew he had dated several women in New York over the last twelve years but she'd never had to see it, apart from the very occasional photo he'd posted on Facebook. Now there'd be no escape from it. He was a good-looking man, incredibly good-looking in fact. He was kind, sweet, funny and very wealthy. He'd be fighting them off with a stick. And she'd have to watch him with them. Even worse, he'd be living next door, his bedroom was next to hers. Although Mrs Wimbledon, who had lived next door before she had sold the house to Dougie, no longer had a sex life after her husband had died several years before, Eden could quite often hear her moving around in her bedroom. Would she be able to hear Dougie having sex with all these women as she lay alone in her own bed? That thought was like a punch to the gut.

'There's that frown again. What's going on in that beautiful head of yours?'

'Just thinking about having to listen to you shagging your way through the female population of the island. It will disturb my sleep, Mrs Wimbledon was a very quiet neighbour.'

'There'll be no shagging, I can assure you of that.'

'Oh really, taken a vow of celibacy, have you?'

'I'm just not interested in having a relationship right now. I have a ton of stuff I need to sort out with work; this move has been a bit tricky to sort out with clients. Isaac is coming to work for me three days a week after Christmas so we'll probably have to sort out an office. I need to get the house finished and I feel a bit done with the dating scene right now. I've had several meaningless encounters and several relationships that were semi-serious but I never loved any of them. Having sex is fun but it just leaves you feeling flat afterwards if it's not with someone you love. I came back to Hope Island because this always feels like my home, because I miss you so much when I'm gone and—'

'You miss me?' Eden swallowed a lump of emotion in her throat.

'Yes, and Bella and Rome of course, and I'm just happy to hang out with you guys. I suppose, eventually, I'll settle down with someone but that's just not a priority for me at the moment. After my parents' marriage ended so badly, I'm not sure I ever want to get married actually.' He paused, staring at her, fondly. 'What about you, are you looking for love?'

She sighed. 'Not really.' She wasn't looking for it, because she had it. It just wasn't reciprocated.

'You haven't been with anyone since Stephen broke your heart,' Dougie went on.

'He didn't break my heart,' Eden said. She would've had to have been in love with Stephen for her heart to break and that wasn't the case.

He frowned in confusion. 'He hurt you.'

'I was sad that it was over.' She had been upset when Stephen had broken up with her, mostly because she knew how much she had hurt him and she never wanted that. But also because

Stephen was perfect in every single way: he made her laugh, he was kind, sweet, attentive, generous, great in bed, completely in love with her. He ticked every single box except the Dougie-shaped one. No matter how hard she tried, she had never fallen in love with Stephen in return. She liked him a lot, she was fond of him, but she had never been in love with him, not in the crazy head-over-heels kind of way that she loved Dougie. And although she'd known that she would never love anyone the way she loved Dougie and had been quite happy to stay with Stephen, it wasn't fair on him and she'd known that. Stephen had been aware of the fact that she didn't love him and had ended it after six months together. And while her concern had mostly been for Stephen and how gutted he was that he wasn't enough for her, she had also been upset because she realised that she was probably destined to spend the rest of her life alone. If she couldn't fall in love with Stephen – who had been perfect – then she had no chance of moving on with anyone unless she could miraculously fall out of love with Dougie and, after twelve or more years, she recognised that was never going to happen either.

'It hurt because I'm clearly rubbish at relationships,' Eden said, skating round the truth. 'And I'm probably going to die alone, getting eaten by a load of cats.'

'That's not going to happen,' Dougie said.

'No?'

'Well you don't like cats, so I can't see that you'd be buying one let alone a pack of them. Dogs maybe, but I don't think death by cat is how you will see your end.'

'Encouraging,' Eden sighed.

'And also because you'll never be alone. You'll always have me.'

'Two spinsters together?' Eden asked.

'I don't think I can be a spinster, I haven't got the right parts for that.'

'You know what I mean. Perpetually single. Neither of us getting married. That's pretty depressing.'

'Well, I don't know if I'll never get married. If my secret crush decides that she loves me too, then I suppose marriage could be on the cards.'

'You have a secret crush?'

'There's a girl I'm crazy about,' he grinned.

Hurt slammed into her stomach as she racked her mind for who it could be. 'You've never mentioned her before.'

'There didn't seem much point, she doesn't see me that way.'

'And… you'd marry her?'

Her voice was suddenly high with anxiety. What would be worse, watching him work his way through half the single female population of the island and listening to him having sex, or watching him fall in love with someone, get married to them and have children with them? She knew the answer as soon as she asked that, panic rising in her chest so hard and fast she could barely breathe.

He shrugged. 'If that's what she wanted… Hey, are you OK?'

'I just need some air, I feel hot,' Eden muttered and quickly removed herself from his arms. He let her go and she moved quickly into the kitchen and out the back door into her tiny garden which overlooked the sea.

The sea was a deep blue today as grey clouds dusted the early morning sky. It still looked beautiful though and it calmed her down. It was cold outside, a shock to the system after being snuggled against the warmth of Dougie's body, and it was enough to make her catch her breath.

She should have told him years ago. She should have made it clear that his frequent visits actually hurt; the ache in her chest always so raw every time he left. But she never had. He'd already broken her heart once when he had kissed her and then moved to America, never mentioning the kiss again. After the kiss, all she'd been able to see was this bright and wonderful future with the man she loved and she'd lost that, which had left a gaping hole in her heart. She didn't want to go through the pain of that again and if she told him how she felt and he rejected her, she knew that pain would resurface. But she didn't want to lose him as a best friend either. He was too important to her for that.

When he'd first mentioned that he was moving back to Hope Island for good, she should have told him then how she felt, she should have selfishly asked him to stay in America, but she couldn't. As much as it hurt her whenever he came home, not seeing him ever again would hurt even more. But could she really watch him get married and have children?

She fingered the star necklace he'd given her for her last birthday. At the time he'd said it was so she would have somewhere to keep all her wishes in the same place and she'd told him she didn't believe in wishes or magic any more. And that was true but as she rubbed it between her fingers now, so that the metal went warm, she closed her eyes and wished as hard as she could that she could fall out of love with Dougie.

'Thought you said you don't believe in wishes any more,' Dougie said and she let the necklace fall back onto her chest.

'I don't,' Eden sighed as she watched the winter sunshine glint off his beautiful red curls. No, she didn't because as she watched him come across the frosty lawn towards her, she knew she was still as in love with him as she'd always been. No wish was going to change that.

'That was such a big part of who you were growing up, you always believed in magic and dreams and wishes coming true.'

'And you were always the one who encouraged me to never give up on them. You told me there was magic all around us if we only know where to look. I remember when all the kids at school stopped believing in Santa Claus and we went down to

Mistletoe Cove, where we would always hang out when it was just the two of us, and we talked about it. You asked if I still believed in him and I said I really wanted to, that there was something wonderful about the idea of this man visiting every child in the world in one night, bringing toys and gifts, travelling across the starlit skies in his sleigh with his magical flying reindeer. I said that I never wanted to stop believing in him and you told me not to, that I was never to give up on believing in magic. And every single year since then, there has always been a gift under my tree from Santa. Every year…' The words caught in her throat as she stared at him. She knew they were really from him. He came home almost every year for Christmas and somehow he always managed to smuggle the present under her tree. Even in the years that he didn't make it home, the present from Santa was always there.

'But you still gave up on wishes. What happened for you to give up on them?'

'They never came true.'

'Maybe you're not asking in the right way.'

'Is there a right way?'

Dougie clearly thought about this for a moment. 'Did you know the patron saint of wishes is Saint Douglas?'

She laughed. 'It is not.'

'It is, I swear. If I had my phone on me, I'd prove it to you, but trust me, it is. You need to tell your wishes to him. As a direct descendent of Saint Douglas, you can tell me your wishes and I guarantee they'll come true.'

She smiled fondly at him and shook her head. 'Not going to happen. Everyone knows if you tell someone your wish, it will never come true, basic wish rules 101.'

'But I'm not just anyone, I'm the great-great-great-great-grandson of *the* Saint Douglas himself. I have the power to make all your wishes come true.'

She rolled her eyes. 'Let me make you some breakfast before I go off to work.'

He snagged her arm. 'OK, don't tell me, but you know the legend of Mistletoe Cove, right?'

'What legend?'

'You mean to tell me that Eden Lancaster, chief wisher extraordinaire, has never thrown a wish into the wishing well?'

'What's the wishing well?'

'The blowhole,' Dougie explained. 'That's what the locals called it hundreds of years ago but its name has been lost over the years.'

On the far side of Mistletoe Cove, there was a hole in the rocks that led to an underwater cave. When the waves hit the sea entrance to the cave, the water would spray up through the hole like a giant fountain. Not many people from the island had seen it as it was so hard to get down to Mistletoe Cove, although the tourist boat trips around the islands always made a point of showing the visitors the blowhole. But Eden had never heard it called the wishing well before.

She decided to humour him. 'No, I've not heard the legend of the wishing well.'

'Well, legend has it that if you write three wishes on a piece of paper and throw it into the blowhole at midnight, all three wishes will come true.'

'So the blowhole can read?' Eden laughed.

'I don't know how the magic works, but I do know that it does work.'

'You have proof of this.'

'Yes, lots of people have done it and had their wishes come true. I did it. I wrote three wishes on a piece of paper on my seventeenth birthday and threw them in the blowhole. They all came true.'

She still didn't believe this but she would indulge him. 'What did you wish for?'

'I wished that I would move to New York, I wished that one day I would own my own gaming company and I wished that I could meet my hero at the time, Harrison Ford.'

Eden laughed, remembering that he had actually bumped into Harrison Ford in a coffee shop in New York a few weeks after he had moved out there. His photo of the two of them together was still one of his most treasured possessions.

'And none of that would have happened if it hadn't been for the wishes I threw into the blowhole.'

'I think the first two would have happened anyway with hard work and determination.'

'Well, how do you explain me meeting Harrison Ford?' Dougie grinned at her.

'Lucky coincidence.'

'Look, what do you have to lose? Come with me tomorrow night, make a wish, see if it comes true. I haven't been back to Mistletoe Cove for years; it'd be good to see it again.'

'I haven't been back there either,' Eden said, knowing full well that she hadn't been there since the night they had kissed just before he had left for America.

'Then let's go there tomorrow, for old times' sake. We'll take a flask of hot chocolate, light a fire and toast marshmallows, just like we used to. And if you're feeling brave enough, you can make a wish.'

'It was minus five last night, I don't think it's warm enough to sit outside.'

'We'll take our sleeping bags, stop making excuses,' Dougie said. 'You just don't want to climb down the devil's stairs. You're obviously too scared.'

She grinned, knowing that was how he had persuaded her to go to the cove with him the first time when she was only eight years old. There was no direct path down to the cove, having to climb down through a cave and then down the rocky cliff face to get to it. Of course she had wanted to show him that she was brave enough to do it with him when she was a child and they had been many times since then as they had grown up together. It had become their special place.

'Fine, we'll go,' Eden said. She couldn't resist going back to Mistletoe Cove with him after all these years. And if the wishing well really did work, maybe her wish to fall out of love with Dougie would finally come true.

CHAPTER 4

Dougie looked down on Hope Island from his position on the highest hill. It was quiet up here, the odd dog walker or runner in view, but most people were already in work at this time. The air was crisp and cold and a damp haze clung to the hillside.

Though many of the trees had died off over the winter, there was still a rugged beauty to the island, the hills that spread across the middle of the island, the long Buttercup beach that still looked golden despite the grey winter sky. Over in one corner he could see the small, pretty Blueberry Bay, one of Bella's favourite places, and in the far corner he could see Mistletoe Cove with the hawthorn trees he knew would be lined with mistletoe. It really was a spectacular place.

He could see the Christmas festival getting ready for the big opening that afternoon and he was pretty sure he could just make out Bella, her long red hair streaming behind her, directing proceedings. He was looking forward to going along this afternoon with Eden.

He stretched his arms above his head and took off at a run as he headed back towards the little town on the far side of Hope Island. He loved to run in the mornings; whether he was in New York or here, it helped to clear his head before he started his day. It gave him time to think. He was definitely going to miss the stunning New York skyline he could see from Central Park on his normal run and he'd miss going to Starbucks after for his regular morning coffee. He'd miss the food, too. New York had the most amazing breakfast places, serving pancakes, waffles, French toast, eggs and their weird-ass bacon which wasn't really bacon in the English sense but was something he had come to love. He'd miss that. He'd miss his car, his Lexus. It wasn't flashy but it was a gorgeous car and drove like a dream. He'd miss his penthouse apartment, with all the space that it had afforded him. He'd miss that the city never stopped. Here many of the shops closed at four or whenever they felt like it really. The island was quiet, almost too quiet. But the views were spectacular, the air was cleaner and, despite everything he would miss about New York, this had always felt like home.

He cut through the park and out into the high street which was decorated with lights and garlands ready for Christmas in just six days' time. He followed the cobbled lane towards Pots and Paints and pushed open the door. Eden was the first thing he saw. She was busy talking to a child as the boy painted a clay model of Santa with purple and green spots. Her long hair was swept back from her face in a little snowflake clip at the back of her head, leaving her glossy black curls to tumble down her back, her eyes were that sweet forget-me-not blue, and when she looked up to see who had walked through the door and her whole face lit up into the biggest smile, he knew he had made the right decision to move back to the island. New York had many amazing things but it didn't have Eden Lancaster.

She stood up as he approached and he immediately enveloped her in a big hug.

'I missed you,' he said.

She laughed as she hugged him back. 'You great daft man, it's been two hours.'

He shrugged. 'It was still too long.'

'Josie has been asking about you,' Eden said, softly, indicating the blonde woman making some half-arsed attempt at painting a mug. 'And Kitty was in here earlier asking after you. You have quite the little fan club.'

Before he could reply to that, Josie tottered over on heels that were ridiculously high. He did like a woman in heels, there was something very sexy about heels. He glanced down to see what Eden was wearing on her feet and grinned when he saw the sparkly pink Converse he'd bought her the Christmas before. These had fairies and unicorns on the side and he'd told her it was so she would always have a bit of magic with her with every step she took. With her snowman jumper and worn jeans with holes in the knees, she was infinitely more sexy than any woman wearing heels.

'What?' Eden said, catching him staring at her.

'You're adorable.'

She frowned and without thinking he bent down and kissed the frown gently away. He pulled back slightly and Eden stared at him with wide eyes.

'Hi Dougie,' Josie said.

Dougie tore his eyes away from Eden and gave Josie his best smile. 'Josie, how lovely to see you. You're looking beautiful as always.'

He heard a little soft sigh of frustration come from Eden as she tried to move away, but he snagged her hand with his own, entwining his fingers through hers.

Josie blushed at the compliment. He genuinely enjoyed making people feel good about themselves. When he was working for Poseidon Games he'd found that compliments went a long way with the men and women he worked with as well as with the clients. Positive comments about their work or even how they looked meant people went away feeling happy. He hated that women always felt so much pressure to look good and how much that affected their self-esteem. Many of them lacked any kind of confidence at all and even the ones that didn't seem to have that trouble were often hiding vulnerabilities or sore spots somewhere else. He'd seen a video online once about all these women and how much they hated their bodies and he couldn't believe it. He thought women were beautiful creatures, and it didn't matter how big or small they were, what colour their hair or skin was, every woman was beautiful to him. Eden accused him of being a flirt and maybe he was but why not make people feel happy?

'Good to see you back, we all missed you,' Josie said, curling a ribbon of hair round her finger. 'Though I think if I was living in New York, I don't think I'd ever come back here.'

'I love Hope Island. The beaches, the views, the people.' He glanced down at Eden and smiled as he said that.

'Well, if you get bored and you want to go out for a drink and have a bit of fun some time you can give me a call,' Josie said, offering out her number with impeccable timing. She didn't even have to find her card in her bag.

He smiled at Josie. 'That's really kind but, well… me and Eden are seeing each other, we have been for a few months. She wanted to keep it a secret, you know what the islanders are like, but now I'm back I don't think there's much point in keeping it a secret any longer, is there honey?'

He grinned at Eden who stared at him in shock.

'Oh, I'm sorry, I didn't realise,' Josie said, the card disappearing so fast back into her handbag that he wasn't sure if he had imagined it in her hand in the first place.

'Don't be sorry, I'm hugely flattered. And you know, I heard that Simon has a massive crush on you. If you're looking for some fun, I bet he'd be happy to oblige.'

Josie's face lit up. 'Simon Broadman?'

'Yes, I just ran into him. It seems you've definitely got yourself a fan.'

Josie smiled then turned her attention on Eden. 'I'm happy for the two of you. When will the mug be ready for me to collect?'

'It'll be after Christmas now, we'll call you when it's ready for collection,' Eden said.

Josie nodded and gave Dougie another smile before walking out.

Eden took a swipe at him as soon as the door closed. 'Why did you tell her that we're seeing each other?'

'Well technically we are. I see you every day, you see me, I think that counts as seeing each other.'

She rolled her eyes and he couldn't help but laugh.

'That will be round the whole island by lunch time.'

'And that will stop people asking me about my love life. I told you I'm not interested in having some meaningless relationship so it doesn't matter what people think about us.'

'And what about me? Just because you're not interested in meaningless sex, doesn't mean that I'm not. I happen to love meaningless sex.'

The customers in the pottery café went silent as they all listened to this conversation. Eden didn't seem to notice.

'You said you weren't looking for love after what happened with Stephen,' Dougie said.

'Stephen hasn't put me off dating. He might have shown me I'm rubbish at it but I've not given up. I know I'm not seeing anyone at the moment and my sex life is a bit sparse of late but that doesn't mean I don't want to date anyone. If someone nice came along and asked me out, I might say yes, I might not, but I'd at least like the option rather than you taking me off the market without my permission.'

He brushed his hand through his hair. He hadn't even thought of that when he'd quickly fumbled for an excuse to give to Josie. And although he hated that he'd upset Eden and she was perfectly right in her outrage, he was secretly very pleased by that outcome. He didn't want anyone to go out with her. The thought of someone else kissing her, making love to her, was not pleasant.

'I'm sorry, but if your sex life is a bit lacking, I don't mind helping you out.'

'You just said you didn't want meaningless sex,' Eden said, clearly exasperated, and he loved to see the fire in her eyes.

He hooked an arm round her waist and pulled her against him. 'Believe me honey, there'd be nothing meaningless about it.'

She stared up at him, her face just a few inches from his, and for a fraction of a second her gaze wandered down to his lips before snapping back up to his eyes again.

'Go on Eden, go for it,' Barbara Copperthwaite from the chemist called across from the corner. 'It'll be the best decision you ever make.'

Eden blushed furiously and disentangled herself from Dougie's arms, suddenly realising that everyone had been listening to them. Well, she'd hardly been discreet.

'Go on, get out, before you completely humiliate me,' she said.

'Can I get a coffee first before you cast me out on the street?'

'Clare, can you get him a coffee, make sure it's extra sweet,' Eden said, obtrusively, knowing full well he didn't take sugar in his drinks.

Dougie smirked as Clare Crissell, Eden's lovely assistant, got his drink ready. He turned his attention back to his best friend.

'Are we going to the Christmas festival together this afternoon?'

Eden sighed and he could see that she was thinking of some excuse. Thankfully Clare came to his rescue.

'There's a couples' snowman-making competition this afternoon, you two should enter,' Clare said, handing him his coffee. 'I know Bella and Rome are entering with their respective partners.

Sounds like a lot of fun. The families' one is tomorrow, my two boys are really looking forward to it.'

'That does sound like fun,' Dougie said.

'And a perfect opportunity for you to show the whole town that we are in fact a couple,' Eden said, pointedly.

'Ah come on, it'll be good to do something with Bella and Rome, and there's no way we can let them win when we both know our snowman-building skills far surpass theirs.'

'Dougie, I think I've made one snowman in my lifetime, we so rarely get a lot of snow here in the Scilly Isles.'

'Well now is the time to start. Besides, I have years of experience building snowmen from the heavy snow we get in New York.'

'That's what you did with your time out there?' Eden said and he could tell she was thawing slightly.

'Oh yes, I've built hundreds. Look, if we don't win I'll do something for you, anything you want, no questions asked,' Dougie said, wondering what he was letting himself in for with that offer.

'Well that's an offer you can't refuse,' Clare said, waggling her eyebrows at Eden in her not so subtle attempts at matchmaking. Dougie wasn't blind to the efforts of the islanders to get them together but it was going to take a bit more than a few comments and eyebrow-waggling to get Eden to fall in love with him.

'OK, deal,' Eden said, suddenly, an evil glint in her eyes. He got the feeling that he was going to have to pull out all the stops to make sure he did win now.

He offered Eden some money to pay for the coffee but she shook her head, so he kissed her on the cheek instead. 'I'll see you here at one, beautiful.'

She smiled at him and he left the shop.

Now all he had to do was look up how to make the perfect snowman.

CHAPTER 5

Eden waved goodbye to Clare and her family as she locked up Pots and Paints. The café was open seven days a week, so it felt a bit strange to be closing halfway through the day, but as all the other shops were shutting for the opening of the Christmas festival and all the islanders would be in the park for it too, there didn't seem much point in staying open.

She looked down the street at all the other shops, lit up with beautiful Christmas decorations. Large oversized snowflakes twinkled from above and multi-coloured fairy lights, strewn across the roofs, danced and sparkled in the light fog that had descended on the island since that morning.

She loved this time of year: the decorations, the festivities and parties, all the wonderful food and delicious sweet treats from the various bakeries and sweet shops in the town. She loved buying presents for her family; finding the perfect gift that she knew would make them smile. She loved the Christmas music and the silly Christmas jumpers. It really was her favourite time of the year. Maybe she should wish for it to be Christmas all year round when she went to Mistletoe Cove the following night.

The last few stragglers were locking up their shops and hurrying off to the park for the start of the festival, when she saw Dougie strolling down the road towards her. As he drew closer she didn't know whether to be delighted or horrified by the fact that he was wearing the exact same Christmas jumper that she was. But as always he had the biggest smile on his face and it was hard to find it in her to do anything to take that smile away.

'What's this?' Eden gestured to his jumper as he bent his head to kiss her on the cheek.

'Team colours,' Dougie said. 'I saw it in a shop in town and knew I had to buy it. I bought supplies too.' He held up a large bag. 'The rules clearly state that couples are allowed to bring their own props and I think our snowman will be the smartest dressed snowman Hope Island has ever seen.'

Nothing seemed to dampen Dougie's spirits, he always seemed to be high on life. Just being around him was contagious; he made her so happy too. And that's why she could never tell him her feelings for him – she never wanted to lose him as a friend or lose this wonderful close relationship they had now.

She had long since reconciled herself to the fact that nothing was ever going to happen between them but as long as she had this, then she would be happy. Well, as long as Dougie stayed single, she would be happy. She didn't think that she could cope with watching him go off and marry somebody else.

He took her hand, linking his fingers through hers as he led her down the street. 'Come on, we don't want to be late.'

Eden looked down at their joined hands and smiled. Maybe pretending to be a couple wasn't going to be the worst thing in the world.

They quickly arrived at the park and it was clear that the Christmas festival was well underway, with hundreds of people wandering around the market, tasting the wonderful foods and enjoying the different activities. Children were squealing and laughing with delight at the ice skating rink or the small toboggan run or excitedly queuing up to meet Santa in his grotto. With the beautifully decorated Christmas trees donated by local businesses lining the edge of the festival and the gingerbread-style houses for the Christmas market, the place looked beautiful and magical. The island had never done anything like this before; it looked like a winter wonderland.

Over on the far side of the park, near the ice skating and sledging, was a small paddock filled with fake snow. The idea being that people could come along whenever they wanted and play in the snow, but for the first two days of the festival there were going to be three snowman-building competitions, one for couples, one for families and one for friends. Crowds were already starting to gather to watch the event and Dougie pulled her over in that direction.

Angela, the new mayor, was directing proceedings, shouting instructions through a megaphone. When the old mayor had stepped down a few months before there had been lots of people who wanted the job, but it seemed Angela got it because she was something of a mini local celebrity, having published a crime story that year. According to Angela's sister, who also had wanted to be mayor, the book had only sold twenty-nine copies but that didn't stop Angela dropping it into the conversation at every available opportunity.

Eden waved at Angela as she and Dougie went over to greet the others. Bella and Freya gave them both a hug and Rome and Isaac wandered over too.

'Good to see you've finally woken up,' Isaac said, clapping Dougie on the back.

'Ah, sorry to fall asleep on you last night,' Dougie laughed.

'No worries, that flight from America is always a killer.'

'Look what a cute couple you two make,' Rome said, dryly, eyeing their matching jumpers. 'And I hear on the grapevine that you two have been a couple for several months.'

Eden laughed, nervously. 'That was just a bit of a misunderstanding.'

'Well, you're wearing matching jumpers, holding hands and entering into a couple competition,' Rome said. He turned to Dougie. 'Are you sleeping with my sister?'

Eden rolled her eyes. She knew Rome was only joking but he did have a huge overprotective streak.

Freya swatted Rome's arm. 'That's none of your business.'

'No I'm not,' Dougie said.

'Good job too,' Rome said. 'She can do better than you.'

Dougie's smile fell off his face and he dropped Eden's hand. Anger flared up in Eden so fast she nearly lashed out at her brother.

'Don't say that, that's a horrible thing to say,' Eden said. 'Dougie is an amazing, kind, sweet, generous and wonderful person and any woman would be lucky to have him. I know you're only joking but that's nasty and absolutely not true.'

Dougie stared at her. They all stared at her. A slow smile spread across Dougie's face at her overprotectiveness, as if he was secretly pleased she'd stuck up for him.

'Well said,' Bella said.

Rome cleared his throat. 'Wow, Eden. I'm sorry, Dougie. I was genuinely joking. No one would be happier than me if you two finally got together, but if you do, and you hurt her, it is my job as her brother to beat you up.'

Dougie smiled. 'Duly noted.'

The megaphone suddenly squeaked as Angela turned it back on. 'Positions please!'

Rome bent his head and kissed Eden on the cheek, squeezing her hand to apologise before they went back to their allocated bays. Dougie went over to the bay next to Bella and Isaac and Eden followed him.

She was still angry at that comment but Dougie didn't seem to be bothered by it any more as he squatted down to feel the snow.

He looked up at her and smiled when he saw that she was still scowling. He stood back up.

'Rome was only joking, you know we have a relationship where we mock each other. It's never meant horribly.'

'I know, but he shouldn't have said it.'

'Remind me never to piss you off,' Dougie said, slinging his arm round her shoulders and kissing her head.

'You should already know that,' Eden said, thawing a little.

'I do appreciate what you said,' Dougie said, quietly. 'You really think any woman would be lucky to go out with me?'

'Yes, stop fishing for compliments.'

'Including you?'

'Dougie!' Eden groaned in frustration.

'I'll take that as a yes.' He moved in front of her, his hands on her shoulders as he dipped his head to look in her eyes. 'Although believe me, I'd be the lucky one.'

Eden sighed. 'You're such a flirt.'

Angela started calling out the rules and Eden moved out of Dougie's arms to listen. It was pretty simple: they had thirty minutes to create a snowman, they could use props and they couldn't hinder another team. There were three other teams apart from Rome and Bella's and she knew them all, apart from one couple who were obviously tourists. Everyone seemed to be taking it very seriously.

'One of these days I'm going to call you out on it,' Eden said, quietly, and Dougie turned to look at her with a big smirk.

'You are?'

'Yes, one day, you're going to offer me a kiss or to take me to bed and I'm going to say yes. Then what will you do?'

Dougie shrugged. 'Kiss you and take you to bed.'

Eden stared at him for a moment and then smirked. He was so full of it.

Angela started doing a countdown and Dougie turned away to look at the mound of snow that each bay had been provided with.

'The key is that we have to make three sections for the snowman, a bottom, middle and the head, because that makes the snowman look more real rather than shapeless. And when we make the three snowballs, we need to pack the snow tightly as we roll it and pack more snow in between each layer.'

'You really know your snowmen,' Eden said, bending to pick up a small snowball and packing it with her hands.

'I looked it up on Google,' Dougie said.

'I thought you said you were the expert.'

'I lied.'

There was no time to be indignant as Angela released the air horn to start the competition.

'I'm holding you to your deal: if we don't win, you have to do anything I ask,' Eden said.

'Will it involve kissing you and taking you to bed?' Dougie said, as he bent down and started forming a large ball of snow with his hands.

'No it will not.'

'Pity.'

Eden shook her head and added her ball to his larger one, packing the snow around his hands and then helping him to roll the ball through the snow, so it picked up weight. It was getting heavier with every second as Dougie deliberately rolled the ball towards Bella and Isaac's area. He winked at her as he 'accidentally' crossed over their line with the ball and stole some of their much needed snow. He was on his way back over the line when Bella spotted him.

'Hey, he took some of our snow,' Bella protested.

Eden quickly packed the contraband snow tighter onto the ball, just in case Bella and Isaac tried to take it back.

They didn't but she felt a thwack against her back as one of them hit her with a snowball.

'Hey!' Eden turned round but when Dougie stopped to see what they were doing she laughed when he got a face full of snow too.

Dougie laughed as he wiped the snow from his eyes. 'I guess I asked for that.'

'There's plenty more where that came from,' Isaac called across.

Eden giggled as she turned her attention back to the giant snowball.

They finally got their snowball back into the middle of their bay and set about making a slightly smaller one for the middle of the snowman. It felt good to be working alongside him.

'Don't make it too big, we won't be able to lift it onto the other one,' Eden said.

'Don't worry about that, I've been working out.'

'I noticed,' Eden said, without thinking.

Dougie stopped what he was doing. 'Oh, you noticed my body then, did you? Do you like my muscles?'

He struck a pose, flexing the muscles in his arms, and Eden burst out laughing.

'Stop that, you look ridiculous.'

Dougie was undeterred as he created several different model poses. 'You can touch my muscles if you want.'

Eden couldn't stop laughing. 'You're so silly.'

He grabbed her into a big hug. 'You love it really.'

She smiled up at him, feeling her heart swell with love for him. 'It's good to have you home. I've really missed you.'

The humour faded from his eyes and he smiled at her, fondly. 'I missed you too.'

Aware that some people were looking at them, Eden removed herself from his arms and returned her attention back to the snowman. 'And that's the only compliment you'll get out of me.'

Dougie joined her at her side. 'I'll take it.'

They worked side by side to create the three large balls and Dougie had no problem lifting them into place. They packed snow in between the different layers and spent a while smoothing out the balls with their hands.

Eden looked over at the other teams and saw that most had just gone with a bottom and a head rather than three separate parts. But whether that would help them to win or not remained to be seen.

Dougie grabbed two thick branches from the small pile that had been provided for them and stuck them either side of the middle ball.

'OK, time for props,' Dougie said as he picked up his bulging bag. 'I visited your aunt's charity shop for a lot of these things.'

'Oh no, you didn't?' Eden loved her aunt Cassie dearly but there was nothing in her charity shop that had ever been in fashion. 'What on earth did you get from there?'

'This.' Dougie pulled out something that was velvet and deep red. He shook it out and Eden could see that it was in fact a velvet smoking jacket, with a black satin collar and a red velvet tie for the waist.

'Oh wow, our snowman is going to look like he belongs in the Playboy mansion,' Eden said.

Dougie pulled out a burgundy cravat, a top hat, a monocle and a pipe as well. Eden couldn't help but laugh.

'When you said our snowman would be the best dressed, I never expected this.'

'I think Hubert will look very dapper,' Dougie said, placing the top hat on the snowman's head with an affectionate pat.

'You have five minutes left,' Angela called out over the megaphone.

'Quick, we need to get him dressed,' Dougie urged.

Eden helped him to get Hubert's jacket on, which was a lot trickier than it looked with his stiff arms. As Dougie tied the belt around the waist, Eden glanced over to see what Bella and Rome were doing with their snowmen. Bella and Isaac had gone for the traditional snowman, twigs for arms, coal for eyes, but had given him a sprig of holly as a button hole and a wonderful green scarf and woolly hat to match. But Rome and Freya had decided to decorate their snowman with glass from their stained glass studio. There was a glass bow-tie, round blue glass beads for eyes and buttons and even an orange glass carrot.

'Oh no, Rome and Freya have made theirs out of glass,' Eden said as Dougie was hurriedly trying to add buttons for the eyes.

Dougie looked over at them. 'That's cheating.'

'And a smoking jacket isn't going a bit over the top?'

'I didn't want Hubert getting cold.'

'Well, looks like you'll have to pay up on our deal,' Eden said, wondering what she could get him to do.

'Not so fast, I have a plan,' Dougie said. 'Here, put the monocle on for me and don't judge me for what I'm about to do next. Hubert won't feel a thing.'

Confused, she placed the monocle over the eye as she heard a cracking. She looked round to see that Dougie had broken one of Hubert's arms in half so he could bend it round in front of the body.

'Dougie!' Eden said, not sure why she was so mortified about Dougie breaking a branch. She had to close her eyes when he did the other one, it looked so brutal. He positioned the arms round so they were just below the snowman's face as Eden tied the cravat round Hubert's neck. As Angela called out there was only thirty seconds left, Dougie pulled a book out of the bag and positioned it in the fingers of the branches so it looked like Hubert was reading. Confused about how this was supposed to make them win, Eden moved round to see what the book was.

'Douglas Harrison, if that's not cheating I don't know what is,' she said as she saw Angela's crime fiction book.

Dougie grinned and shrugged and Angela let off the air horn to signify the end of the competition.

One of the teams had somehow lost their snowman's head and another hadn't brought any props with them at all, but had managed to carve out what looked like arms and legs in the snowman.

Angela paraded up and down the line, claiming how wonderful they all were, but Eden could see she was torn between Rome and Freya's glass work snowman or Eden and Dougie's playboy Hubert.

'Has she seen the book?' Eden murmured.

'I don't think so.'

As Angela walked back towards Hubert again, Dougie tweaked the position of the book slightly. This time Eden knew that Angela had seen it as her whole face lit up.

'Oh, ha ha, very good, very good indeed,' Angela said. She looked back over to Rome and Freya's snowman but Eden could see her mind was made up.

Angela raised her megaphone. 'The winners are… Eden and Dougie!'

The crowd cheered and Angela strolled over and pinned the rosette to poor Hubert's chest. Angela's assistant handed over a box of mulled wine chocolates, a box of mince pies and a tub of white hot chocolate.

The crowd dispersed, going off to explore the delights of the rest of the Christmas festival, and Bella, Isaac, Freya and Rome came over to inspect Hubert for themselves.

Bella spotted the book. 'We were robbed.'

'Isn't that called bribery?' Rome said.

'You're all just jealous that we won,' Dougie said.

'Our glass creation should have won,' Freya said, as she stared at Hubert with a smile. 'Though I do love that your snowman has a monocle and a pipe.'

'Very clever, my friend,' Isaac said, staring at Hubert with admiration.

Dougie opened the box of mince pies and offered them to his friends and they all took one, any animosity over Dougie's cheating quickly forgotten.

Just then Angela came back over to them.

'I do love your snowman, I think he looks very smart and, um… if you want me to sign your book for you, I'm more than happy to do so.'

Dougie gave her a winning smile. 'Angela, I would be over the moon if you would.'

As Angela rushed off to get a pen, Eden smiled at him and shook her head. It really was good to have him home.

CHAPTER 6

Eden walked up the hill with Dougie at her side. Every Friday she, Rome and Bella went for dinner at their parents' house. Over the last few months, Freya and Isaac had come along as well. Dougie always came when he was on the island; her parents adored him. It didn't matter that she wasn't with him; he belonged with her and her family.

She knocked at the door and heard footsteps thundering down the hall as if someone was excited to see them. She loved her parents but they had only one setting: completely overenthusiastic about everything.

The door was flung open and her dad Finn, with a big grin on his face, enveloped them both into a big bear hug, squashing Eden and Dougie together against his chest.

'Ah Dougie, it's so good to see you again, we've all missed you.'

Finn pulled back to look at them both and Eden smiled at the bright red Christmas jumper with the gormless Rudolph staring out from the middle of it.

'Come in, come in,' Finn ushered them into the hall and closed the door behind them. 'We heard that you two had finally got together, but Rome said that you hadn't and it was a big misunderstanding, but Lucy and I were talking and we think that you really are together and just pretending that you're not because you want to keep it secret.'

'No it's not—' Eden tried before Finn continued.

'And quite rightly so. When you first get together it's all new and wonderful and you just want to keep it between yourselves for a while. Sometimes, I've walked through the park and seen a couple kissing and it's been so passionate that I've thought they should perhaps take it somewhere a bit more private. Not that there's anything wrong with kissing in public or showing your love with holding hands or a cuddle, but this couple I saw the other day, he had his tongue so far down her throat it could have choked her and his hands were not exactly in a respectable position either.'

Eden chanced a glance at Dougie, who was grinning like an idiot at Finn's monologue.

'I mean, I like kissing with tongues as much as the next man,' Finn said. 'But some things should be done in private, don't you think? Myself and Lucy weren't exactly discreet when we first got together, she loves a bit of outdoor sex and we were caught in some compromising positions around the island, let me tell you, and there's nothing wrong with that, if the mood takes you, but you don't want to be an exhibitionist.'

Her mum, Lucy, suddenly joined him and Eden was relieved that this embarrassing conversation would be over.

'Well of course you might like that sort of thing,' Finn went on. 'Voyeurism, I think they call it. Where you enjoy people watching you having sex.'

'No, voyeurism is where you enjoy watching other people having sex,' Lucy interrupted.

'Oh.' Finn looked thoughtful. 'What's it called when you like people watching you?'

'Dogging, I think,' Lucy said and Dougie snorted so hard that he ended up coughing. 'But I think you need a car for that.'

'Why do you need a car?' Finn asked.

Eden could see Rome, Freya, Bella and Isaac all peering round the kitchen door, laughing at them.

'So you can have sex in the back of the car and then people watch through the windows,' Lucy patiently explained.

'That sounds a bit creepy,' Finn said and then turned back
to Eden and Dougie. 'But if that's what makes you happy, then
we're happy,' he said.

'Are you two dogging?' Lucy asked and Eden wasn't sure
whether to laugh or die of embarrassment. Dougie was in full-
blown fits of giggles now and was clearly not going to step in and
help her anytime soon.

'No, we're not,' Eden said, firmly.

'Well we don't have many cars on the island,' Finn said. 'Might
be a bit difficult if you did want to. We have golf buggies, I guess
that would work in the same way.'

'Bit small though,' Dougie said and Eden looked at him
incredulously. Why was he joining in? 'You might have to get
creative about the positions you used.'

Finn nodded. 'Yes that's true.'

'And where would you do it? I can't see the mayor being happy
about you doing it in the main high street,' Lucy said.

'We're not having sex,' Eden blurted out. 'We're not together,
we've never even kissed and if we were together we certainly
wouldn't be doing it in the back of a golf buggy so the whole of
Hope Island could watch.'

Lucy and Finn stared at her.

'Well dear, if you want to keep your relationship to yourselves
then we will of course respect that,' Lucy said and Finn gave a
theatrical wink. 'We'll say no more about it. But don't knock
outdoors sex until you've tried it.'

'Though maybe wait until the summer,' Finn said. 'Bit cold at
the moment and certain parts shrink in the cold and we wouldn't
want that, eh Dougie?'

'No, quite right,' Dougie said.

Lucy walked off back into the kitchen and Finn followed,
leaving Dougie and Eden alone in the hall.

'I love your parents,' Dougie said, grinning at her.

'They don't need any further encouragement from you.'

'I wasn't encouraging them, I was just… agreeing. Come on, I don't want to miss any other hilarious conversations.'

He took her hand and led her into the kitchen where Bella, Isaac, Rome and Freya were already sitting at the dining table grinning at them. Clearly they had heard every word. Dougie sat down at the bench and patted the place next to him. She smirked and sat down beside him.

Lucy brought over a huge cooking dish piled high with food.

'Finn has made a delicious monkfish curry but as always he's made too much, so I hope you're all hungry,' Lucy said, placing serving spoons inside the pot and then sitting down as Finn brought over a large bowl of steaming rice.

It was quiet for a moment as everyone dished up the food onto their plates. Finn was a great cook and his curries were the stuff of legends.

'How are the wedding plans going?' Lucy asked Bella before she took her first mouthful.

If Eden hadn't been watching Bella she would have missed it. She had just happened to glance over at her as Lucy had asked that question and saw Bella quickly plaster a fake smile on her face.

'Great, really great,' Bella enthused. 'We're having the most beautiful ice sculptures. Isaac's PA, Claudia, has found the most fantastic ice carver from White Cliff Bay and she's going to do us some ice dolphins and seals to represent Hope Island – as we were having this wedding in London, Isaac and I wanted to take a little bit of Hope Island with us. And because originally me and Isaac wanted a Christmas-themed wedding but now the wedding is going to be end of January, Claudia thought that we should have a winter theme as a compromise so everything is going to be silver with snowflakes and Claudia even found a place that will do snowflake cupcakes.'

'Sounds like this is Claudia's wedding, not yours,' Rome said and Eden smiled with love for her brother. Being the eldest out of the three of them, he was so protective and especially of Bella who'd had such a hard time before she was adopted by Finn and Lucy. He was desperate to see Bella happy, they all were, and Isaac had made her happier than she had ever been, but they could all see this wedding was not what she wanted. Only the rest of them were too tactful to tell Bella this whole event was turning into a farce. Rome, it seemed, didn't have these scruples.

Isaac's smile was strained. 'Claudia is very efficient and also very overenthusiastic about this wedding. But Bella, if there's anything you don't want, you must tell her.'

'Likewise, if there's anything about this wedding you don't like then you need to tell her too,' Bella said.

Eden bit her lip. Why couldn't they see that this wedding was making them both miserable?

Isaac stroked Bella's cheek. 'I just want you to be happy.'

'I want you to be happy too, I want to give you a wedding you can be proud of,' Bella said.

Isaac frowned slightly at her choice of words. 'I will be proud to have you by my side, anything else is just aesthetics.'

Bella smiled and Eden willed her to tell him the truth but she didn't and, as she turned her attention back to her curry, Eden saw how sad she looked.

Eden opened her mouth to say something, though she wasn't sure what she should say, but Lucy got in ahead of her.

'I have to say that this Kensington Tower Hotel looks very fancy,' Lucy said. 'Not the sort of place I ever dreamt I would stay in. But our room for the night has its own lounge and a balcony with views over the Thames. It's all very exciting.'

'We have the biggest ballroom in the hotel, to accommodate all the guests,' Bella said. 'It has the most gorgeous chandeliers and you should see our cake.' She grabbed her phone from her pocket and pressed a few buttons then passed it round to show everyone.

'Wow, that's huge,' Finn said. 'Seven tiers. That's a lot of cake. What will you do with it all?'

'Well, all the guests will have a slice,' Bella said.

'How many guests do you have coming?' Lucy asked.

'Presently, four hundred and eighty-two.'

Isaac choked on his drink and the table fell silent.

'Four hundred and eighty-two?' Eden said. 'How do you know that many people?'

'I don't. They are all Isaac's colleagues and associates,' Bella said, the smile fixed on her face.

'I had no idea it was that many people,' Isaac said. 'I just let Claudia handle the guest list. The only ones I wanted there was these guys and my mum. Why so many people?'

'Claudia said these were people that we had to invite.'

'Well, I suppose there are some colleagues that I would invite but that many people seems a bit much.'

'Everyone who was invited is bringing their partners or wives or husbands. If you're not happy I can try to cancel some of them,' Bella said.

'No, no, it's OK. Don't do that. God, I feel awful, this is turning into such a big event and I feel like I've not done anything to contribute in the organisation. Selling off BlazeStar and SparkStar is taking a lot longer than I anticipated and I just want to be done with that and be here for you instead of travelling backwards and forwards to London all the time.'

Eden knew Isaac had been really stressed recently. He had accidentally fallen into making computer programs and phone apps for companies when he had graduated from university and built two very successful companies out of it but it wasn't what he really wanted to do. Being with Bella had made him re-evaluate what he wanted from life and he had started to take a step back from his computer companies, eventually deciding to sell them completely so he could work with Dougie on making computer games which he loved but the sale had involved countless trips to London and too many meetings to count.

'I'm an events manager, this is what I do,' Bella said. 'Besides, Claudia has been… very helpful.'

Eden saw Isaac frown and she knew he had noticed the pause as much as everyone else had.

'Look, why don't we try to scale it down a bit? There's still a whole month until the big day and after Christmas I should be able to help you some more.'

'No, it's fine. Weddings are always stressful. It's going to be beautiful,' Bella said.

Isaac kissed Bella on the cheek and she smiled. 'It will be, I can't wait to see you in your dress.'

The dress had arrived a few days before and it looked stunning. Bella was thrilled with it and at least that was one thing she was happy about.

'You know, we nearly missed our wedding,' Finn said, as he poured water into everyone's glasses.

'You did?' Bella asked, clearly glad of the distraction.

'Don't tell them that story,' Lucy said, flapping her hands ineffectually at Finn when he leaned back in his chair ready to impart the details anyway.

'Well as you probably know, we got married here on the island. I was at the church waiting for the guests and my lovely bride to arrive and most of the guests had already got there when I realised that I had on the wrong shoes. I'd worn trainers that morning because the bloody wedding shoes were so uncomfortable and I was going to change before I left the house and completely forgot. Knowing that Lucy probably would be a little late anyway, I figured I had time to nip back to the house and get them. So I ran across the town and back to her mum's house and grabbed the shoes and I figured that Lucy was upstairs finishing getting ready so I wouldn't disturb her – bad luck to see the bride before the wedding and all that. But then, as I went back into the hall to leave, Lucy walks down the stairs. She looked so beautiful, so utterly incredible, and I felt so overwhelmed that she was about to be my wife. She must have seen the look in my eyes because the next thing she was pushing her sisters and mum out of the door saying she was going to help me look for my shoes and would meet them all there. Well, I won't go into details but we had the most amazing sex up against the wall and then again over the back of the sofa. The carriage driver came and knocked on the door and we were way too busy to answer it. Finally we stopped and realised that we were nearly an hour late by that point. We went outside and the carriage driver had gone so we had to run across town together. Well, the priest thought we weren't coming; guests had started to leave because they thought the wedding had been cancelled. And to top it off, it was quite obvious what we had been doing: Lucy's hair was a mess, my clothes were rumpled and I was still wearing my bloody trainers. Luckily the priest had time to give us a quick ceremony before he had a christening to take care of, but we nearly missed the whole thing. Her mum wasn't happy with me, I can tell you. So as long as that doesn't happen on your wedding day, I'm sure it will be a big success. Well unless you want to, of course. I'm sure lots of couples have sex on their wedding day.'

'Normally afterwards, Dad,' Eden said as Dougie laughed by her side.

'Yes, well of course after,' Finn said. 'But before too. The whole "don't see the bride before the wedding day" malarkey is just a load of codswallop. If you want to have sex before the ceremony, you go right ahead.'

'Thanks for your approval,' Bella said, smiling.

Eden smiled and shook her head. At least Bella was smiling again but Eden knew she was going to have to do something about this wedding.

CHAPTER 7

Dougie walked into the lounge after wrapping up some Christmas presents upstairs. They'd left Eden's parents early as Lucy and Finn were going to Cornwall the next day, so it was still relatively early in the evening. Eden was staring at the flames in the fireplace as they danced and swirled. The fairy lights twinkled and sparkled from the tree in the corner, where there were already presents for all her family neatly wrapped and covered in pretty bows and for a moment he was struck with this sweet moment of domestic bliss.

His family life had never been particularly idyllic. As a child, his parents had… ticked along. He'd presumed at the time they were happy, though in reality he'd never seen any sign of that. Then again, he'd never seen any sign of unhappiness either. They weren't married back then, and it never really occurred to him to wonder why at the time. They'd married when he was thirteen and, while he wasn't sure what made them tie the knot at that point when they had already been together for so many years, what he was sure of was that that was when it had all gone wrong, as if a switch had been flicked and they suddenly hated each other. His parents had argued constantly after that. They mostly fought about his dad not being good enough for his mum, which she had proved to him shortly after moving to America by leaving his dad for someone far richer and more successful.

Although they had celebrated Christmas together when he was a teenager, the day had invariably been ruined with rows; the presents his dad had bought for his mum weren't good enough, the turkey was overcooked or undercooked, his mum could always find fault in everything his dad did. It had been something of a relief when they had finally divorced when Dougie was nineteen. It had just been him and his dad for many years. The only advice his dad ever gave him, and he gave him it frequently, was to never get married, never get tied down, 'as women will suck the life out of you,' and 'you'll never make them happy, no matter what you do'. It was no surprise then that, although Dougie had never been against marriage, he'd never actively looked for it either.

But staying with Eden every few months for the last twelve years had always felt like coming home, there was peace and contentment here. He loved spending time with his best friend and he didn't think he would ever get tired of that. He watched her, obviously deep in thought as she watched the flames flicker, and wondered, not for the first time, what it would be like to be married to Eden, to spend every night with her for the rest of his life and he couldn't help the huge smile that spread on his face with that thought. Marriage scared him, but forever with Eden didn't.

She looked up at him and smiled but he could see the worry in her eyes. He sat down in the corner of the sofa next to her and put his arm around her and without question she snuggled into his chest. He liked that.

'You OK?'

She nodded. 'I'm just worried about Bella.'

'And the wedding? Yes, I'm worried too.'

Eden was so protective over her adopted sister. Bella had not had an easy start in life. His uncle had had an affair with Bella's mum, a summer fling that had happened purely because Bella's mum wanted to get back at her husband for having his own affairs. It resulted in an unwanted pregnancy and an unloved child. Bella had eventually been adopted and raised by her aunt Lucy, Eden's wonderful mum, but not before Bella had endured the first few years of her life without any love from her mum or her mum's husband, who Bella had assumed was her dad. Bella believed she was unlovable and Eden was fiercely protective of her because of it. It wasn't until Isaac came along that Bella finally believed in love again and everyone wanted this marriage to work out and for her to be happy.

'She doesn't want this wedding, I can see that. Don't get me wrong, she wants to be married to Isaac, she loves him with everything she has, but this wedding is getting bigger by the day and I just don't think she really wants any of that. Knowing Bella, she would probably be happy to have a quick registry office ceremony and then go to Rosa's after for some pasta and some wine.'

'You know what, I don't think Isaac wants this wedding either.'

'I thought that too. But she is doing all this for him. She's having it in London for him, she hates the place.'

'Isaac has never been in love with that place. There are things he misses, of course there are, just like there are things I miss about New York, but being here is far far better.'

She smiled at that. 'You really think so?'

He stared at her denim blue eyes, her long dark lashes and the tiny smattering of freckles on her nose. 'I know so.'

Her smile grew and then she looked away back into the fire. She was silent for a moment. She was thinking about something else and he suspected it wasn't to do with Bella and Isaac.

She cleared her throat before she spoke as if trying to get back on topic. 'Well, if neither Bella or Isaac want to get married in London, why are they getting married there?'

'He thinks she wants the big fairy-tale wedding, the hotel they are doing it at is very posh, there's a big ballroom with chandeliers and gold ornate mirrors. And he wants to pull out all the stops to give her the wedding he thinks she wants.'

'She doesn't want any of that. All those hundreds of guests, she doesn't know any of them.'

'Isaac's colleagues and business associates. That's his assistant's fault, Claudia. I think she's brilliant and Isaac does too; she is a machine when it comes to organising anything, but she always has an eye on business opportunities and networking and any chance for hobnobbing is a good thing in her books. A lot of those corporate bigwigs in the city will have big society weddings; Isaac has been to enough of them over the years, and I think Claudia thinks that's the socially expected thing to do. Isaac is going along with it because he thinks Bella wants a big wedding and Bella is going along with it to make Isaac happy.'

Eden groaned. 'They need to talk to each other.'

'I know, I think they both are at that stage of the relationship where they just want to make the other person happy.'

'Should we say something?' Eden said.

Dougie realised that he was playing with the ends of her hair, letting it run over his fingers. He quickly let go but Eden hadn't seemed to notice at all. He wasn't sure if he was relieved or disappointed by that. How could he ever get close to her if his affection was always seen as just the norm?

He realised that she was waiting for an answer.

'I was thinking the same thing, I don't want to interfere but they can't see what we can see and I don't want either of them to be unhappy. Maybe we'll get Christmas out of the way and talk to them about it then. I know Bella is still busy with the Christmas festival so maybe now isn't the best time,' he said.

Eden nodded and leaned her head against his shoulder for a moment. 'Oh, I'm so glad you feel the same way and that I've spoken to you about this. I didn't know what to do, but now I have you on my side too I feel better about tackling it.'

'I'm always on your side,' Dougie said softly and she looked up at him.

Neither of them said anything for a while and then she gently pulled out of his arms as if the intimacy was too much for her.

'So tell me about your new venture with Isaac. He'll be working with you three days a week after Christmas?' Eden asked.

Dougie nodded. 'Yes initially. I think he would like to do more, but he is still heavily involved with the Umbrella Foundation charity. I think he likes working there because he gets to work alongside Bella every day but I think eventually he will come and work with me full-time.'

'Are you looking forward to working with him?'

'Yes, very much. Working alongside him was part of the reason why I came back to Hope Island. He has skills and knowledge that I just don't have. He has a lot of imagination too. We're starting a new project actually. A lot of the computer games are quite violent and though children love them we thought we would make something sweeter and cuter for those children with a… gentler disposition.'

'You mean computer games for girls?' Eden said, smiling. 'Nothing like a bit of gender stereotyping.'

He laughed. 'Believe me, that's the last thing I want to do, but girls love playing computer games too and so many of the games are geared towards… well, boys. Blowing things up, killing people, riding fast cars, sword-fighting – the bloodier and gorier the better. And girls love playing those games too but there are a lot of girls and boys actually who are more delicate. On test audiences we ran in the States a lot of the girls we tested didn't like to shoot the "poor animals", even though those poor animals were savage beasts trying to kill them, and they winced when there was a lot of blood. In quest games the girls were more likely to pick up pretty jewels, animal sidekicks or magic potions rather than many of the boys who were mostly choosing big scary weapons. So we wanted something a little gentler, something still fun, quests, challenges to overcome, jewels to collect, magic potions, flying unicorns and dragons to ride on, but no killing. So we've come up with some ideas for fairy games. There will be a series of different fairy games all set in the same fairy kingdom. The players will get to choose who their characters are, and yes, there will be an equal amount of boy and girl fairies to choose from to avoid any gender stereotyping. There won't be an abundance of pink either, but hopefully a lot of children will like it. Feedback from parents shows they would like this sort of thing too as many of them don't want their children playing violent games.'

'This sounds right up my street,' Eden said. 'I love the idea of flying on the back of a unicorn and collecting magic potions. Children will love that. Adults too.'

'I had you in mind when I was thinking of this; you were always obsessed with fairies and unicorns growing up. The fairy I've used in all the simulations and while I've been designing it is called Eden.'

Her whole face lit up. 'You named a character in one of your games after me?'

'Yes, of course. Would you be willing to test it out once I've finished it?'

'Absolutely. This sounds amazing.'

He smiled, somehow needing her approval on this and relieved that he'd got it. In truth the game had been made for her, so it was important that she liked it.

'Well I'm not remotely tired, do you want to watch a movie or something?' Eden asked. 'I have loads of cheesy Christmas films we can watch.'

'I think if I was to watch a film now, I'd probably fall asleep as I'm still a bit jet-lagged and I'd rather spend the night talking to you than fall asleep again on the sofa. Do you fancy playing a board game?'

From the huge smile on her face he knew immediately that he'd said the right thing. She loved playing games: Pictionary,

Trivial Pursuits, Risk, even Snakes and Ladders. The rest of her family didn't really have any interest in it, they just did it for her once a year at Christmas. So the only other time she got to play was when he came home to visit. He loved it too, they both got highly competitive and would ruthlessly cheat to outdo the other and spend the night laughing so hard. He liked to think that's why she enjoyed playing games so much – because she had so much fun with him. It was definitely the reason he liked playing games with her.

'We could play strip poker,' Dougie suggested as he got up and moved to the cupboard where all her games were kept.

She laughed as he knew she would. 'We are not playing strip poker.'

'Strip Trivial Pursuits then?'

'No, no strip games at all.'

'Damn it. OK, Cluedo then?'

'Oh yes, I haven't played that for ages.'

The cupboard was right next to where her tree was and he had to open it through the branches, the tree ornaments hitting him in the face as he tried to reach through the leaves to get into the cupboard.

'I like your tree ornaments,' Dougie said as one clonked him painfully on the head. 'Bit heavy though.'

Eden giggled. 'They're pottery ones; these are ones I've hand-painted myself. But next year I'm hoping I might have some decorations on my tree that I've hand-made as well as hand-painted.'

Dougie sat back on his heels to look at her as excitement creeped into her voice.

'We had a pottery wheel delivered this morning. I want to take the pottery painting café in a new direction and offer pottery-making workshops too. If it proves popular then I'll buy some more pottery wheels. But my plan is it won't just be teaching people how to use the wheel, I want to run pottery-making classes, teaching coiling, sculpting and various other techniques. I want to teach people about glazing and how to make their own glazes too. I learned all this stuff at college and never used any of it. I really want to be able to offer workshops to children especially. There is nothing really for the children to do here on Hope Island. The school offers lots of sporting extra-curricular activities but a lot of the children are just not into sports. They hang around in the parks and beaches because they have nothing else to do with their time and then they leave the island as soon as they can. And I know there's nothing I can do to stop them leaving, exploring the world, discovering life outside of the Scillies. Hell, a younger more adventurous me would have gone off and explored the world too, but I want to inspire them to be creative, to show them there are things they can do that aren't academic or sporty. I've been talking to Rome about it and he and Freya are keen to get involved too. They are going to offer stained and fused glass workshops as well, the kids will love that.'

He smiled at her, loving her passion. 'That sounds like a wonderful idea.'

'I have a large shed out the back of the shop. It's filled with junk at the moment but I'm going to clear it out and do it up, and I'll run some of the classes back there so it's more private and won't get in the way of the regular customers who come into the café.'

'I could help you, I have some time. I'm a dab hand at painting and decorating,' Dougie said, wanting more than anything to make this dream come true for her.

'You painted your penthouse apartment, did you?' Eden smirked.

'Well, no, it was already decorated when I moved in but I used to help Dad on some of his decorating jobs when I was younger.'

Eden grinned. 'I'd love that.'

'Or if you needed money to help start this side of your business up, I could help…' he trailed off as she shook her head as he'd known she would. His mum had once told him he needed money to impress women and he'd worked really hard over the years to get into a position where he would never need to worry about money again, and with this wealth he loved being able to help others, give financial support where needed, surprise his friends with gifts. But Eden seemingly didn't want any of that. She wasn't impressed with money, which meant he'd have to impress her another way.

'I don't want your money, you work hard for that. If using the pottery wheel becomes popular and I have to get more, it will be expensive but I have money squirrelled away that will help to cover that. Although I have to learn how to use it myself first.'

'You don't know how to use a pottery wheel, but you work in a pottery café,' Dougie teased.

'I know, I feel thoroughly ashamed. Besides, everyone comes in to paint the things, not make them.'

'I can teach you,' Dougie said as he turned his attention back to the games, freed Cluedo from the contents of the cupboard and passed it to her.

'You know how to use a pottery wheel?'

'Just one of the many things I've learned at my night classes over the years. I can't say I'm an expert but I can certainly teach you the basics.'

'I'd really like that. I was just going to watch some videos on YouTube and hope for the best, but I'd love it if you could teach me. We could have our own *Ghost* moment,' she giggled.

Dougie stood back up. 'What's that?'

He was surprised to see her suddenly blush.

'Oh nothing, just a scene from the film *Ghost* involving a pottery wheel. Patrick Swayze wasn't very good at it, it was funny.' She waved her hand dismissively and he knew there was something she wasn't saying.

'Well, we can do it one of the nights this week if you want, after the shop has closed,' Dougie said as he followed her to the kitchen to set up the game on the dining table.

'That would be great, who would you like to be?' Eden said, referring to the characters in the game.

'I'll be Professor Plum.' He looked over at her and saw her cheeks were still pink from the thought of that scene from *Ghost*. 'And I think you should be Miss Scarlett.'

She blushed again but didn't say anything as she sorted through the cards and set the game up.

He vowed that when he got a chance, he was going to look up that scene to see for himself exactly what it was about it that had made her blush.

🌲🌲

Eden lay on the sofa and watched the fairy lights dance across the ceiling. Dougie had already gone on up to bed a while before, though she could still hear him moving around upstairs.

They'd played games all night, drank mulled wine and laughed so much that her face had started to ache. She wasn't drunk, she was a long way off from that, but she was feeling completely and blissfully happy. And that was a dangerous place to be.

Because while she was lying there, warm and cosy with a big grin on her face, she would let her mind wonder about what life would be like if Dougie lived with her all the time and how utterly fabulous that would be. They would spend their evenings like they had tonight, talking, laughing, playing games or watching movies and they wouldn't need to be together or even married to enjoy that. She would have her best friend living with her and nothing could be better than that. Well, apart from if they were married. That would be pretty bloody spectacular because then they'd get to kiss and make love and some nights he would carry her to bed. And that would be pretty bloody spectacular indeed. She frowned slightly. If everything was pretty bloody spectacular she probably was the teeniest tiniest bit drunk.

She heard footsteps on the stairs as Dougie came back down and then he was there standing in front of the sofa wearing only his Rudolph pyjama bottoms. She had already got changed into her pyjamas a few hours ago. Which ones had she worn? Were they the pretty ones? She tried to look down but she couldn't see much when the room was lit only with fairy lights.

'You OK?' Dougie asked.

God, his chest was a glorious thing, all big and yummy.

She grinned at him and gave him a salute. Yep, probably a little bit drunk.

He smirked at the salute and with good reason. She'd never saluted anyone before in her life.

'I thought you might have fallen asleep down here,' Dougie said.

'Nope, just enjoying smiling.'

Just enjoying smiling? What kind of weird-ass answer was that?

He snorted at that and then changed it into a cough to cover it up. He bent down and scooped her up into his arms.

'I can walk, you know,' Eden said, wrapping her arms round his neck, purely to keep her balance and not for any other reason. 'You don't need to carry me to bed.'

'I know I don't need to, but I want to.'

She didn't really have anything to say to that as he carried her up the stairs and into her room.

'I've been thinking,' Eden said as he laid her down gently on her bed. She rolled over on her side and snuggled into her pillow.

'About what?'

'I think you should stay with me,' Eden said. It made sense. Otherwise they'd be two lonely people living next door to each other instead of two happy people living with each other.

'OK.'

Dougie slipped into bed behind her and covered them both with the duvet. Eden frowned for a moment and then nearly laughed. He'd completely misunderstood. But as he curled himself around her back and wrapped his arms around her, any comments she had been about to make dried in her throat.

She closed her eyes and relished in the warmth of his body next to hers.

'I didn't mean tonight, I meant forever,' Eden murmured as she started to fall asleep.

'OK,' Dougie said, without any hesitation.

She smiled. It didn't hurt to imagine what forever with Dougie would look like for just a little bit longer. She drifted off to sleep thinking that enjoying smiling was pretty bloody spectacular actually.

CHAPTER 8

Eden was shaken gently awake the next day. She woke up blearily and noticed that it was still dark outside.

Dougie was standing next to the bed holding out a bacon sandwich and a mug of tea.

She sat up and looked at him in confusion. 'What time is it?'

'Half past seven, I'm going for a walk on the beach to watch the sunrise, thought you might want to come with me before you go to work. Of course you might want to stay in bed for another half hour; I can always go on my own.'

'Oh, I'd like to come.'

'Good. I've missed that sunrise – it's just not the same watching the sunrise through a ton of skyscrapers as it is watching it over the sea. Sunrise is at twenty past eight, so you've got a bit of time to eat your breakfast.'

She took the sandwich from him and propped herself up against the headboard. She took a bite and watched as Dougie settled himself next to her as he opened his newspaper. It was such a coupley thing to do, as if he was just contented to be with her, rather than going off to read it in the kitchen or the lounge.

Memories of the night before came back to her as she chewed, how much fun she'd had with him playing the games and then how he'd slept in her bed with her.

'We slept together last night,' Eden blurted out.

Dougie put his paper down and turned to face her with a big grin on his face.

'Yes we did.' He stroked his finger up her arm. 'Was it as good for you as it was for me?'

She ignored the innuendo. 'Why did you sleep in here?'

'Because you asked me to.'

She put her sandwich back on the plate and thought back to the night before.

'You asked me to stay with you,' Dougie explained, his eyes alight with amusement.

It all came back. She *had* asked him to stay with her.

'But I didn't mean that, I meant…' she trailed off because what she actually meant was probably even more embarrassing.

'You explained what you meant; you said you wanted me to stay forever.'

Eden picked up her sandwich and took a big bite, while she played for time. He was still watching her, waiting for some kind of explanation, though she could see he wasn't taking this remotely seriously.

She swallowed. 'I didn't mean… That makes it sound a lot worse than it is. I just meant…' She sighed. 'I like having you here, it's nice to have some company and we get on so well. All I meant was that it would be fun if we actually lived together. But not as a couple, just as two friends. You'd be my lodger, nothing more.'

The smile on his face faded away. 'Your lodger?'

'Yes, exactly.'

'Nothing more?'

She could see that she'd hurt him with that comment. 'No, I didn't mean that. You're my best friend, there is no one in the entire world I would rather spend my time with than you. That's why in my mulled-wine-addled brain last night I was proposing that we live together. Which is ridiculous, you wouldn't want to live with me, I know that, but I did really mean just as friends.'

'Got it, just friends, nothing more.' Dougie picked up the newspaper and carried on reading.

Well, this was suddenly awkward. And Eden had no idea what was the right thing to say to make it better. She could hardly tell him that as she had thought about how wonderful it would be to live with him the night before, what she'd really wanted was to be married to him and live the rest of their lives as husband and wife. But in trying to convince him that her comments of the night before didn't mean that she had feelings for him, she'd gone too far and hurt his feelings instead.

'It was nice having you sleep in my bed last night,' Eden said quietly, focussing her attention on the remains of her sandwich.

Nice?

That didn't even come close to describing how it had felt to have his body wrapped around hers as she fell asleep.

He didn't say anything for the longest time and when he did speak he didn't look at her either.

'I thought so too.'

What did he mean by that?

He folded the newspaper and climbed off the bed. 'You need to get dressed, we have to leave shortly.'

And with that he left the room, leaving Eden feeling more confused than ever.

By the time she had got dressed and gone downstairs, Dougie seemed to have forgotten their previous conversation and was back to his normal happy self. He passed her scarf and coat to her and then pulled her woolly pompom hat on over her head. A few moments later they were out on the street and Dougie took her hand again as he led her down towards Buttercup Beach.

'I'm looking forward to going with you to Mistletoe Cove tonight,' Dougie said. 'Have you thought any more about your three wishes?'

They walked down the steps onto the beach as the sky in front of them turned an inky blue in preparation for the day.

'There's only one thing I want.' The same thing that she had wanted all her life but it was an impossible dream.

'Wish for it at Mistletoe Cove and it will come true.'

Eden sighed. She definitely wasn't going to get her hopes up.

'And it needs to be three wishes for it to work. Apart from the one thing that you really want, what else would you like?'

'There's nothing I want as much as that.'

'A sports car, a holiday home in the Bahamas?'

'Are they the kind of things you want? I know you could probably afford those things.'

'No, I don't.'

'I don't either. Why would I need a sports car? Hope Island is probably only two miles all the way round. And I don't want a holiday home in the Bahamas either. I live in one of the most beautiful places in the world. It might be hotter in the Bahamas right now, but I'd take Hope Island any day. Besides, if I did have a holiday home in the Bahamas, how would I fly there? My pottery painting café is doing very well, but I'm no millionaire. I certainly don't have the money to fly to the Bahamas on a regular basis.'

'There's got to be something.'

'It's hard really. I'm very happy with my life – as I said, there's only one thing that would make me happier. What would you wish for?'

'I've already had my three wishes.'

'But if you hadn't, what would you wish for right now?'

Dougie was quiet for a while as they walked hand in hand along the shore. 'I guess I would wish that it was the right decision coming back here.'

That was like a kick to the stomach and so unexpected. He'd only been back a few days and he was regretting it already.

'You don't think it was the right decision to come back here?'

'No I do, Hope Island has always felt like home, I love it here. And regardless of what happens I think it will always be home for me. And if I'm going to be working alongside Isaac in my company, I can't do that as easily if I'm in New York and he's here, but…'

She waited for him to finish but when he was still silent she prompted him. 'But what?'

'There was another reason I wanted to come back here. Well, quite an important reason actually, and although coming home to Hope Island felt like the right thing to do and working with Isaac is reason enough to make that change, in my heart I know that it was the other reason that brought me here.'

'What was that?'

'I can't tell you, not yet. But right now, I want that to work more than anything else.'

They were silent for a while and Dougie sat down on the cool sand, so she sat next to him.

'If it doesn't work out, will you go back to New York?'

Out on the horizon a fragment of rose gold lit up the midnight sea. They watched it for a moment, the beauty of it silencing them both.

Dougie slipped his arm around her and she rested her head on his shoulder.

'Right now, I don't want to be anywhere else but here,' he kissed her on the head. 'But who knows what will happen in the future.'

She swallowed down the pain of the thought of him leaving again.

'Well in that case I know what my wish will be.'

'What's that?'

'That your wish comes true and whatever brought you here works out for you, so you can stay.'

'You want me to stay?'

She looked out at the line of gold that was growing, sending its sparkling blanket over the waves.

'More than anything.'

'More than the thing you were going to wish for?'

She didn't dare tell him that the two were irrevocably linked. But in actual fact she wanted him here more than she wanted to be with him so she nodded.

He looked out over the sea and they watched the sun until it was too bright for them to stare at any more. Then Dougie stood up and pulled her to her feet. He wrapped his arms around her and held her. She wished that this gesture meant as much to him as it did to her, but he had always been a very tactile person.

'If me staying makes you happy then I'll stay.'

'You will?'

Dougie was such a generous person, but she never expected him to alter the course of his whole life just to make her happy.

'I want to make you happy and I don't want you to waste a wish on me. I want it to be something you want for you, not for me.'

'Wishing for you to stay here is for me, it's completely selfish, believe me. I have my best friend back and I don't want to lose you again.'

'You won't, I promise. It was silly of me to say that. I will be disappointed if it doesn't work the way I want it to work, but I won't leave because of it. You're too important to me for that.'

She leaned her forehead against his chest and he cupped the back of her neck. God, why couldn't he be hers? This wonderful, kind man, she loved him so much. And they'd be great together, she knew that. Why couldn't he see it? How could he hold her like this and not have feelings for her? It was beyond heartbreaking. But if this was all he was willing to give her, then she'd take it over not having him in her life at all.

'We better go back, you've got to go to work and I've got some things to take care of. Think about your wishes,' Dougie said.

She sighed because no amount of wishing was going to change what they had between them and it was futile to hope for that. She nodded anyway because there was no point telling him any of that.

But regardless of the wishes, she was looking forward to spending the night with him at Mistletoe Cove. They would have fun, talk, laugh, toast marshmallows by the fire and she would try really hard not to remember that that was exactly how it had been the night they had first kissed.

CHAPTER 9

Dougie stood on the shores of Mistletoe Cove and looked up at the hawthorn trees that jutted out from the steep grassy banks above him. It was a magical place, a secret secluded haven that hardly anyone ever came to. The hawthorn trees were heavy with mistletoe, making them look as if they had been decorated especially for Christmas. He knew that on occasions people looking for an easy buck would come by boat to the cove and climb up to the trees to get the mistletoe to sell but it wasn't as easy as it looked to get up there, and he was proof of that. He licked his fingers to wipe away the bloody scratches on his arms. Most people now were happy to leave the mistletoe alone and without interference it grew in abundance.

Water spraying out of the blowhole at the far side of the cove drew his attention, sending water some ten or twenty feet up into the air. The blowhole was going to be even harder to get to, situated at the top of a tall standing rock. But he had already had a good look round the rock and found a slightly easier route to the top on the far side.

He and Eden used to do a lot of rock climbing and coasteering when they were younger, using the rocks and coastlines as their adventure playground. She was as nimble as a mountain goat, jumping from rock to rock with apparent ease and completely without fear. They used to challenge each other to do some ridiculously stupid and crazy things, which was why they had first decided to venture to Mistletoe Cove. The fact that the police on the island had banned anyone from going down to it after a few horrible accidents meant, of course, that it was more attractive to Eden and him. It was a miracle that both of them were still alive and had escaped their childhood and teenage years relatively unscathed. He wondered if she was still as brave and fearless now or whether she had lost that along with her belief in magic and wishes.

It broke his heart that she had lost that wonder and hope. She had been such a happy girl growing up; it just sparkled out of her. But in the months just before he had left for America, after he had announced he was leaving, he had watched that sparkle slowly fade away. Maybe it was just growing up, becoming an adult and letting go of those childish ways, or maybe it was something else that had dulled her shine. He knew she had a job she loved, she was happy in her little cottage with its sea views from the back of the garden. She had a wonderful family and a close group of friends. She loved living on the island but something was missing from her life. He wanted her to sparkle again and he had no idea how to give that to her but he was going to give it his best shot.

He looked back up at the trees and smiled, then climbed back up the large boulders to the cave entrance and scrambled up the rocks and through the cave until he hauled himself out in the grassy meadow. Then he took off at a run heading back to the town. He didn't want to admit that the coffee he'd got from Eden's café was better than the stuff he had been drinking in New York for the past twelve years but he knew it was likely to become a daily habit.

As he reached the park, he spotted Rome out for a run too. Normally Rome would be at work by now, creating stunning glass pieces with his wife Freya. Although as it was Saturday it was possible that the glass studio was opening a little later. With only a few days left until Christmas a lot of the shops were now on reduced opening hours as they wound down for their festive break. Most shops, once they closed on Christmas Eve, wouldn't open again until the New Year, and some had closed already.

He waved at his friend and Rome came running over to talk to him. Rome stopped in front of him trying to catch his breath for a second before he spoke.

'How's it going?' Rome asked. 'Does it feel good to be home?'

Dougie thought back to spending the night with Eden and how wonderful it had felt to wake up and find her in his arms this morning.

He thought about how good it had felt to walk hand in hand with her along the beach and hear her say that she wanted him to stay.

'Yeah, it feels pretty bloody fantastic to be home actually.'

Rome nodded and indicated that they should carry on running so Dougie fell in at his side and they jogged around the perimeter of the park.

'How's married life treating you?' Dougie asked.

A huge smile spread across Rome's face, which caused Dougie to smile himself. He loved seeing his friend happy. After Rome's fiancée had died in a horrible accident six years before, Dougie had thought that Rome would never find love again but then Freya had come along and saved him in more ways than one.

'Getting married to Freya is the best thing I've ever done. Do you know what it feels like to wake up every morning with a huge smile on your face, to find the woman you love with everything you have lying asleep in your arms? I can't even begin to describe how happy I am. And yes, I know I sound like a complete girl, feel free to take the piss out of me, I would if I was you, but I don't even care.'

And normally Dougie would. Rome was one of his closest friends, they had grown up together and theirs was a relationship where they would wind each other up constantly, always knocking each other or trying to outdo the other, but Dougie couldn't because he wanted all of that too.

'And how do you feel about becoming a dad?'

'I am so excited, you wouldn't believe it. I'm probably more excited than Freya at the moment and she's over the moon. You know we spend most nights cuddled up in bed, reading baby books together. I could tell you more about that baby than I could about stained glass. I'm so ready for the baby to come now, frustrating that she has to keep it in there for another five months.'

'I'm envious of you,' Dougie said and it was a few seconds before he realised that Rome had stopped dead. He stopped running and turned to look at him. 'What? Are you OK?'

'I just never thought I'd see the day that Dougie Harrison was ready to settle down and have kids. You've never been the settling-down type.'

'This is my home now, probably for the rest of my life. It stands to reason that at some point I'm going to get married and have children one day. I see you and Bella so happy in your own relationships and I want that too.'

Rome stared at him as if he didn't recognise him. 'And has this change of heart got anything to do with Eden?'

Dougie sighed. He didn't want to talk about him and Eden. That felt private, even though nothing had really happened between them. 'I've got stuff to do, so I'm going to head back. I'll see you later.'

He turned to go but Rome snagged his arm. 'Look, I'm sorry if I was out of line with my comment the other day about you not being good enough for her. I was only joking, you know that, right?'

Dougie nodded.

'I would be delighted if you two got together.'

'The whole island wants us to get together, I'm not sure why.'

Rome grinned. 'Because that's what they do, the islanders have always been the same. But you stay at her house, everyone sees how close you two are, it's the natural progression in everyone's minds. Do you not see her that way?'

'She's my best friend.' He left it at that.

Rome studied him for a moment. 'Just… don't hurt her.'

'I have no intention of doing that.'

'Good. Because I really don't want to have to beat you up.'

Dougie grinned. 'I'll catch you later.'

Rome nodded and Dougie ran off in the opposite direction towards town.

He pushed the door open on Eden's pottery café and saw that she was struggling to do a painted footprint of a small baby boy. There was a young girl who couldn't have been older than thirteen years old holding the screaming baby and she didn't seem to be having much luck in quietening him either. Eden was desperately trying to get paint onto the baby's foot but the boy was kicking and screaming so much that she could barely get anywhere near him.

Dougie moved closer.

'Hey, what's going on here?' Dougie said in a singsong voice he hoped would distract the baby. It didn't work. He looked at the young girl who was looking very stressed and embarrassed about the situation. He winked at her. 'Is he yours?'

The girl laughed. 'No, he's my little brother. I was hoping to get a plate with his footprint on as a Christmas present for my parents but he just won't stop crying. He doesn't need changing, he's just been fed, but he still keeps crying. Maybe I should come back tomorrow and we can give it another go then.'

'No, don't go. Why don't we just leave him for a few minutes to calm down and we can try again in a while,' Dougie said.

'Have you tried Clare's amazing chocolate and ginger cake, it's to die for. Let me buy you a slice of that and once you've finished it we can try again.'

'Thank you,' the girl said, quietly.

He waved at Clare and she nodded.

'Here, why don't I hold him while you eat? What's his name?'

'Jake,' the girl said. She looked relieved to hand him over for a few minutes' reprieve and Dougie took the screaming bundle of arms and legs and held him up in the air, smiling at him as he brought him back down and then swung him back in the air again.

Jake, obviously shocked by the motion, momentarily stopped crying to stare at him. Dougie repeated the motion again and then brought him back down to cradle him in his arms. He looked at Jake, two huge angry blue eyes staring back at him. Dougie saw the lip quiver a little and Jake took a big in-breath so he could continue his wailing. Dougie quickly grabbed his foot and blew a raspberry on it, which had the effect of shocking the baby into submission again. Jake scowled at Dougie as if he couldn't quite believe that Dougie had the audacity to do such a thing to him, so Dougie did it again, this time aiming the raspberry onto Jake's toes. This elicited a little giggle so Dougie did it again. Then he did it on the other foot and Jake giggled again. He repeated this several times, breaking up the raspberry-blowing with puffing on Jake's feet too.

'Do you have a clean paintbrush?' he said softly to Eden. She quickly handed it to him and he used it to tickle across Jake's toes and then sweep across the feet. He could see Jake wasn't entirely happy with this new sensation, so he alternated blowing raspberries on Jake's feet and tickling him with the brush until the baby was used to it. Jake was still giggling intermittently, as if not entirely convinced that the whole thing was amusing, but at least he wasn't crying any more.

While bouncing him up and down in his arms, talking to him in a soft voice, he dipped the paintbrush into the water and then swept that across the feet too. Jake barely seemed to notice so Dougie decided to take his chances and dip the brush into the paint, sweeping it quickly across one of Jake's feet while talking to him, pulling funny faces and bouncing up and down.

Dougie looked at the foot and saw that there was enough paint on there and he nodded to Eden who quickly got the plate and held it against the foot to capture the print.

Jake protested a bit but the deed was done and Dougie soon distracted him with raspberries over his tiny little fists. Jake relented and laughed at Dougie's attempts to cheer him up. As Eden quickly wiped the foot clean Dougie picked up a toy crab from the table and shook it at Jake. Jake reached for it with his little chubby hands and Dougie passed it to him and then placed him down in the pushchair. Jake seemed quite happy now, playing with his crab and the other toys that were attached to the sides. He probably wouldn't stay quiet for long but at least the print was done.

'Thank you so much,' the girl said, as she finished her cake. She jiggled the pushchair a bit but Jake seemed more settled now.

'No problem at all.'

He turned to look at Eden who was staring at him in a mix of awe and frustration.

'You really can charm the birds from the trees, can't you?'

He shrugged. 'I have the magic touch.'

Eden just shook her head.

He looked over at Clare. 'Can I have a gingerbread latte to go?'

She nodded and set about making it for him. He turned his attention back to Eden.

'I have a meeting tonight with Isaac, so would you be able to meet me at the entrance to the meadow at around eleven o'clock?

I'll have everything ready for our *date*, so you don't need to bring anything other than your lovely self.'

Eden sighed and he could see she didn't really want to go. He had to admit sitting on a beach in the freezing cold in the middle of the night didn't exactly fill him with a warm glow either.

'Dougie, do we have to go through all this façade, you and I both know this isn't real. We could watch movies and cuddle on the sofa instead.'

Now that did sound very tempting but he had a plan and he meant to carry it out.

'Look, I promise it'll be worth it,' he said, fixing her with his best puppy dog eyes. 'Besides, you owe me for the baby-whispering.' He indicated Jake, who was now fast asleep.

She smiled and rolled her eyes and he knew he had won.

'Fine,' Eden said. 'I'll be there.'

Clare came round and gave him his coffee and again waved away his attempts to pay for the coffee and the cake. She hurried off to go and serve another customer and he turned back to face Eden.

He bent to give her a kiss on the cheek. 'I'll see you tonight.'

She smiled and he waved at Clare and at the girl then left.

He just had to hope that Eden would be as impressed with his efforts tonight as Jake had been with his raspberry tricks.

🌲🌲🌲

Eden watched him go and then went behind the counter with Clare. It was ridiculous but there were times he actually made her legs shake like jelly. It was such a cliché but seeing him holding Jake so sweetly pressed every emotional button inside her.

She let out a huff of breath and tried to ignore that Clare was staring at her with a big grin on her face.

'You ever been to Mistletoe Cove?' Eden asked, trying to change the subject.

'No, only crazy people go there, you'd cut yourself open on the hawthorn trees trying to get down to the beach. And the cliff side is so steep, so many people have hurt themselves trying to get the mistletoe and falling onto the shore.'

'There's a hidden cave that bypasses the hawthorn trees, I don't think many people know about it. There's still quite a climb down but it's not as hard as it first looks.'

She and Dougie had never seen the danger when they had been kids. The more they had been told to keep away, the more determined they had been to go there. They had found the cave by chance one day and although the rocks down to the beach on the other side of the cave were jagged and hard to navigate, they had faced them in that fearless way that all children seem to have and, after many visits, found the best possible route down to the sand.

Clare shook her head. 'The boys wanted to go down to it in the summer, but I told them that I'd like to keep them alive and intact, thank you very much. Of course that has made Bradley want to go down there even more.'

Eden smiled. That was exactly how she and Dougie had been as kids, always going where they shouldn't have gone.

'Have you seen the blowhole?' she asked.

'The wishing well, yes we saw it from the boat. Matthew loved it, he kept on cheering every time it erupted.'

Eden stilled in wiping the counter down. 'It's really called the wishing well?'

'Yes of course, many a wish has been granted from the wishing well.'

'Come on, you're having me on.'

Clare shook her head. 'No, I'm really not. Not every wish comes true but lots of people have had their wishes granted at the wishing well.'

Eden stared at her in disbelief. 'Why have I never heard about this before?'

'It was years ago that it was popular for people to go down there and make their wishes – before the war, I think. My gran used to tell me all about it. But then the hawthorn trees got really big and out of control and there was that horrible incident with Bill McKenzie and no one has ever really been back there since. But my gran had wishes come true after she threw them into the wishing well. She told me you have to write three wishes on a piece of paper and throw them into the well at midnight.'

This was a joke. Dougie had told Clare to say this to her. Clare was the most level-headed, rational person she knew. She was the least likely person in the world to believe in magic and wishes coming true, but she was saying it with such sincerity.

'What were the wishes?'

'She wished that her husband would come home safely from the war, she wished that her baby would be born healthy and – because those were the only two things she wanted and she knew it wouldn't work unless she had three wishes – she wished for something ridiculous.'

'What was that?'

'That'd she'd win the best in show for her cake at the summer fair.'

Eden laughed.

'All the wishes came true. My gran was a lousy cook. Her cakes were like biting into stones but that year, and only that year, her cake was amazing. Or so she says.'

Eden shook her head. She didn't believe it for one minute. Dougie's wishes and Clare's gran's wishes were all simply coincidences. Sure, meeting Harrison Ford was a pretty big coincidence, and making the best cake on the island when all your cakes had been disasters before was very lucky, but they weren't exactly impossible wishes.

'My gran wasn't the only one who had wishes come true,' Clare insisted, clearly seeing the doubt on Eden's face.

'If it really was a magical wishing well, people would be coming from all over the world to try it.'

'It was always supposed to be the island's little secret. As much as we love the tourists coming here, the islanders didn't want them arriving in their thousands back then. Apparently there was a town council meeting about the wishing well once it was found to be granting wishes. It was agreed by everyone on the island that we would never tell anyone off the island about it. And after Bill's accident and the police banned people from ever going there, it was almost forgotten by the locals over the years. Most of the people that were alive when the wishing well was popular are no longer with us, but my gran told me many stories about it before she died. I was always tempted to try it myself, but I don't have a death wish.'

Eden watched Clare carefully. She wouldn't be surprised for one minute if Dougie had told her to say all of that so that Eden would go that night. He had left the house for a run before Eden had left for work; maybe he'd gone down to see Clare then and told her all this rubbish to tell Eden. He was up to something, she was sure of it.

Clare shrugged. 'I know you don't believe me but if you're going down there, what have you got to lose? Just promise me you'll be careful.'

'I will.'

'And wish for something amazing. If you can get Ben Affleck to come to the café I'd love you forever.'

Eden laughed. 'OK, deal.'

CHAPTER 10

Eden stomped her feet and blew into her hands, pulling her hat down tighter onto her head. She looked across the meadow to see a golden orb of light was travelling quickly towards her. As it got closer she realised it was Dougie carrying a torch.

'Hello beautiful.' He bent and kissed her on the cheek. 'I've lit a fire on the beach so you'll soon be warm.'

He slung an arm round her shoulders and started guiding her back across the meadow, using the torch to light their way. Even though it was pitch black either side of the torch beam, she felt so completely safe in his arms.

'I know you talked to Clare,' Eden said as they walked up the hill. 'About what?'

'About the magic of Mistletoe Cove, all that rubbish about her gran's wishes coming true. I know you told her to say all that to get me to come with you tonight.'

'I haven't spoken to Clare. The legend of the wishing well at Mistletoe Cove is true and I knew you'd doubt it so I did some research into it.'

He dug his phone out of his pocket and pressed a few buttons and then passed it to her. She could see it was a page on Wikipedia titled 'Mistletoe Cove, Hope Island'. It was a really long article and she wasn't able to properly read the tiny print as they walked along but there was a huge section about the wishing well and the legend associated with it, giving some examples of when bizarre wishes had come true.

'Clare said that the islanders agreed they would never tell anyone about the magical powers of the wishing well, how then is it on Wikipedia?' Eden said, as she passed the phone back to him. She didn't believe any of this. There was no such thing as magic.

'You know what the islanders are like, they've never been able to keep a secret. Come on, watch your step, the cave entrance is just ahead.' He shone the torch and, hidden behind a large rock, she could see the darkness of the cave beyond. Except it didn't look particularly dark – golden shadows of light flickered from within.

She looked at Dougie in confusion. Mistletoe Cove was not known for its electrical supply.

'It's magic.'

She laughed.

'I'll go first,' Dougie said. He passed her the torch and then lowered himself into the cave. 'OK!' he called up to her.

She tucked the torch into her pocket and then lowered herself into the entrance. Immediately she felt his arms wrap around her legs and let go of the edge of the hole. He lowered her slightly so her face was level with his. She didn't need help getting in and out of the cave and he knew that; they'd done it hundreds of times as kids.

She rested her hands on his shoulders as he held her there against him.

'Don't get any ideas,' Eden said.

'I have lots of ideas,' Dougie said, as he leaned forward slightly and placed a tiny kiss on her nose. He was always doing something like this, hugging her, kissing her cheek, kissing her forehead. In her rose-tinted world she liked to imagine it was because he had feelings for her too, but this had long become the norm.

He lowered her to the floor and Eden looked around to see there were large white candles in various-sized storm lanterns leading down the cave. It looked beautiful.

'So these candles are magic candles?' she asked.

'Of course.'

He took her hand and led her through the cave just like he'd always done when they were kids. A nervous excitement rushed through her as she remembered the last time they had come to the cove and the kiss they'd shared. She knew it would never happen again but she couldn't help but smile at the memory. The path through the cave was uneven and they sploshed through several puddles as they clambered over rocks, slowly heading downwards towards the cove. Up ahead she could see the silvery ribbons of the moonlight dancing across the waves and the glow of the fire from the beach cast flickering golden shadows across the cave mouth.

She walked to the entrance of the cave and stopped as she looked down on Mistletoe Cove. There was a great big roaring fire in the middle of the small beach with blankets laid out on the sand to the back of it but... She hesitated as her eyes became more accustomed to the bright lights of the fire. The flames were blue. Not just blue – as they danced and twirled in the night sky, she could clearly see hues of lilac, green and turquoise too.

'How did you do that?' Eden said. She had never seen anything so beautiful.

'It's not me, it's the magic of Mistletoe Cove,' Dougie said.

Eden laughed and then moved to climb down the large rocks that actually looked like giant steps cut into the rock face.

Dougie moved ahead of her. 'I'll go first.'

She followed him down and smiled when he kept looking back to check on her. They finally made it down onto the beach and Dougie took her hand again and led her to the fire. She sat down and he wrapped a thick fur blanket around her shoulders then sat down next to her. The heat from the fire was intense and she soon forgot the cold of the night as she stared at the blue flames. They sat in silence for a while, watching the flames dance and change colour against the inky backdrop of the sky. They didn't need to say anything. Being together was enough. His arm was around her shoulders, holding her against him, and for a short time everything was perfect with the world.

'Come on then, tell me how you did it?' Eden said.

Dougie pulled his phone out of his pocket and passed it to her again.

'Scroll down past the stuff about the wishing well, there's stuff about fires in there too.'

She rolled her eyes but did as she was told. She found the part of the article he was talking about and started reading aloud.

'"Because of the high level of fairy dust in the air surrounding Mistletoe Cove, lighting a fire can cause a chemical reaction with the fairy dust and cause the flames to turn blue…"' Eden read. 'You've written this Wiki page, haven't you?' she laughed. 'The wishing well, now the fairy dust in the air. All of this is your doing. You're up to something, Douglas Harrison. What is it?'

'It's not me,' Dougie laughed. 'If it's on Wiki, it must be true. I wouldn't have the first clue how to create my own Wiki page.'

'Says the computer geek,' Eden said.

'It's obviously based on factual evidence; scientific tests have clearly been done on the high level of fairy dust in Mistletoe Cove and—'

'You're such a liar,' Eden laughed, launching herself at him and poking and tickling everywhere she could reach through his thick coat. He fell back on the sand and took her with him. He wriggled and screamed and laughed as she continued to poke him, then he rolled on top of her and pinned her hands above her head.

'Stop poking me,' he laughed as she looked up into his beautiful green eyes that sparkled in the light of the fire.

Suddenly the humour died as they stared at each other and he gently brushed a strand of hair from her face. He didn't say anything, just stared at her and for one wonderful blissful moment she was sure he was going to kiss her, before he suddenly leapt to his feet.

'You need to write your wishes, it's important you throw them into the wishing well at exactly midnight.'

She sat up, feeling suddenly embarrassed and vulnerable over the moment that had passed as quickly as it had arrived.

'Fine, come on then, let's get this nonsense out of the way and then you can toast me some of those marshmallows I can see in your bag,' Eden said, holding her hand out for the pen and paper that Dougie had just pulled out of his bag.

He passed it to her.

'I wish for a magical flying unicorn,' Eden said, putting pen to paper.

Dougie suddenly knelt down in front of her, putting his hand out to stop her writing. 'It has to be something that's possible. The wishing well can't bring people back from the dead, it can't give you super powers or give you a magical flying unicorn. And it has to be something you really want, something you want more than anything in the world.'

'Dougie, this is ridiculous, me throwing a scrap of paper into a blowhole is not going to grant me my wishes. There is no such thing as magic. There is no special force in the world, no fairies or deities or angels or lucky pennies or stars that will be able to grant me my wish. All this,' she gestured to the fire, 'and the Wiki page and the candles and Clare's story about her gran is lovely but it's all rubbish. None of it is real and I'm going to throw this piece of paper into the sea and nothing will happen, nothing will change.'

'Look, I might have put on a bit of a show for you tonight with the fire and the candles, and I may have edited the Wiki page about Mistletoe Cove to mention the fairy dust, but the legend surrounding the wishing well is true and I promise you that whatever you wish for, as long as it's in the realms of possibility and doesn't include flying unicorns or dragons, I promise you, it will come true.'

Eden sighed.

'You have nothing to lose, and everything to gain.'

'OK, fine.'

'And please, make sure it's something you really want.'

Eden nodded. 'Well, I'm not doing it with you sitting there watching me. I don't want you to see my wishes.'

'I have that covered.' He handed her an envelope. 'Write your wishes and then put it in that and then seal the envelope so I can't see it.'

Eden took it and Dougie moved away. 'And it has to be three wishes or it won't work.'

She rolled her eyes. To prove to him that this was all nonsense she wrote down the first two ridiculous things that came into her head.

I wish I had a million pounds.
I wish Hope Island had a white Christmas.

That would prove almost impossible for the wishing well. It so very rarely snowed in the Scilly Isles, the warmer coastal weather put a stop to that. And blanket snow like in those old Christmas card scenes was never seen, especially at Christmas.

She held her pen over the paper again and thought about something else ridiculous to ask for to prove to Dougie that wishes didn't come true.

She looked up at him and he was watching her with such hope in his eyes. This was important to him and she didn't know why. He had gone to a lot of trouble tonight to get her to make these wishes – what would he possibly gain when none of them came true?

She looked over to the blowhole as it sprayed water into the night sky, the droplets sparkling in the moonlight like…magic.

What if it was true?

There were so many unexplained occurrences in the world, strange coincidences that couldn't possibly be dismissed. Could there really be little pockets of magic in the world too?

She shook her head. No, that was ridiculous.

She looked back at Dougie and he nodded at her encouragingly. He really wanted her to do this.

Eden put the pen back on the paper and decided to just do it. What did she possibly have to lose? She would wish for the one thing she wanted most in the world.

I wish that Dougie would love me as much as I love him.

'There, three wishes.'

Dougie smiled with relief as she folded the paper and slid it into the envelope. She licked across the top of the envelope and sealed it up tight.

He held out his hand for it and she gave it to him and watched as he pulled out a pot of what looked like gold glitter from his pocket and sprinkled some over the envelope.

She laughed. 'What was that?'

'Fairy dust.'

She laughed again as he shoved the envelope in his pocket. 'Come on then, we need to get up to the top of the blowhole before midnight.'

He held out his hand for her and then helped her to her feet, leading her to the back of the standing rock.

'I got us some head torches, although the light of the fire will help. But there's lots of handholds round this side so it should be quite easy.'

He passed her a head torch and she turned it on and pulled it over her head. The top of the rock wasn't high, probably no more than ten or twelve feet. If she fell, she might have a few broken bones to contend with but nothing life-changing. Besides, she and Dougie used to do this sort of thing all the time as kids.

She started climbing, testing each hold before putting her weight on it, taking her time to get a good grip and find the perfect place, and every step of the way Dougie was right behind her.

She climbed onto the ledge just as the blowhole sprayed water up in the air and she squealed as the cold water sprayed down on top of her. Dougie laughed as he joined her.

'Couldn't I have wished on a star instead?' Eden said, shaking the water off her.

'The problem with wishing on a star is the stars are trillions of miles away and it takes many many thousands of years for the wish to get to them and then many thousands of years for the wish to come back. The wishing well can grant your wish straight away.'

He pulled the envelope out of his pocket and passed it to her. The glitter sparkled in the light of their head torches.

'You have to hold your wishes, close your eyes and say, "I believe in magic."'

Smiling, Eden shook her head but decided to just humour him. 'I believe in magic.'

'Three times,' Dougie insisted.

She laughed and said it two more times. This was getting more ridiculous by the minute.

She opened her eyes. 'Happy now?'

He was grinning at her so she guessed he must be. He checked his watch. 'OK, we have a minute, let's get a bit closer.'

'You just want to get me wet again.'

He laughed. 'No, we have to get closer to throw it in.'

Dougie guided her nearer, with his arm round her back, and she peered tentatively into the blowhole, not wanting to get a face full of water.

'OK, this is it,' he said, looking at his watch. 'Five, four, three, two, one. Throw it in.'

Eden obliged, tossing the envelope into the hole and with impeccable timing the blowhole suddenly erupted with a huge spray of cold water and she squealed, quickly stepping back out of the way. Her envelope was tossed into the air but as it came back down it fell straight back into the hole again and as the last of the water settled she hurried to the edge of the hole to see if she could still see her envelope but it was gone.

CHAPTER 11

Dougie watched as Eden stared into the hole and smiled. Despite all her protests he knew there was still a tiny part of her that still believed in or at least hoped for magic. He was glad he brought her here tonight to be able to, in some very tiny way, give that back to her.

He was nervous about the next part, it could all go very wrong. But he had sold his home, a huge penthouse apartment, sold most of his belongings, bought a tiny cottage and moved thousands of miles to a tiny island. He had made such massive changes in his life that there was no point in quitting at the final hurdle.

'Come on, we should toast some marshmallows before the fire goes out,' Dougie said.

Eden turned round and smiled at him. 'What happens now with my wishes?'

He walked to the edge and eased himself over. Once he'd found a good foothold, he moved down a few metres and waited for Eden to do the same.

She lowered herself over and climbed down just in front of him.

'You have to be patient, sometimes the wishes come true straightaway, sometimes it takes a while longer for the magic to happen.'

He climbed down carefully, making sure that Eden had a good grip before he moved down again until they were both safely on the beach.

He took her hand and led her over the rocks back towards the fire. His heart was hammering against his chest.

'Do you remember the last time we both came down to Mistletoe Cove?' he asked as he stopped her, pulling her towards him.

'Hmm, vaguely,' Eden said, noncommittally.

That wasn't the answer he was hoping for. Their kiss, their one and only kiss, had been seared on his brain ever since.

He wrapped his arms around her but she steadied him with her hands on his chest to stop him getting too close.

'Do you remember our kiss?'

She didn't answer at first and a hundred different emotions played across her face.

'Yes, it was nice.'

Nice wasn't exactly encouraging either. Christ, was he making a terrible mistake? Her eyes were wary now, not filled with amusement as they had been before. With the stunt he had pulled with the blowhole, he'd pushed her buttons and not in the right way. Maybe he should wait and try this another time. He surreptitiously checked his watch. He had about thirty seconds until the next part in his plan happened. It had to be here. And he was unlikely to get her to come back to Mistletoe Cove anytime soon.

He shifted her closer to him and her eyes became guarded.

'I thought it was magic,' Dougie said, softly.

Suddenly the cove was lit up, thousands of fairy lights hanging from the hawthorn trees glowing brightly over the cove.

Eden's eyes lit up with awe and wonder and she gasped softly. 'How did you do that?'

'Magic,' Dougie said and then bent his head and kissed her.

The taste of her on his lips was heaven and the soft little moan of need that fell from her mouth was a kick straight to his stomach. Her sweet marshmallow scent surrounded him, god this was everything he had hoped it would be and more.

Suddenly Eden made a tiny noise of protest and pushed him away.

He let her go, pushing a hand through his hair. She was staring at him with hurt and anger and confusion in her eyes. He hadn't expected that reaction. He had thought that when he kissed her she might not be willing to kiss him but he hadn't expected her to be hurt by it. That was the very last thing he wanted.

She stood there staring at him for a moment. Her breathing was heavy then she put her fingers up to her mouth, as if remembering what it felt like. She ran her tongue across her lips, tasting his kiss, and in the light of the fire he saw her blue eyes darken with need.

She took a step back towards him but he met her halfway, gathering her in his arms. He wasn't sure if she kissed him or he kissed her but they were kissing again and that's all that mattered. Her hands slid up behind his neck, caressing his hair. He slipped his tongue inside her mouth, tasting her, and it sent a jolt of need and desire for her spiralling through his stomach. God, it hadn't been like this the first time. It had been wonderful and sweet but this was so much more than that.

He lifted her against him so her feet were dangling off the ground and she didn't even seem to notice. Without taking his lips from hers, he shuffled her back a bit and then gently lowered her to the blanket so he was on top of her. He wanted to stroke her and touch her but as he ran his hand down her side, he was met only with her thick coat and by the feel of it several other layers underneath that. With a desperate need for her, he moved to unzip her coat but she stopped him again. He cursed his lack of control. He had never meant for it to happen like this. He had wanted to give her a gentle kiss to see if she had any feelings for him at all, not pin her to the ground and kiss her like his life depended on it.

He pulled back slightly to apologise but she stroked his face, her touch on his skin stalling any words in his throat.

'As much as I want to do this with you, and I *really* want to do this with you, there's no way you're taking any of my layers off here. Blue skin is really not an attractive feature.'

He laughed as he suddenly remembered where they were. She was right. The fire took the edge off the coldness of the night but there was still a noticeable nip in the air which they definitely would feel more once they started taking off clothes. It was probably for the best anyway. He wanted to take things slowly with her. He had no idea what her feelings were for him. She liked him, that much was clear, but was it more than that or just friendship and a need for sex?

She ran her thumb gently over his lips and he kissed it. 'Shall we go home?' she said.

So much was left unsaid with those words. What would happen when they got home, would it be more of this, would they make love?

He got to his feet and held out a hand to help her up. She took it and he pulled her up against him. He bent his head and kissed her again, just briefly.

'I can't believe this is happening, it's like a dream come true,' Eden said and then she frowned, the smile slipping off her face. She glanced up at the blowhole and then back at Dougie. What was she thinking? He quickly kissed her again before any more doubt or fear could creep in and, while she was hesitant at first, she soon melted into him.

'Come on, let's go,' he said. He made a half-hearted attempt to kick sand over the fire, but it was already on its way out. He then stuffed everything in his bag, grabbed her hand and started climbing back up the rocks towards the cave.

'What about the candles and the fairy lights?' Eden protested.

'I'll come back for all the rest of it later, or I'll ask the fairies to deliver them back to our house.'

Despite the wonderful tension of the moment he was relieved to hear Eden giggle at that.

They hurried back through the cave and when they got to the opening he gave her a leg-up and then pulled himself out into the meadow too. As soon as he was standing next to her he kissed her again, afraid that without the magical atmosphere he had created in Mistletoe Cove they would lose the magic between them too.

They hurried along the meadow holding hands and by the time they had made it back to the high street they were practically running flat out.

Eden fumbled for her key and opened the door to her cottage and as soon as they were inside he pinned her to the door and kissed her again. He unzipped her coat and let it slide off her shoulders onto the floor and she wrestled him out of his. He gently pulled off her woolly hat, letting her black curls tumble over her shoulders.

He kissed her for the longest time, then pulled back slightly, rested his forehead against hers and closed his eyes, just breathing her in.

'What happens now?' she asked.

He opened his eyes, not entirely sure how to answer that question. He knew what he wanted to happen but he had no idea if she wanted that.

'How about I light a fire?' Dougie said, playing for time. He felt so out of his depth with Eden. With every other woman he'd been with he'd known exactly what to say and do to charm them, exactly what move to make and when. He'd always had a natural affinity with women; growing up, he'd always preferred being friends with them and being nice to them than pulling their hair or being cool and aloof. For reasons he'd never know, women would flock round him. But Eden was so different to all of them.

'That sounds good,' Eden said. He kissed her briefly before stepping away from her. He didn't want this bubble around them to burst and he sensed that soon it would. He moved over to the fireplace. 'And then you can explain why you kissed me?'

He smiled. He could at least answer that. 'Because I wanted to.'

'Dougie!'

'Eden.' He mirrored her body language and her tone of voice.

'Is this a game to you? Just another little joke to mock me?'

It was safe to say the bubble had burst. He should have just kept kissing her then they wouldn't be having this discussion. They could both be half naked by now and then their actions would have done all the talking. He was also hurt that she thought he would do something like this just for a laugh. He knew that he had a reputation for never taking things seriously but he would never do anything to hurt her.

'Definitely not a joke.'

'So what was it then?'

'You kissed me as well, honey, it wasn't completely one-sided. Why did you kiss me?' Dougie asked.

'Because you kissed me?'

'Is that how it works, anyone comes up to you and kisses you and you just kiss them back?'

God, this wasn't how he imagined it at all.

'You're an ass,' Eden said and turned to walk out the room but Dougie moved to stop her, snagging her around the waist.

'Look, I'm not sure why we're shouting at each other. We both clearly enjoyed the kiss, I was there, it got pretty heated for a while. Why don't I light a fire and we can cuddle on the sofa and just carry on where we left off rather than ruining it with discussing the whys.'

Eden looked away and he caught her chin to get her to look at him, trying to read what was going on inside her head. 'I would never do anything to hurt you.'

She stared at him for a moment and then shook her head. 'I can't do this.'

'Why not? You seemed to be enjoying it on the beach.'

'Because I have no idea what this is for you. Is this just another friendly kiss that we'll never mention again after tonight? Is this kiss just because you haven't been involved with anyone for a while and you're feeling a bit sexually frustrated? Is this kiss because you feel sorry for me because I've been single for a while? Or is this kiss a prelude to something more? You say you won't do anything to hurt me but you will. When you wake up tomorrow morning and regret the kiss and pretend that it never happened like you did last time, it will hurt. If you can't tell me what this is, then I can't do this. I need to protect myself.'

He sighed. She was right, he owed her an explanation. He felt sick. It was never meant to happen this way – he had never imagined it would happen at all – but a little over forty-eight hours after he had arrived on Hope Island, he was being forced to say something he'd never thought he'd say.

He swallowed. 'You want to know why I kissed you? Because I love you.'

CHAPTER 12

Eden stared at him, hearing his words echo in the silence. The words she had been waiting over twelve years to hear, the words that she never imagined she would ever hear had just fallen from his lips, and she couldn't think of one word to say in reply.

Tears formed in her eyes, emotion clogging in her throat.

He loved her.

Despite her best efforts the tears spilled over onto her cheeks.

'Hey, don't cry. God, that's the last thing I want. If you don't feel the same way, that's OK, we can still be friends. Nothing has to change.'

He had no idea. And she couldn't even find the words to tell him.

Dougie pulled her to the sofa and sat down and then tugged her onto his lap. He wrapped his arms around her and held her against him.

'What's wrong, tell me what's wrong?' he said, stroking her back.

Eden shook her head.

'Something has upset you.'

She looked at him; he looked so concerned for her but she couldn't tell him. He gently wiped her tears away, cupping her face with his hands.

'I've told you why I kissed you. Why did you kiss me?' Dougie asked softly.

Over twelve years she had been in love with this man and she had kept her feelings for him hidden, locked in her heart, being careful never to reveal how she felt for him. She was so used to keeping that part of her locked away that it was impossible for her to admit the truth even after he had bared his soul to her.

'Because I wanted to,' Eden answered, obtrusively.

Dougie let out a small sigh of frustration as he continued to stroke her face.

'Well, would it be OK if I kissed you again?'

Eden didn't hesitate this time. She nodded.

He smiled and slid his hand round the back of her neck and kissed her tenderly. This was so different to how it had been before. On the beach it had been passionate and needful but this was altogether sweeter.

He pulled back slightly. 'Let's go to bed.'

A soft gasp escaped her lips. God, she wanted that but she was also scared of it too.

'We're not going to do anything,' Dougie reassured and she felt a kick of disappointment in her stomach. 'But if I'm going to hold you in my arms while I fall asleep, like I did last night, I'd like to do so in the comfort of the bed again. This sofa is not great for sleeping on.'

She clambered off him and held out her hand. Taking it, he led her up the stairs and straight into his room.

He turned to face her, resting his hands on her shoulders. 'I don't want to push my luck as tonight has already far exceeded my expectations but can I undress you?'

Her heart was already beating so hard against her chest and at those words it broke into a gallop. She had never seen this side of Dougie before. He was normally so confident, funny and charming, but right now he was quiet, serious and seemed to be nervous and second-guessing his every move. She knew he had been with quite a few women in New York but she would never have imagined that someone as flirty and confident as Dougie would ever ask permission to kiss a girl or undress her. She'd imagined he would just do it.

She nodded.

He slowly unzipped her hoodie and let it slide off her shoulders, not taking his eyes off hers for a second as he went to work on her cardigan.

Should she be undressing him too? She'd had a few boyfriends herself over the years, not as many as she'd like, and she definitely didn't have the experience that Dougie had, but she had never second-guessed her way around the bedroom either. But what even was this? They weren't going to make love but they were going to cuddle in bed, he'd told her he loved her and she damned well loved him and now he was undressing her. She didn't know the rules for this. This was Dougie, her best friend, and they were going to see each other naked.

They were going to see each other naked!

Her greedy fingers reached out to the bottom of his jumper, found the hem of his t-shirt and dragged both items off in one quick sweep. He chuckled at her impatience but all she could do was stare at his chest. She'd seen it before. Many times in fact as he didn't have any scruples about wandering around her house half naked and once she'd even seen him completely naked. But every time she had quickly looked away, not wanting him to see her staring with hunger in her eyes. But now it seemed she could do what she wanted. He loved her. So she could stare at him all night if she so wished. She could even touch him. He was gloriously beautiful, his smooth chest and arms were so big and strong, he had these big thick shoulders that looked like he could take on the weight of the world. Her eyes drifted down to his flat toned stomach and then even lower to where his jeans hung on his waist.

He dispensed with her cardigan and gave a soft sigh of frustration at the shirt she was wearing. He started work on the buttons.

'Just out of interest, how many layers are you wearing?' Dougie said.

She giggled. 'Sorry, it's freezing out there. I figured if we were going to be sitting on the beach for a few hours then I'd need to wear some layers or die of hypothermia.'

'So do I need to go and get a snack or something to keep my energy up while I dispense with all these clothes? I'm presuming there's flesh under there somewhere.'

'Keep going, I'm pretty sure there's only four more layers.'

'Four?'

'After the shirt.'

He smirked as he slid the shirt to the floor.

'Or maybe I'll just take a leaf out of your book.' He grabbed the bottom of her clothes and hauled them all up together.

'No wait—' Eden tried to stop him but it was too late. The jumper, the two t-shirts and the vest came to a halt around her neck but over her face. Dougie tried to free her by pulling harder on her clothes but that didn't do anything. 'Stop, you're strangling me,' she said, her voice muffled through all the layers of clothes. 'One of my t-shirts has a drawstring collar.'

'Of course it has,' Dougie said.

God, there was nothing sexy about this. She was standing there in her bra and jeans with the rest of her clothes hanging over her head like some weird kind of headless monster.

Suddenly she was acutely aware he was staring at her. She didn't know why, but she was sure he was. This was not how she wanted him to remember seeing her naked for the first time.

What bra was she wearing? She hadn't put any thought into her underwear when she had got ready that evening. It was the pink one, which definitely wasn't the worst of her bras, but probably not the best either, though it did have that cute bow at the front that looked like it was the only thing holding the bra together.

Dougie must have thought so too as he suddenly gently tugged at the end of the bow, obviously hoping that her bra would suddenly come undone and her breasts would come tumbling out.

'Douglas Harrison,' she laughed, her hands on her hips, though she knew there was nothing formidable about her in her current position. 'If you think you can pull my bra off and cop a feel of my breasts when my clothes are hanging over my face like this, you have another think coming.'

He laughed. 'Sorry, I was trying to be efficient. Does that mean I can't take your jeans off either?'

'That's exactly what it means. Your impatience got me into this situation, you can damned well get me out of it.'

He sighed dramatically. 'In all my meticulous planning for this evening, never in my wildest dreams did I see it panning out like this.'

'What was your plan for the evening?' Eden said as she tried to fight through her layers to find the drawstring.

'To make you smile,' Dougie said, without missing a beat.

She smiled with love for him. 'Well, you definitely achieved that.'

'Does that mean I can cop a feel now?' he said as he tried to pull her clothes back over her head and onto her body.

'No it does not.'

'Spoilsport.'

'Pervert. Look with your eyes, not your hands.'

'Oh believe me, I was,' Dougie said, pushing her clothes back down and she was able to see once more. His face was filled with amusement and, although she liked it a lot better when he was looking at her with hunger, this had to be a very close second.

'You find this funny?'

'I find this hilarious. We've not even had sex and this is already ranking as one of the best nights of my life. Who wears drawstring t-shirts anyway?'

'It was cold!' Eden said. 'I didn't want any draughts getting in.'

'Or anything else for that matter. When we do make love, I'm going to have to give over an extra few hours in my schedule to get you undressed. How about we have dinner at four o'clock that night? That should give me enough time to get through the hundred layers of clothes and get laid sometime before midnight.'

'Well, if you take me out to somewhere warm and inside, instead of a beach in the middle of December, then I might even wear a few less layers that night. And I promise no drawstrings.'

They were talking about this like it definitely was going to happen and she liked the thought of that. Even if it wasn't going to happen tonight. Hell, it definitely wasn't going to happen tonight, she had killed any passion dead.

Finally she found the drawstring and released it. 'Now you can take my clothes off.'

Dougie rolled his eyes but she could see he was loving every minute of this. He pulled her clothes gently over her head and let them drop to the floor. His eyes roamed over her body.

'Can I cop a feel now?'

She laughed. God, she loved this man so much and whatever this thing was between them, whether it was one night or a few weeks of fun, she knew they would be OK. He was her best friend and nothing was going to change that.

She leaned up and kissed him and he smiled against her lips as he kissed her back. She ran her hands over his chest and round his back, enjoying the feel of his smooth skin over rock-hard muscle, and then her hands met the waistband of his jeans. She hesitated for just a second before she slid her hands round the waistband and undid the button on the top of his jeans. He continued to kiss her, holding her face in his hands, but when she slowly undid his zip, he took a little intake of breath.

He pulled back slightly to watch her and she moved her hands back to his hips and pushed the jeans down over his huge muscular thighs. He quickly wriggled out of them and kicked them to one side.

'Do I take that as a yes?' He reached his hands out in a breast-grabbing motion and she laughed hard because he wasn't taking this remotely seriously.

'Nope, but if you're good I'll let you take my jeans off.'

Dougie rubbed his hands together as if about to get his hands on a fabulous prize. He was going to be so disappointed.

He popped open the button on the top of her jeans and, echoing her moves, he slowly undid her zip. His eyes were on her face as he did it, gauging her reaction so he missed what he was unveiling. His eyes cast down appreciatively, obviously hoping he was going to see some sexy knickers. Eden could barely keep the laughter inside.

He frowned in confusion. 'What is that?'

'Tights,' Eden said, proudly. 'Navy blue, thick, woollen tights.'

'God, you know how to turn a man on.'

'Keep going, there's more where that came from.'

Dougie got to his knees, slowly peeling her jeans down her legs and gradually revealing a pair of green- and purple-spotted knee-length socks over the blue tights. She kicked her shoes off, stepped out of the jeans and struck a pose like a model on the catwalk as she stood before him in her bra, thick blue tights and spotty socks.

Dougie laughed and she started parading round the room singing Rod Stewart's 'Do Ya Think I'm Sexy?'

He stood up and moved towards her but at the last moment he ducked down and threw her over his shoulder. She squealed and then he tossed her down on the bed and came down on top of her.

'As a matter of fact, I do,' Dougie said, before kissing her again.

She hooked her legs around him, holding him to her as she kissed him back but he quickly sat up and straddled her instead. 'Sorry honey, I really can't kiss you in these things, they're so scratchy. They're going to have to come off.'

He peeled them away and the socks came off with them so she was only in her underwear and he was just in his boxer briefs as he lay back down half on top of her and kissed her again. The humour was gone now; it was just the two of them kissing, their hot bodies sliding against each other. It was everything she had hoped it would be and more. It really was a dream come true. Something jolted in her head but she pushed any doubt aside. She was enjoying this kiss too much to worry about the whys.

She pulled back slightly and he looked down at her with complete and utter love in his eyes.

'So we're really not going to make love tonight?' Eden asked.

'Not tonight. When you're ready I'm going to make sure it's perfect for us. There'll be candles and wine and a whole string quartet standing in the corner playing beautiful music.'

Eden giggled. 'Voyeurism, that sounds super romantic.'

'I thought so. Now as it's almost two in the morning, I think I'd better let you get some sleep, otherwise you'll be exhausted at work tomorrow.'

'I have the day off,' Eden said.

He grinned. 'You do?'

'Yeah.'

'Well in that case I think I might enjoy kissing you for the rest of the night.'

'I think I'd like that too.'

He kissed her again and this time he didn't stop.

CHAPTER 13

Eden woke with a big smile on her face and the smile grew even wider when she saw Dougie fast asleep in bed next to her, his arm wrapped around her waist. He had the hugest grin on his face, as if he'd spent the night having the best sex of his life instead of just kissing, and she liked that she had made him smile so much.

It was four days until Christmas and the thought of waking up in his arms on Christmas Day, of being with him and probably making love to him, filled her with so much excitement. It was the best Christmas present she could ever hope for.

She hadn't expected any of this to happen when Dougie came home. They were friends, they'd always been friends, and nothing had ever happened apart from that one kiss on Mistletoe Cove twelve years before. There had never been any sign from him that he had feelings for her. Not just feelings – he loved her. It was so completely out of the blue, almost as if a switch had been flicked in his head, and suddenly those feelings were there when they had never been before.

She felt the smile sliding off her face.

Those feelings *had* never been there before and mere minutes after she had wished he loved her, he was kissing her like his life depended on it.

Was it the wish that had made this happen? No, that was ridiculous. There was no such thing as magic. There was no such thing as fairies or fairy godmothers for that matter; there was no magical school of witchcraft and wizardry hidden from the muggles in the Scottish Highlands. Those were stories, nothing more. There was no way that writing her wishes on a piece of paper and throwing it into the sea could ever possibly make her wishes come true. But if he really did love her then why had he never said anything before?

She was so confused and as she lay there staring at him, the fear started creeping in too. What if this wasn't real? What if Dougie didn't love her and it was all just some stunt to make her smile? What if it was a temporary thing and, just like Cinderella's wish to go to the ball had started to unravel after midnight with the golden carriage turning back into a pumpkin, what if Dougie's love for her faded away too? What if she fell into this relationship with Dougie – or whatever this thing was between them – and then one day he decided he didn't love her any more? Was it better to not enter into it at all? Because having a relationship with Dougie and then losing him had to hurt more than not having him at all.

She sighed with frustration. In her dreams, whenever Dougie told her he loved her and wanted to marry her, there had never been this fear and doubt. Why was she letting this ruin her happiness now?

She carefully got out of bed, needing some time away from him to think. She quietly threw on some clothes and left him smiling as he slept.

She slipped out onto the moonlit street. There was not a sound or any sign of movement at all. It wasn't even six o'clock yet and the sun wouldn't be up for hours. She walked down the high street towards Buttercup Beach and as she got closer the gentle lap of the waves on the beach was soothing. She sat down on the sand, and closed her eyes, trying to let nothing but that sound fill her head.

In her pocket her phone buzzed with a notification. She normally put it on silent at night because Bella had been up very late and very early over the last few months as she prepared for her wedding. Eden was in a texting group with Bella and Freya where Bella would post pictures all hours of the day and night about ideas for the upcoming wedding. Eden knew that Bella wasn't expecting a response at those times but the pictures were there for when Eden or Freya could get to them.

Eden pulled her phone out and inspected the picture of the five-tier chocolate fountain that Bella had just posted with the word 'thoughts?' next to it followed by a crying emoji. There had been lots of these emojis lately and Eden knew that Bella was getting very stressed out by all the planning. Eden and Freya had offered countless times to help with some of the organising but Bella was keen to do it all herself.

But if Bella was posting pictures of chocolate fountains then she was clearly awake.

Eden quickly typed out a message.

Fancy a coffee?

Eden waited. It was just coming up for six o'clock in the morning and it was a Sunday. Bella was most likely looking forward to some kind of lie-in and spending the day with her wonderful fiancé as she wasn't working. She really wouldn't want to get up and out of bed when it was dark to meet her for a coffee.

She could see Bella was typing.

Of course. Are you OK?

Eden smiled with love for her sister as she typed back. *Rosa's?*

Rosa's was open all hours of the day and night – the fishermen came and went very early in the morning, either before a day's fishing or after a night out at sea, and Rosa had lots of different staff working throughout the night to cater for them.

Give me ten minutes Bella wrote.

Suddenly Eden noticed Freya was typing too. She definitely hadn't expected Freya to be awake at this time.

I want to come too.

Why are you awake? Eden wrote back.

Because this baby makes me pee every hour.

Eden smiled. *Come on then, my treat.*

She got to Rosa's just before Freya, and Bella arrived a few minutes later, both of them hugging her as they arrived.

'What's going on, are you OK?' Bella asked as she sat down in the booth opposite Eden. 'It's your day off today, isn't it? I didn't expect to see you up this early.'

'Is this about Dougie?' Freya asked, tucking into the delicious chocolate pastry Rosa had brought over on a plate with other sugary delights.

Eden nodded. There was no point beating around the bush. 'He told me he loved me.'

There was absolute silence from Bella and Freya, no squeals of delight or claps or cheers, just absolute silence as they stared at her. Maybe they needed more details.

'We ended up going to Mistletoe Cove last night where we kissed, we came back to my house where we kissed again. A lot. And… he told me he loved me.'

More silence. They clearly hadn't been expecting it either; it wasn't just her that thought this was completely out of the blue.

Freya finally found her voice. 'Eden, I'm so happy for you. It's a little unexpected and sudden but I'm really happy for you.'

'Is it sudden?' Bella argued. 'It's been twelve years. It's about time he made a move. I've always thought that he had a thing for you.'

'No, Freya's right,' Eden said. 'It's sudden because he's never shown any sign of having feelings for me in the past. And now he's been back three days and he's declaring his undying love for me. It feels odd.'

'What do you mean, he's never showed any sign of loving you before? You hug, hold hands, he kisses you on the cheek. You're more affectionate together than most couples. You've been in love with him for almost all of your life, why are you not happier about this?' Bella said.

'I just don't know if this is some stunt that he is trying to pull, you know what Dougie's like. I've never known him to be serious about anything.'

'Dougie wouldn't do that to you.'

'I don't mean something nasty, I just wonder if he is doing it simply to be nice. He said last night that he just wanted to make me smile, I wonder if this is something like that…' Eden trailed off because in her heart she knew Dougie would never do something like that to her. He might switch the sugar for the salt or change her voicemail message to something silly but he'd never do anything like this.

Eden stalled over telling them the next part because it sounded insane just thinking about it.

'Do you guys believe in magic?' she said, quietly, focussing her attention on a custard pastry on the plate in front of her.

'Um, well… I suppose it was magic the way that Isaac and I met,' Bella said, desperately trying to help. 'If he hadn't come to see what my reaction was to having a homeless person outside my house, if I hadn't invited him in, I'd probably just be his employee by now instead of his fiancée. Some things happen for a reason.'

Eden smiled at her. She couldn't be happier that Bella had found love when she hadn't even been looking for it. Her sister deserved it.

'Are you talking about a connection between two people, that thing that only soul mates share?' Freya asked. 'When Rome and I made love for the first time, we shared the most incredible connection that was magical. Do you mean something like that?'

Eden shook her head. 'No, I'm not talking about serendipity or lucky coincidence or an intense emotional connection. I'm talking spells, magical powers and wishes coming true.'

Bella and Freya stared at her in surprise and confusion.

'I know it sounds crazy…'

'I think there are lots of things in this world that can't possibly be explained. If you go on YouTube there are thousands of videos of ghosts, weird creatures, strange floating balls of lights in the sky, furniture that moves by itself, people that can supposedly move things with their minds, there are even videos of people flying. A lot of that is faked or can be explained but some of it can't. I do think there's lots that we just don't understand about our world,' Bella said.

'What's this about?' Freya asked, gently.

'Have you guys ever heard about the legend surrounding Mistletoe Cove?'

They both shook their heads.

'I have,' Rosa said, arriving at their table with their drinks. 'I can't say I hold much stock in it myself, I've never been one to believe in fairy stories. But I've heard that if you throw wishes into the blowhole they come true. Load of old rubbish if you ask

me but the rumour says it's especially effective for young lovers.'
Rosa raised her eyebrows pointedly in Eden's direction, unloaded
the drinks from the tray and walked off.

Eden stared after her. 'I can't believe I've never heard of this
legend before, I've lived here my whole life, but Clare has heard
about it too.'

'I've never heard of it either,' Bella said. 'What happened?'

'Dougie persuaded me to go with him to Mistletoe Cove last
night, told me all this rubbish that if you write three wishes on
a piece of paper and throw them into the blowhole then they
would come true. I'm sure he primed Clare to agree with him
and tell me this story about her gran's wishes coming true, he'd
even created some Wikipedia page detailing about the legend of
Mistletoe Cove to back up his story. I didn't believe any of it, but
he was so adamant that I should make the wishes that in the end
I did it just to humour him and…' she trailed off.

Bella reached across the table and took her hand. 'Did you
wish that Dougie loved you?'

Eden sighed and nodded. 'That's the only thing I've ever wished
for. It's crazy, wishes don't come true, no amount of birthday
wishes, wishes on a star or lucky pennies in a wishing well will
ever make your dreams come true. I know, I spent years trying.
But minutes after I threw my wish in the blowhole, he was kissing
me and telling me he loves me and I know this sounds stupid
but… what if it was the wish that did it?'

'Look, I think Dougie has always loved you, and maybe he
didn't realise it until he moved to America and left you behind,
but I think those feelings for you have always been there. Why
do you think he visited so often?' Bella asked.

'Well, to see all of us, me, you and Rome.'

'And you were always the first person he went to see whenever
he came back. Why did he always stay with you and not me or

Rome? Rome would be the much more logical choice, he has a bigger house and his guest bedroom has an en-suite.'

Eden thought about this. She'd never really questioned why she was always the one he insisted on staying with. She'd always been happy to have him stay with her in the past even though it had tortured her having him walk around with hardly any clothes on.

'How many texts or messages or emails do you get from him when he's in America?' Bella persisted.

'Well, probably only two or three a day,' Eden said.

Bella's eyebrows shot up. 'I get maybe one a week, if I'm lucky. I'm sure Rome doesn't hear from him that often either.'

'But they're just silly messages, jokes, meaningless comments, nothing serious.'

'But it shows he's thinking of you,' Freya said.

'Well I guess. But if he loved me why hasn't he moved back here before now? It's been twelve years.'

'You've never given him any sign that he had anything to come back for,' Bella said. 'Besides, he moved with his parents, he didn't really have any choice with that, then he was at university over there, got a job with that gaming company; it would have been hard to work for a gaming company over here while living on Hope Island. He would have had to move to London to do that and that wouldn't have helped you guys to have any kind of relationship either.'

'Bella's right, it wasn't the right time for him before. I've always thought he's had a soft spot for you,' Freya said. 'Everyone on the island thinks he has come back here for you, there's even a bet that you'll be married by this time next year.'

'The islanders see what they want to see,' Eden said.

'All we're saying is, it isn't that implausible that he does love you. He adores you, you know that. It's not a far stretch that that adoration would turn into love at some point. And if he does love you and he has come back here for you, then it makes sense that he would want to make a move straight away. Why waste any more time?' Bella said.

'OK, there are three solutions to this scenario,' Freya said, practically. 'Firstly, as Bella says, he genuinely does love you, and he'd always planned on coming back to Hope Island with the hope of starting something with you and it's just coincidence that he told you he loved you after you wished that he did. Secondly, it could be some big Dougie trick, although to what gain, I don't know, unless, like you say, it's his attempt at doing something nice. Is there any way that Dougie could have seen your wishes?'

Eden shook her head. 'He wasn't anywhere near me when I wrote the wishes and I put them in a sealed envelope. I threw the envelope into the blowhole myself and watched it get sucked away into the sea. There's no way he could know.'

'So we know he isn't just saying he loves you because he saw it was your wish.'

'Dougie is not going to say he loves Eden for a joke,' Bella insisted. 'I know he never takes life seriously but he would never hurt Eden like that.'

'OK, so if it's not a stunt it's either that he does genuinely love her or… the wish came true.'

They sat there in silence for a moment. They all knew how unrealistic that was.

'OK, let's say for one moment that the wish did really come true. You said there were three wishes. If one wish comes true, I think it's merely a coincidence rather than magic, but if the other two come true too, well then maybe there is something else going on. What were the other two wishes?' Freya asked.

'They were silly wishes, just something I wrote down to prove to Dougie that the whole Mistletoe Cove legend was complete rubbish.'

'And how likely is it that they would come true?' Bella said.

'Not likely at all, almost impossible I'd say.'

'Well then we'll soon see,' Freya said.

'I still think it's option one,' Bella said. 'That's much more realistic.'

'I suppose,' Eden said, breaking off a chunk of the pastry and putting it in her mouth.

'What are you so afraid of?' Freya asked.

'That it will end. I'm afraid of letting myself believe in this relationship and then watching it get taken away from me if Dougie changes his mind or reveals it's all some big joke or if... the wish stops working after midnight.'

'There are no guarantees in love, Eden,' Bella said. 'But that's why you should enjoy what you have now because who knows what's around the corner.'

Eden wasn't convinced. She felt like she needed to protect herself from Dougie and not entering into a relationship felt like a good way to do that.

'OK, let's imagine that throwing wishes into the blowhole does make them come true, but instead of wishing that Dougie loved you, you wished you could fly. And it came true. But with a limited time,' Bella said. 'Would you just never fly, knowing how disappointed you would be once the wish ended, and then you'd never experience that heart-soaring joy of flying through the air, dancing on the clouds and swooping through the skies? Would you keep your feet on the ground, too afraid to make that leap, and then, after a few weeks or months, you just watch that wish fade away?'

Eden smiled as she thought about this. 'No, I'd fly everywhere, over the seas and mountains, over foreign lands and then I'd do it all over again.'

'Well then. Go and enjoy being loved by Dougie for however long that it lasts. This is what you've wanted for your whole life, go and experience it, kiss him till your lips are numb, take him to bed and enjoy that amazing sex you want so much, take baths with him, go for walks or picnics or whatever else was on that list you gave me the other night.'

Eden's grin grew as she realised Bella was right. This was everything she ever dreamed of. And if it was going to come to an end then she needed to enjoy it now.

'I need to go and talk to him.' She stood up and rooted around in her bag to pay for the coffee and pastries.

'No, my treat,' Bella said. 'I was glad of the distraction from the wedding planning.'

Eden paused. 'Bella, are you OK? You seem so stressed out about this wedding. With all the big charity events you've organised in the past, I've never seen you like this before.'

Bella sighed. 'It's turning into a complete nightmare if I'm honest. But look, let's not talk about this now. Go get your man and I'll tell you all about it at our weekly dinner on Tuesday.'

'OK, if you're sure?' Eden said.

Bella nodded. 'Go, I'm fine.'

Eden hugged them both and had turned to go when Freya snagged her arm.

'Tell him you love him. Believe me when I say there is nothing worse than telling someone you love them for them not to say it back. If you love him, then tell him.'

Eden nodded, not really sure if she could find the courage to do that, but she would give it her best shot.

CHAPTER 14

Dougie stared at the piece of paper in shock. He couldn't believe what he was seeing. But as he read the words for what felt like the hundredth time he couldn't help the huge grin that spread across his face. This was quite possibly the best news that he'd ever had.

No, it wasn't all good news, certainly some of it was going to cause him a bit of a headache, but that last line on the page made the rest of it feel completely doable.

He had woken up that morning to a cold and empty bed, which was hugely disappointing since he had hoped to carry on where they had left off the night before. The fact that Eden wasn't even in the house showed that she was probably having some regrets about what had happened. He had told her that he loved her and she hadn't said it back. But she had spent the night kissing him in his bed which showed she had some feelings for him. He guessed she was just scared. Somehow he had to get her to trust him.

He heard the front door slam open and he quickly threw the paper into his bag before running downstairs to greet her.

She ran straight to him, throwing her arms around him and hugging him tight. He hugged her back.

'Well that's the best greeting I've ever had.' He tilted her chin up to face him and, cupping her face, he kissed her sweetly on the lips. A huge smile spread across her face.

'Do you still love me?' Eden said, doubt filling her eyes.

He smiled and kissed her again. 'Of course.' He paused, waiting to see if she would say it back, but she was too busy smiling to say anything. Happiness shone from her. It had been way too long since he had seen her smiling this much. He stroked her cheeks with his thumbs. He didn't want her to lose that smile but he needed to know how she felt, he needed to hear the words. 'Do you love me?'

As expected, the smile faded away. Fear and worry filled her face and she looked down, staring straight at his chest before she took a deep breath and answered.

'Yes, I've always been in love with you. Years before our first kiss, I was in love with you then. And that love has never gone away. In fact, it has only deepened over the years.'

Euphoria like he had never known filled him, quickly followed by acute pain. He knew what it felt like to love somebody but not be with them. That pain in his chest had never gone away. Eden had been in love with him almost her entire life, she'd experienced that pain too, and the worst thing was he'd done that to her. His parents emigrating wasn't his fault, realistically he couldn't have stayed on Hope Island without them at the age of eighteen. He had no house, no job and it had always been his dream to live in America, but maybe he could have come back sooner. God, if he'd known that she felt this way, he would have.

'I'm sorry.' The words weren't enough but how did he even begin to apologise for causing a lifetime of hurt?

She looked up at him and smiled sadly.

'Don't apologise, it's not your fault. Well, it's a little your fault but I still love you.' She laughed.

He smiled. 'Well I'm here now and I intend to make up for lost time.'

He bent his head and kissed her, that incredible feeling of joy spreading through him as soon as their lips touched. She moved her hands from his back, sliding them round to his hips and then gently caressing his ribs. He was suddenly really pleased he hadn't had a chance to get dressed yet, her soft touch against his skin was pure heaven. He slid his hands to her shoulders and realised with frustration that she was wearing way too many clothes again. It didn't matter though, the kiss was more than enough. God, he was never going to tire of kissing her, even if she was completely overdressed.

The kiss quickly escalated from being sweet and tender to something much more heated. He found himself unzipping her coat again and slipping it off her shoulders. He wanted to touch her, feel her warmth next to him.

She pulled back slightly to look at him. 'Make love to me,' she said against his lips.

Oh god. The thought of that was enough to bring him to his knees.

'I can't.'

Her face fell, her beautiful smile fading away.

'Honey, it's not that I don't want to, believe me I do. But I was planning on wooing you first.'

'Wooing?' The smile was back.

'You know, flowers and—'

'You've brought me flowers.' Eden nodded towards the white roses he had bought for her a few days before, sitting pride of place on the mantelpiece.

'Dates then. Restaurants, fine wine, fine food.'

'And that sounds lovely but we can still do all that and make love.'

He pretended to be shocked. 'I'm not making love to you in the restaurant, honey, I'd like to do that somewhere a little bit more private.'

Eden laughed. 'Well that would certainly give the islanders something to talk about if we did.'

'When I make love to you for the first time, it's just going to be me and you.'

'And the string quartet,' she said.

'Yes, them too.'

Eden giggled and leaned her head against his chest. 'Oh god Dougie, you have no idea how much I want you. Twelve years and this all felt like an impossible dream. And now it's happening I don't understand why you want to wait.'

'I don't want to rush things.'

'Twelve years, Dougie! I hardly think that we can be accused of rushing things. Besides, you hadn't even been back three days and you told me that you loved me. That's a little fast, don't you think?'

'Yes, I hadn't planned on doing that. I'm not sure what came over me.'

Eden frowned slightly and he leaned down and kissed the frown between her eyes.

'I want to be the man that you deserve; I want to do this right.'

'What does doing it right mean?'

'Well, I want it to be romantic.' An idea came to him. 'I want to make love to you in front of the fire in a room filled with candles.'

Eden's eyes lit up and he knew he'd said the right thing. 'That does sound lovely.' She ran her fingers down his chest. 'We could do that now.'

Dougie groaned. 'You're killing me. How about tonight?'

Her whole face lit up with a huge smile. 'I can wait until tonight. But I do have the day off today, so how do you plan to woo me in the meantime?'

He thought about it for a moment and another idea came to him. 'I have some ideas but why don't we start by taking a bath?'

The smile on Eden's face grew even bigger. 'Now that sounds like an excellent place to start.'

He took her hands in his and kissed them both. Then, with her hand still in his, he led her upstairs and into the bathroom.

Fortunately Eden had a large corner bath which looked like it might be big enough for the both of them. He put the plug in and started running the water. Eden had lots of different-coloured bottles lining the edge of the bath and he picked up a creamy-looking one and realised it was marshmallow bubble bath. He smiled; this was where she got her wonderful scent from. He unscrewed the top and took a sniff, the smell sending a kick of desire straight to his gut. He poured some under the hot running water and immediately bubbles started to form on the surface. She had quite a few candles on the edge of the bath and, wanting to add to the romance of the moment, he set about lighting them. Noticing there was a jar of what looked like rose petals, he unscrewed the lid and poured a few of those into the bath too. He stepped back slightly to view his efforts and, pleased with what he had achieved at very short notice, he turned back to face Eden.

His eyes nearly popped out of his head when he saw that she had got completely undressed and was standing before him stark naked. Words failed him. She was the most beautiful woman he had ever seen, she was his best friend and she was offering herself to him on a plate. She looked vulnerable, awkward and a little scared and his heart ached for her. He knew there was a part of her that didn't believe that he loved her, that was expecting him to tell her it was all a joke at any moment – he could see it in her eyes, he knew her so well. He quickly moved towards her, gathering her in his arms and kissing her hard. There was no better feeling in the world than her warm naked body against his. He lifted her and she wrapped her arms and legs around him as he pinned her to the door, not taking his lips from hers for even a second. Waiting until tonight was a terrible idea.

He shifted her tighter against him and she gave a little moan of protest against his lips. He pulled back slightly.

'The bath,' Eden said, breathlessly.

'To hell with the bath,' Dougie said, moving to kiss her again.

She giggled. 'The water.'

'Oh crap,' he said. He turned around to see that the water level was rising fast. He quickly lowered her to the floor and ran to turn the taps off. It was quite obvious from the huge mountain of foam in the bath that he had used too much bubble bath as well. He would quite likely lose Eden in there. 'Well, the bath is ready.'

'Shall we get in?'

Dougie had just been about to make love to her against the bathroom door so he was glad of the distraction. He didn't want that for their first time together. Remembering his plan to woo her, he nodded.

He looked down at his boxer briefs and wondered whether to take them off. She was naked so should he be too? Although if they were both naked, cuddling in the bathtub, any restraint he did have would quickly vanish. He looked at her and she arched an eyebrow at him, obviously knowing what he was thinking.

'I think I'd better leave them on,' Dougie said. 'I don't want you taking advantage of me.'

Eden laughed. 'It will take more than a piece of black cotton to stop me from taking advantage of you, but if it makes you feel safer then go ahead.'

He smiled and then turned back to the bath. He clambered over the edge and got in and immediately got back out again.

'Jesus Christ that's hot!' Dougie said, jumping around on the cold tiled floor to try to cool his feet down. God, nothing was going smoothly. He hadn't planned for any of this to happen. He was simply going to kiss her on Mistletoe Cove and see what she did and now it had escalated in the most wonderful way but he wasn't prepared for it and everything was going wrong.

Eden, giggling at his antics, moved to the bath, pulled out the plug to let a little water out and added more cold to cool it down. She swirled her hand around inside the bath, and when she was happy with the temperature, she turned the tap off and then nodded for him to get in.

He climbed back in and now he was more comfortable with the temperature he lay down. She clambered in too and he opened his legs so she could sit between them and rest her back against his chest. But to his surprise she was facing towards him as she kneeled down and then lay down on top of him, leaning her face on his chest.

She was submerged, almost to the top of her shoulders, so he lapped water over her to make sure that she was warm. Her black curls fanned out in the water behind her, making her look like some kind of beautiful mermaid. He ran his fingers through her hair relishing the feel of it, then he wrapped his arms around her and held her tight, leaning his head on top of hers.

'Is this what you want, is this OK?' Dougie asked.

'This is perfect,' she said, quietly.

He got the feeling that this made her sad but he didn't know why. The very last thing he wanted to do was hurt her.

'Are you OK with this, with us?'

He stroked her hair from her face and she looked up at him.

'Yes, it's just so unexpected, it's hard to get my head around. You've never shown any feelings for me before.'

'I've always had feelings for you.' Had those feelings always been love? They probably had, only he had never realised it until he had left her behind. Living in New York, to his mind the greatest city in the world, had always been his dream, but when he'd first moved and he should have been having the time of his life, all he could think about was her. Those feelings had never gone away. But he knew she was right: he'd never told her how he felt so all this must have come as a bit of a shock to her.

'I was over there, you were over here, I didn't see how we could possibly make it work. And there was no way I was going to come over here on holiday, kiss you, make love to you and then leave again, no matter how much I wanted to. I couldn't be that man. You're my best friend and I would never do anything to hurt you.'

'But having feelings for somebody and being in love with them are two completely different things. It feels like a big leap. Is this anything to do with last night?'

What was the right answer here? He needed her to believe that this thing between them was real, he needed her to trust in him, but equally he wanted her to believe in magic again and here was his opportunity to do just that.

'Last night was magical. When I kissed you underneath the fairy lights and a thousand stars, I never wanted anyone or anything as much as I wanted you right then.'

She stared at him, confusion and doubt filling her eyes, and he decided to change the subject slightly.

'Look, I know this all feels sudden for you as I never told you how I felt but you were in love with me for twelve years too and you never made your feelings clear either.'

'I was scared, I still am. I didn't want it to change things between us. I didn't want you to stay away because you were avoiding me. And I guess, ultimately, I didn't want to face the rejection. If I never told you then I'd never have to be rejected by you because that would hurt too much. Not knowing was far easier.'

He stroked his hands down her back. 'Well, if this relationship is going to work then we need to be honest with each other.'

He looked away for a moment because part of his plan involved not being honest with her at all. Even if it was for the right reasons.

'OK, complete honesty going forward,' she said.

He smiled. He felt like this was going to come back and bite him if she found out but he was hoping she would understand.

She rested her cheek back on his chest and sighed happily. 'You know, having a bath with a man is on my list.'

'What list?'

'Things I'd like in a romantic relationship. It's silly really, most men don't care about any of that romance stuff. Cuddling, going for walks on the beach, taking baths, going on dates, yet you seem quite happy to do all of that stuff. I never figured you for a cuddling-in-the-bath type of guy.'

'What kind of guy did you think I was?'

'I don't know, I imagined that you would be very confident with women, passionate, someone who likes sex a lot. I never had you down as much of a cuddler.'

'It's different with you. I want all of that and I want to make you happy, so it's not exactly a hardship. And we can still have all of that and have the passionate sex too.'

She ran her hand down his belly towards his shorts. 'Well we could have the passionate sex now.'

He caught her hand to stop it going any further, linking his fingers through hers to soften the blow. 'I want our first time together to be perfect and at the moment you don't really trust me. Sex when you trust the other person is infinitely better than when you don't.'

'I just keep waiting for this to end. The last time you kissed me it was never mentioned ever again.'

'That was because I found out that I was going to America straight after our first kiss. It wouldn't have been fair to start something with you then, knowing I was leaving a few weeks later. And I never knew that you felt that way about me.'

'Would it have changed things if you had?'

'Honestly, I don't know. But I wouldn't have left it so long to come back if I had. But I promise you now, I'm never leaving you again.'

He saw her smile and she closed her eyes with a look of complete contentment on her face.

'If this is a dream, I don't ever want to wake up.'

Dougie held her tighter. 'Not even when your prince gets here?'

She looked up at him and smiled. 'Oh, you're too smooth. Go on then, Prince Charming, you can kiss me.'

He grinned and bent his head to do just that.

CHAPTER 15

Eden wandered through the gingerbread houses that made up the Christmas market, each selling their individual and beautiful wares. Large oversized iced sweets decorated the tops of the houses, along with snow lit up with tiny LED lights that made it look like it was sparkling. Wonderful smells of delicious sweet treats and savoury snacks hung in the air and she wanted to try them all. Christmas trees, snowmen and reindeer decorated the gaps in between the little houses and holly, ivy and mistletoe garlands were strewn from the rooftops, lit up with fairy lights. It looked magical and she couldn't help but smile.

She glanced down and knew that, charming and beautiful as the Christmas market was, the thing that was making her smile so much her face was starting to ache was that she was holding hands with Dougie Harrison.

The reaction of the islanders made her want to laugh. Some of them stopped and stared, some pointed and whispered, some nodded to her knowingly, but every single one of them was over the moon about it. She wasn't sure if there had been the same reaction from them when they had turned up to the snowman competition hand in hand and she just hadn't noticed. But they'd just been friends then and now they were... well she wasn't really sure what they were now. Boyfriend and girlfriend? Lovers? Except they hadn't even done that yet. But it didn't matter what they were, because they were something and she wanted to shout it out to everyone.

'What are you smiling at?' Dougie said, drawing her to one side as a child wearing a flashing reindeer antler headband and carrying a sticky toffee apple in one hand came charging through the marketplace, his harried-looking mum chasing after him.

'Just this,' she indicated their joined hands. 'Us. I don't think I will ever stop smiling about this. For so many years I've had comments from the islanders about us, about me being in love with you and you being in love with me and I've just dismissed them all. But now we're together I kind of want to tell everyone. I know you probably don't want that and you probably want to keep it private but, well, I will just continue being happy that we're holding hands.'

She knew she was rambling. Everything had changed between them and she wasn't sure what the rules were any more.

Before she had a chance to say anything else, Dougie bent his head and kissed her, stalling all other words in her head.

It was the sweetest, gentlest of kisses and she smiled against his lips. He clearly didn't care who saw or what they thought, he was just happy to kiss her.

He pulled back slightly.

'I'm happy about this too; I never thought it would happen either. Never doubt that I'm not as excited as you are. If you want, I'll go up to everyone here in the market and tell them personally.' He turned to the nearest passers-by, who happened to be her dad's friend Roger and his girlfriend Elsie. 'Excuse me, I just wanted to say that me and Eden are together now, we love each other and we're going to get married and have babies.'

Eden blushed, furiously. OK, maybe she didn't actually want to tell everyone at all.

'Oh, that's wonderful news,' Roger said.

'We always knew you two would get together,' Elsie said. 'We couldn't be happier for you both.'

They hurried off, no doubt to impart this wonderful gossip to everyone they could find.

'I can't believe you just did that,' Eden said.

'Who else would you like me to tell?' Dougie said, looking around for his next victim.

'No one. Kissing me is more than enough.'

He grinned. 'Well I can do that.'

He bent his head and kissed her again and Eden forgot her embarrassment with her lips against his. A giggle bubbled inside her and she pulled back slightly so she could laugh. 'I can't believe you told them we were going to get married and have babies. You couldn't have just left it at telling them we're dating?'

'Well I didn't want there to be any doubt.'

'I think you succeeded with that. The whole island will believe we're engaged within the hour and most of them will think that I'm already pregnant, despite you not having been here since the beginning of September.'

He smirked. 'How would that work exactly?'

'I'm sure the islanders will have their own theories. You being a computer geek, you probably emailed me your sperm and sent me a 3D printer to print it out on.'

He laughed loudly. 'That would be pretty amazing.'

'Can we just slow this courtship down a tiny bit, before you whisk me down the aisle?'

'We can take it as slow as you want, we can date for the next six months before we even sleep together if that's what you want.' He bent his head and kissed just below her ear, somehow knowing from the short time they had spent together the exact place to kiss her that made her go weak in the knees. She immediately wanted to drag him back to her house and make love to him as soon as they closed the door behind them. And she knew he knew that. He trailed his hot mouth lower and she closed her eyes before she remembered where they were and she pushed him gently away.

She cleared her throat before she spoke. 'I don't think we need to go to that extreme, but let's not go to the other extreme either.'

'OK, honey, whatever you wish. Now let's have a look around the market and maybe if we're lucky we might be able to get matching tattoos, or one of those heart necklaces where the pendant is split in half and I'd wear one half of the heart and you'd wear the other and then everyone would know we are two halves of the whole.'

'You're so cheesy, it's unreal.'

'I know, but you love it.'

'No, you can keep your cheesy tattoos and necklaces.'

'How about some cheesy Christmas cushion with a motto about love like, "I love winter because it gives us more reason to cuddle" or "If kisses were waves I'd give you the ocean"?'

Eden laughed. 'No, no cushions either.'

'Wow, you spoil all my fun.'

He gave her another brief kiss on the lips, as if he couldn't be parted from her, and a few feet away she heard a little squeal of excitement.

She pulled back slightly and saw her mum and dad staring at them as if all their Christmases had come at once.

'So you are together,' Finn squealed like an overexcited teenage girl.

Eden smiled as she pulled out of Dougie's arms slightly.

'Yes, we are but—'

'We couldn't be happier,' Lucy said, running forward and pulling them both into a big hug. 'We just saw Roger and Elsie and they said you'd told them you were engaged and pregnant. Are we really going to be grandparents again? This is so exciting. Your child will only be a few months younger than Freya and

Rome's. They can grow up together and play together and that's so important to have family that will look out for each other, don't you think? There was quite a big gap between me and my sisters and, as you know, I don't even speak to one of them any more and—'

'Wait, I'm not pregnant,' Eden said, before it got too far out of hand, although it seemed a bit late for that. She passed Dougie a glare though he seemed to think the whole thing was hilarious. 'And we're not engaged. We only got together last night. This is still really early days for us.'

She watched her parents' faces fall.

'You're not pregnant?' Finn said, looking like he was about to cry.

'I'm sorry, that was my fault,' Dougie said, finally speaking up. 'We were just getting a bit carried away with our excitement about being together and I told Roger and Elsie that we were going to get married and have babies. I meant eventually, umm… not now.'

Lucy and Finn stared at them for a second before Finn started smiling again. Nothing could dampen their spirits for long.

'The important thing is that you're together,' he said. 'We always knew you two would end up with each other. You see that sometimes, soul mates, two people that were born to be with each other. It took you a lot longer to come back for Eden than we all would have liked but sometimes you have to go away to see what you're missing, otherwise you just take it for granted and you don't want to do that. I was young once and I know you want to sow your seed, have some fun, have lots of sex. I used to love sex when I was young, still do if truth be told, but Lucy knows she wasn't my first. I wasn't her first either. We both had lots of partners before we found each other and I think you have to do that sometimes, try on different pairs of shoes to find the one that fits. It's a bit different for you two as Lucy and I hadn't met so we didn't know the other existed until we did meet. You knew Eden was here but you didn't know you were in love with her so you had to try on all those other women to see if they turned out to be the one. Eden was trying on lots of other men too. Well not lots. Not as many as you. To be honest I think she only slept with those other men because she couldn't have you. None of them lasted very long because none of them were you.'

'Dad—' Eden tried. This was getting more awkward by the second.

'The important thing is that it doesn't matter that you've had lots of sex with lots of different women, what matters is that you're here now and you two are together, where you should be. The fact that you have sold your house and moved to a different country to be with her is all the sign we need that you're serious about her. And now it's time to let go of your pasts and embrace your beautiful future together.'

'I am very serious about Eden,' Dougie said. 'I know I took my time coming back but—'

'You had to sow your seed. I understand,' Finn said.

'No, it wasn't quite like that—'

'The thing about being with your soul mate is that it's so much better, so much more incredible than anyone you've been with before. And you know, in your heart, this is forever. This is the person you're supposed to be with for the rest of your life. And you two have that connection, everyone can see that, it shines from you. You were supposed to be together. Soul mates always find their way back to each other eventually.'

There was silence for a while and Eden didn't know whether to laugh or cry.

Dougie cleared his throat. 'I'm going to try my very best to be the man that Eden deserves.'

'You already are, son,' Finn said, patting him on the shoulder. 'You make her happy, anyone can see that. That's all you need to do, keep making her smile.'

'I will, I promise.'

'And don't be too long about getting that ring on her finger either,' Finn said.

Finn and Lucy gave them both big hugs and left them alone, whispering excitedly between them as they walked off.

Eden waited for them to get out of hearing distance before she spoke. 'I'm sorry about them.'

'Don't be, your dad has a point. Those other women—'

Eden pressed a finger to his lips. 'I don't need to hear it. Dad was right, our pasts are just that. You are here now and that's all that matters. Don't let him pressure you into doing something you're not ready for.'

Dougie stared at her for a moment, and placed a gentle kiss on her forehead.

They wandered through the market for a while, smelling the amazing dried orange garlands, tasting the warm apple cider, feeling the velvety warmth of the brightly coloured hats and scarves and listening to the fantastic carols that were being piped out of the speakers. It was wonderful and filled her with a warm festive glow.

They stopped at the pancake stand and looked at all the fillings, which all looked and smelt delicious.

'Oooh, mince pie pancakes, they sound amazing,' Eden said as she read the sign offering a wide variety of flavours. 'Is that actually crushed mince pie pieces?'

The stall holder shook her head. 'Warm mincemeat served with brandy cream.'

'Oh, that does sound good.'

'One please,' Dougie said, handing over the money and Eden watched as the stall holder poured the batter onto a hot plate and then flipped it when it was ready.

'Are you not getting one?'

'I thought we could share. After that massive lunch you cooked for me, I'm still feeling stuffed and I'm cooking dinner for you tonight so I want us to have some kind of appetite for it.'

The stall holder handed over the warm, rolled pancake and Eden eagerly took a bite as they moved away. It was fruity and sweet, the spices of the mincemeat blending wonderfully with the warm brandy cream.

She offered it out to Dougie to take a bite but instead of taking some, he bent his head and kissed the corner of her mouth.

'Mmm, tastes delicious.'

Oh god, this man was so bloody sexy. How was she going to last until that evening?

He pulled back slightly to look at her and she could see his eyes were dark with desire.

'Behave, you were the one that wanted to wait until tonight.'

He shrugged. 'Doesn't mean we can't start the foreplay now.'

She offered out the pancake again, almost holding it as a barrier between them, and he smirked as he took a bite.

'Oh, that does taste good. Although my first taste of it was infinitely better.'

Eden took another bite, watching him as he gazed at her. The tension bubbled in the air between them. She offered out another bite and he took it, not taking his eyes off hers. He swallowed it and licked his lips in a manner that was about way more than just getting the crumbs off them.

She laughed. 'Dougie, you're such a flirt.'

'These are my best moves, you're not supposed to laugh,' Dougie protested though she could see he wasn't taking this remotely seriously. He never did.

'I can only ever laugh at you, because you are just ridiculously silly. But that's one of the many reasons why I love you.'

He grinned. 'Come on, let's go on a horse sleigh ride.'

He took her hand again and led her to the far end of the market where a jaunty red and gold sleigh – on wheels – was waiting to be pulled by a white shire horse, wearing a red harness with bells on. It was adorable.

Eden rooted in her bag for her purse. 'Let me pay for this as you bought the pancake.' She sighed as she watched Dougie hand over the money for the ride. 'I can pay for myself, you know. I'm not expecting you to pay for everything.'

'My dad always paid for my mum; well she pretty much demanded it. I grew up thinking that's how it should be. My mum said as much to me before she left, that if I ever wanted to get married, I was to stop messing around with computer games and get a proper job as women would only marry wealthy men.'

Eden stared at him in shock. 'Your mum said that?'

'Well in my experience, most women do like rich men. My dad plied my mum with gifts in a desperate attempt to get her to stay but it was all in vain.'

'You listen to me. I am not "most women". I wouldn't care if you didn't have two pennies to your name. You don't need to buy my love. I loved you when you had nothing and I still love you now, regardless of how much money you have in the bank.'

'You always said you wanted to marry a prince and live in a big castle overlooking the sea.'

'Dougie! I was a child who believed in magic and fairy tales. And do you know who I always imagined when I pictured my prince? You. That was the fairy tale, not the castle or the royalty. It was always you. The castle was just the backdrop because I didn't know any better, but the dream was always you.'

He stared at her. 'I just want to give you the best.'

She leaned up and pressed a hand against his heart. 'This is the best part of you and you've given me that.'

He nodded and then smiled, the seriousness of the conversation suddenly gone. 'Doesn't mean I can't treat you to a pancake and a horse sleigh ride once in a while though. Shall we go and meet the horse?'

Eden sighed with frustration but followed Dougie round the front of the sleigh anyway. She realised that the harness had the horse's name printed on it in gold and she smiled when she saw his name was Saint Nicholas. The Christmas festival was definitely going all out to make sure every element of the event was ticking the Christmas box.

She stroked his velvety nose and he whickered softly then licked her hand, obviously smelling the remains of the pancake.

They walked back to the sleigh, Dougie holding out his hand to help her aboard, and they settled themselves under a large silvery fur blanket.

The sleigh started moving, a gentle rocking motion as Nicholas started plodding around the park.

Dougie put his arm round her and she snuggled against him. There was a small course laid out, seemingly made of ice sculptures though Eden knew they were made from glass. The ice carvings would last only a few hours before they started to melt and these had been here the day the festival opened, though she hadn't yet had a chance to look at them properly. There were statues of snowmen, angels and elves playing and gambolling in the snow. It was all so well put together, Bella had completely outdone herself.

'Now we're under this blanket I can do rude and dirty things to you and no one would know,' Dougie said, snaking his hand over her thigh.

Eden giggled and batted his hand away. 'Stop that, Hope Island is a respectable place, we are not getting up to rude things in a one-horse open sleigh.'

'*Dashing through the snow,*' Dougie suddenly launched into song, drumming out the beat of the song on her thigh and slowly drifting his hand up towards the top of her jeans, singing loudly to distract her from where his hands was going. '*Oh what fun it is to ride in a one-horse open sleigh.*' he finished, putting extra emphasis on 'fun' and 'ride'.

'You're pure filth,' Eden said, wriggling out of his greedy hands. 'There will be no fun in this sleigh.'

'You're such a spoilsport,' he said.

'If you're good, I'll let you ring my bells on bobtails tonight.'

'I have no idea what that is, but I definitely want part of it.'

She smiled as she snuggled back against him and he wrapped his arm round her and kissed the top of her head. She closed her eyes for a moment, relishing in his warmth, his body against hers. She looked up at him and realised he was watching her.

'Enjoying the ride?'

'Very much.'

'With your eyes closed?'

'I'm enjoying being with you.'

He grinned and held her closer as he looked out over the park and at the sea beyond which was twinkling gold in the late afternoon sun.

'You know, a horse carriage ride is on my list,' Eden said.

'It is?'

'I thought it would be romantic and it really is.'

Dougie slid his hand back up her thigh. 'It could be more romantic.'

She laughed and snagged his fingers with her own.

'I'm not doing too badly on this list of yours, am I?'

'You're doing well so far.' She leaned up and stroked her hand through his stubble. 'If it all ends at midnight tonight, I'd still have the biggest grin on my face for the rest of my life.'

He frowned. 'You'd be happy if things ended between us?'

'No, I'd be gutted about that, but I would be happy about what we'd had. I couldn't be happier than I am right now. This is everything I ever wanted and if it ends I would still be happy that I experienced it all.'

'I don't intend to let it end,' Dougie said.

'You won't turn into a pumpkin at midnight?'

'I can promise you that.'

'Just promise me we'll make love before midnight, just in case.'

'OK, straight after dinner, I promise.'

'Straight after the wooing?'

'That's right. Well, the whole thing is the wooing, this, dinner, doing rude things to you in the back of a sleigh, shame I didn't get to do that one.'

'Yes it is. You'll just have to try harder with the rest of the wooing to make up for it.'

'OK, I will.'

They came back to where they started and the driver pulled the sleigh to a halt. Dougie immediately hopped out and held out a hand to help her down.

She smirked at his charm and manners.

'What would my princess like to do now?'

Eden looked around and up at the ride called Icy Extravaganza, where people were sliding down an icy ramp in giant, inflatable doughnuts, whooping and screaming as the inflatables bumped down the ice and deposited them on a crash mat at the end, most of the people failing to stay in the doughnut by the end of the ride.

'That.'

He smiled and rolled his eyes. 'There's nothing romantic about that.'

'True, but it does look like a lot of fun.' She quickly walked off in that direction and he caught up with her and snagged her hand. 'And I'm paying this time, or they'll be no nookie for you tonight.'

'Then you can definitely pay.'

CHAPTER 16

Dougie looked down at Eden as they waited in the queue for the ice slide. That conversation in the sleigh had put him on edge.

She was expecting it to end between them.

As far as she was concerned she was enjoying it all now because it would end in the not-too-distant future.

She didn't trust him and that hurt.

They'd both said they loved each other and in his book that meant forever for them. Why did she doubt that?

He'd hurt her after their first kiss on the beach all those years before, he'd hurt her by never mentioning it again as if it meant nothing to him, when nothing could have been further from the truth. He'd never told her how he felt, never given her any indication that he had feelings for her over all the years he had been away. This was all out of the blue for her, so maybe he just needed to give her time to get used to the idea. It hadn't even been a day since he'd told her he loved her.

He hadn't planned for any of this. He thought he would kiss her and if she kissed him back he might pluck up the courage and ask her out. They'd date for a few weeks, maybe months, while he tried to get her to fall in love with him and he tried to convince her that he was good enough for her and then eventually he would tell her how he loved her. But now they'd both said they loved each other, it seemed they had skipped ahead several months in his plans. And it was wonderful and it was everything he had ever imagined it would be and so much more and a little scary if he was honest. He'd only been back four days and he was in a full-blown relationship already.

There was no way he was walking away from it though. He wanted forever with Eden and that was scary too because could love really endure, could it really last for the rest of their lives? His parents were proof that love wasn't everlasting. His uncle had had an affair with Bella's mum even though he was supposedly happily married. What if he was like his mum and ended up just walking away from the marriage? What if he was like his uncle and wasn't content to stick to one woman for the rest of his life? He had never been in a relationship that could be considered serious, he'd never wanted forever with anyone before. Could he really give Eden that?

She looked up at him and smiled and he felt a surge of love for her. Yes he could. He would do everything he could to keep her, to make her happy, to make her trust him so she would believe in forever too.

What would it take for her to believe in them, to trust in their future together?

She wanted marriage and children and though the marriage part scared him, the children part didn't. The thought of her carrying his baby made him smile, he loved the idea of raising a child with her; he felt ready for that stage in his life. However, his parents' marriage had been enough to put him off that aspect for life. They had been happy before they got married and it was only after tying the knot that cracks had started to show. But maybe that was more to do with them than the act of marriage. Being with Eden forever didn't scare him; it was just the getting married part. But if that would make her feel more secure and happy then he'd give her that too.

She reached up and stroked his face and he wrapped one arm around her, holding her against him.

'Why are you frowning?' she asked.

'Just thinking how I can make you trust me.'

Her eyebrows lifted in surprise. 'I do trust you.'

'Enough to trust in us forever?'

She hesitated and his heart dropped.

'This is just going to take a bit of getting used to. Never in my wildest dreams did I ever think this would happen. I hoped for it, but I knew in my heart that it wouldn't. Before you came home I was so excited and so desperately sad all at the same time. I wanted you home and I was so looking forward to seeing you every day but I knew it would be even more painful to have you here all the time and know you would never be mine. And now here we are and I'm still finding it hard to believe. I trust you but there is a small part of me that is fearful of hoping for a future together because what if you change your mind and don't want to be with me any more? It's easier for me to take each day as it comes at the moment rather than believing in that future like I did when we first kissed and then having it snatched away again.'

'I'm not going to let you down again, I promise you that.'

She smiled and reached up to kiss him. 'Let's just enjoy what we have now and don't make promises you can't keep.'

He sighed. He was going to have to pull out all the stops to get her to trust him but in the meantime he had every intention of enjoying himself.

The people in front of them paid to go on the ride and they moved forward to pay themselves. Knowing how important it was to Eden to pay, he didn't even attempt to this time, though she was so quick in producing the money that he wouldn't have stood a chance even if he'd wanted to.

'Come on.' Eden grabbed him by the hand, dragging him up the stairs, and he couldn't help but smile at her enthusiasm.

They reached the top and waited a while for the slide to become free. He watched the other people as they hurtled down the icy slide, most being thrown up in the air as they got to the end.

'If I break any bones on this, it won't exactly be conducive to a romantic night.'

She grinned at him. 'Don't worry, I'll protect you.'

The ride attendant gestured them to come forward as he held the large oversized doughnut at the top of the slide. Dougie got in and Eden sat between his legs. She turned round to face him with a huge smile on her face.

'Don't be scared.'

He looked at her smiling face. Love was scary, for them both, but he was prepared to take the risk for her because the reward of being with her was definitely worth it.

'I'm not.'

She grinned and gave the thumbs up to the ride attendant. Dougie wrapped his hands around her waist and the attendant pushed them over the edge.

Eden whooped and screamed and he yelled as they hurtled towards the end. As they hit the crash mat the doughnut stopped and they both flew into the air. Eden landed face down on the crash mat and a second later he landed face down on top of her.

Immediately he was worried he might have hurt her by landing on her so hard and tried to scramble up, but she was giggling and laughing so hard he knew she couldn't be in any pain so he stayed where he was for a few seconds as he caught his breath and realised his groin was pressed against her bum.

He leaned over to whisper in her ear. 'I've changed my mind, this ride is very romantic.'

He flexed his hips a tiny fraction and her laughter went up an octave.

'Get off me you great big pervert,' Eden said and he climbed off her.

She rolled onto her back and swept her curly hair off her face and she was still laughing. He held out a hand and pulled her to her feet and they struggled to get off the crash mat together.

'That was so much fun,' Eden said.

'I particularly liked the end,' Dougie said and she just rolled her eyes at him. 'What would you like to do next?'

The sun was starting to set and it wouldn't be long before it got dark. He was hoping to get home soon so he could start the preparations for the evening, though if Eden wanted to stay on a bit longer then he was happy to do that.

Eden looked around. 'Oh, the ice hockey shoot-out.'

Now this was something he was definitely good at, having been a member of an amateur club on and off for several years while in New York. Maybe he could get something out of this.

'Sure, want to make it interesting?'

'A bet?' Eden asked.

'Yes, not for money though.'

She looked up at him, narrowing her eyes with suspicion. 'Then what?'

Remembering his promise to make her trust him, he decided to forego any suggestion that would take her out of her comfort zone.

'If I win, you have to make love to me tonight.'

She laughed. 'Oh, you brute. OK, what do I get if I win?'

'I'll make love to you.'

Eden pretended to think about it as they walked closer to the ice hockey stand. She sighed theatrically as if he was coercing her into it.

'OK, but if I win, you better make sure the sex is absolutely bloody amazing.'

'Oh, I will.'

He reached into his pocket to pay but Eden had already whipped out her money. He was going to have to be faster than her in the future, but he'd let her have that for today.

The ice hockey shoot-out was like a shooting range with cans or targets or buckets to hit. In fact, judging by the tiny holes in some of the targets, it had obviously been used for a shooting game before and had been converted into use with hockey pucks instead. The stall holder explained that the different targets were worth different points depending what colour they were and their difficulty rating. It was quite obvious the gold ones would be the ones to get the most points, but Dougie noticed that most of those were moving targets.

He gestured to Eden that she should go first. They had three pucks to get the most points.

Eden missed with her first attempt, got ten points with her second puck and probably by sheer fluke got fifty points for her third puck. She leapt up in the air, overly impressed with her score. And then with a sassy, cocky little swagger, she handed the hockey stick to him.

He grinned as he examined the stick. It was a lot lighter than the one he was used to but he knew he could probably hit quite well with it.

He looked over at the silver star in the top left-hand corner and slammed the puck straight into that, scoring fifty points. He glanced over at Eden and her smile had vanished.

'Let me guess, you took night classes in ice hockey too?'

He laughed. 'I've played a little.'

'You never mentioned that.'

'You never asked.'

'You could have asked for something much more than what you did ask for then,' Eden said.

'There's nothing I want more.'

He watched her smile before he turned his attention back to the targets. Deciding to ramp up the tension a little, he deliberately missed with his second puck and he smiled when she laughed triumphantly.

He aimed for another silver star but as a small gold reindeer came flying out at the top of the shooting area he slammed the puck into that, netting him another hundred points.

He turned to face Eden and to his surprise she was still smiling.

'Well it looks like you won.'

'Yes it does.'

'Well I think we better go home so I can pay up.'

He grinned. 'That sounds like an excellent plan.'

CHAPTER 17

Eden was lying on the bed waiting for Dougie to tell her that she could come downstairs. He was preparing some big meal and over-the-top romantic gesture in his attempt to woo her. She wanted to tell him that he didn't need to bother with all this romance, he already had her heart and no amount of 'wooing' would make her fall any deeper in love with him, but she was actually rather enjoying the amount of effort that he was putting into this.

She sighed as she fingered the beautiful snowflake bracelet that he had bought her just as they were leaving the Christmas market earlier that day. None of this made sense but she was going to take Bella and Freya's advice and just enjoy it while she could. She still didn't entirely believe that Dougie was telling the truth about loving her – he was up to something and she didn't know what. But she had bared her soul to him now and he hadn't run away. There was no going back. If he changed his mind he would always know how she felt. But maybe that was a good thing. After twelve years of hiding her feelings, she felt nothing but relief at finally having them out in the open. She didn't have to pretend any more. Besides, even if Dougie didn't love her, she did trust that he would never do anything to deliberately hurt her. But if this was some big trick how far was he going to take it? Would they actually make love? Dougie had said they would do it tonight but she couldn't even begin to imagine they really would and what that would actually look like if they did.

She laughed. She felt as awkward as a virgin at the thought of having sex with Dougie. She had been with quite a few men over the years and had never really felt awkward or nervous before. Even her first time she hadn't been nervous, although that probably had something to do with the half a bottle of wine that she'd consumed beforehand. Maybe she should try that again tonight, otherwise she would be trembling like a leaf by the time the main event arrived. Although knowing Dougie and his role as sweet, gentlemanly Prince Charming, he'd probably make some kind of excuse to not make love to her if he thought that she was under the influence of alcohol. And actually, if it really was going to happen and maybe it would only ever happen once, then she wanted a clear head for it so she could always remember it in glorious high definition.

But god, it needed to happen soon. Kissing him was an incredible drug she was never going to get enough of. The taste of him, the feel of his body against hers, it had been a wonderful, delicious, tantalising appetiser and now she was ready for the main course. But that was crazy because she'd never jumped into bed so fast in a relationship before.

Her stomach rumbled hungrily. Thoughts of enjoying the main course had got her brain thinking about food and, coupled with the gorgeous smells that were drifting from downstairs, she tried to put thoughts of making love to Dougie to the back of her mind and started thinking about dinner instead.

Dougie had been busily preparing for the evening for the last few hours while she had been relegated to the bedroom. Surely dinner had to be ready soon or maybe she could call downstairs and ask for some kind of snack.

A thought occurred to her that maybe she should dress for dinner. He was making all this effort so perhaps she should make an effort too. With that in mind she quickly leapt off the bed.

She opened her wardrobe and looked inside. She wanted something that said class, sophistication, romance and happy-ever-afters. Hell, what she actually wanted was something that said to Dougie, 'Take me now.' Sadly, her wardrobe was lacking anything that would say any of those things. She rifled through the coat-hangers hoping that something magical would leap out at her but nothing did. And then she spotted it. The pretty bright blue satin dress that had unicorns flying all over it. It had been a gift from Dougie and something that she loved but had never found the right time to wear it. It was so crazy and whimsical and she loved that he had thought of her when he saw it.

She quickly pulled it out and put it on. Then she swept her hair up into a high French roll and clipped it into place with some sparkly grips. There was just one more thing to complete the outfit. She'd rushed to the cupboard to try to find it when there was a knock at the door.

'Just a minute,' Eden called as she rummaged around in the boxes, trying to find the perfect accessory.

'Are you naked in there?' Dougie asked, mischievously rattling the handle. 'Because I've already seen that so there's no point in hiding.'

Eden laughed. 'Just give me a second.' And just as she was about to give up she found the box with the pink crystal-studded tiara, yet another gift from Dougie. If this really was a fairy-tale romance then she might as well play the part of the princess.

She didn't have any heels so she pulled on her sparkly unicorn Converse instead as at least they matched the dress. She rushed to the door to answer it and was wonderfully surprised to see that Dougie was wearing a suit. God, he looked so sexy, he was so broad and he filled the suit perfectly in every way. The suit had been made for him, making him look like some rich CEO, which she supposed he was since he owned his own gaming company now. Her eyes cast down to his powerful thighs and then up over his large chest and strong muscular arms. She looked up at his face, at his warm cheeky smile, his beautiful clover green eyes and his mop of red curls that never seemed to be tidy but didn't detract in any way from his sexiness. She loved this man; she loved every single thing about him.

'You look beautiful,' Dougie said, his eyes roaming appreciatively over her dress. His eyes caught the pink tiara and he smiled.

'You look pretty bloody sexy yourself, Prince Dougie.'

He grinned at her and then offered her his arm. 'Princess Eden, can I have the honour of escorting you to dinner?'

'Of course.'

She took his arm and he led her down the stairs and into the kitchen. She paused at the bottom of the stairs, noticing that the room was lit only by a candelabra in the middle of the dining table. Golden shadows flickered up the walls, making it look magical. Dougie reached out and passed her a bouquet of lilies.

'Oh Dougie, you didn't have to buy me flowers, you already bought me those roses the other day.'

'Yes but that was before I knew we were going to have sex. Those were friendship flowers. These are I-can't-wait-to-get-into-your-knickers flowers.'

Eden laughed. 'At least there's no misunderstanding.'

'Yes by accepting these flowers, you are committing yourself to a night of nookie.'

'I agree to those terms. In fact we can just skip dinner and go straight for *dessert* if you want.'

'No, I've told you, you have to let me woo you first.'

'OK, OK. You may commence wooing.'

Dougie took the flowers back off her and turned to put them in a vase.

'Ah you see, you've taken the flowers off me now, I'm not sure our contract still stands.'

'You can't eat while you're holding the flowers. I'll give them back to you to hold during the sexy times if you want.'

'I might be busy holding other things.' Eden smirked at him.

He stared at her and shook his head. 'I think this might be the fastest dinner I've ever eaten.'

'Well, we don't want to get indigestion or heartburn, so I think I'd better take my time over this meal that you've lovingly prepared.'

Dougie groaned as he pulled out the chair for her. 'You're killing me.'

Eden settled herself at the table while he went back to the oven. Wonderful smells filled the air and, despite what was going to happen after dinner, she couldn't wait to eat some of Dougie's home-cooked food. He was a fabulous cook, knowing almost instinctively which flavours and ingredients went best together. Over the years, he had gone on many different courses and classes, constantly trying to better himself. He had learned Spanish, how to play the guitar, he'd done a plumbing course, an archery course and learned how to paint. Cooking was another thing he had taught himself to do and something that he was really good at.

He returned to the table with two small plates and presented hers to her with a flourish.

'To start with this evening we have creamy garlic mushrooms. They were sautéed in garlic butter and then cooked with parmesan and cream.'

They looked amazing. Eden picked up her fork and speared one of the mushrooms. 'Garlic? We're going to be kissing each other later, you didn't really think this through.'

'Yes, but we'll both stink of garlic so it won't make any difference.'

Eden nodded to concede this. Dougie could eat a whole clove of garlic and it wouldn't make any difference to their plans for that evening.

She popped one of the mushrooms in her mouth and the wonderful creamy flavours combined with a slight tang of garlic exploded on her tongue.

'Oh god, these are amazing.'

Dougie grinned as he tucked into his own. 'It's worth a bit of pong when it tastes like this.'

He poured some red wine into her glass and she took a sip. The flavours combined perfectly.

'I could get used to this kind of treatment.'

Dougie flashed her a winning smile. 'Well when we get married, I'll cook for you every night.'

He turned his attention back to the mushrooms and Eden stared at him over the table, her fork frozen halfway to her mouth.

When.

When we get married?

As if it was already a foregone conclusion. This was their first date and he was already talking about marriage. There had been some mention of it before but that never seemed serious or real, now it suddenly seemed very real. She couldn't even imagine that far ahead. They had been friends for so long that it was hard to conceive that this was going to be forever. She tried to picture that in her mind, coming home to Dougie every night, making love to him, raising their children together. God, she wanted that but it seemed so ridiculous to even begin to hope for it. At the moment this all seemed like a bit of fun. Was that really where this was going?

He must have felt her watching him because he looked up and then cocked his head slightly, clearly confused by her expression.

'What's up?'

'When we get married?'

He swallowed a mushroom too quickly and then took a long slug of red wine. 'We both love each other, you want to get married. So I imagine we will get there eventually.'

'When you first came back to the island you said you weren't interested in having a relationship with anyone, you said that you weren't sure you ever wanted to get married, and now you're talking about us getting married as if it's the most normal thing in the world?'

'I said I wasn't interested in having a relationship with anyone but you.'

She frowned. 'That's not what you said.'

'Yes it is. I said no relationships unless my secret crush suddenly decides that she loves me.'

'I'm your secret crush?'

'I've told you, I've been in love with you for years.'

Eden stared at him. Why could she not believe him? 'It just seems a little fast.'

Dougie smiled.

'"Twelve years, Eden! I hardly think that we can be accused of rushing things",' he quoted her own words back at her.

She smiled. He was right, she supposed.

'Look, don't worry about any of that now. When it's the right time for us, we'll talk about it then.'

She popped the mushroom in her mouth and chewed thoughtfully, not taking her eyes off him.

He reached for her hand. 'Stop looking for flaws in this. It is what it is, no scam, no joke, I love you. Just enjoy what we have and stop waiting for it to end.'

She looked down at her fingers entwined with his. They looked so right there. This thing between them felt so right as if they'd been doing it for years and in many ways they had. This was her dream and, as she'd told Dougie today, it was time to enjoy it.

She lifted her glass and held it across the table towards him. 'To us.'

He smiled and lifted his glass to chink against hers.

This was Dougie, her best friend. Whatever happened they would be OK.

CHAPTER 18

Eden placed her spoon carefully down inside her bowl. That was it. Three delicious courses had been eaten and, unless Dougie wanted to prolong the evening with coffee, cheeses or after-dinner mints, they were about to have sex for the first time.

Before dessert had been served, he had disappeared off to the lounge, closing the door behind him so he could get ready for the rest of the evening, though she wasn't sure what preparation was needed. Whenever she'd had sex in the past, there had been very little preparation. In fact bringing a condom along to the evening was probably as prepared as it had gone with the men that she had dated. She had no idea what to expect.

Dougie reached across the table to hold her hand, stroking his thumb over her knuckles.

'So…?' Eden said, still not quite believing this was about to happen.

He grinned, waggling his eyebrows mischievously. 'So?'

'How do we do this?'

He smiled. 'Well, first of all we have to get naked and then there'll be a lot of kissing, touching, in, out, in, out, shake it all about.'

He stood up and took the bowl over the dishwasher as he hummed the 'Hokey Cokey'.

'Interesting technique.'

He shrugged. 'It's worked for me before.'

'So women like the shake-it-all-about approach?'

'They love it.' He closed the dishwasher door and moved back towards her.

'And the "Hokey Cokey" part?'

'The women go crazy for that.'

Dougie held out his hand and she placed hers inside it. He gently pulled her to her feet and kissed her cheek.

'Should we start ripping each other's clothes off?'

Dougie looked down at her clothes. 'This dress is way too pretty to be ripped, besides I don't think the unicorns would like that. But if you like that sort of thing I can certainly rip your underwear off.'

Eden giggled. 'I've never had a conversation like this before sex.'

Dougie nodded. 'It's certainly lacking the spontaneity of my previous sexual experiences. But a little bit of preparation is sometimes a good thing.'

Still holding her hand, he led her to the lounge door and pushed it open. Eden followed him inside and stopped when she saw that every surface was covered in flickering candles. There had to be easily a hundred candles lighting the room along with the twinkling fairy lights. The log fire was burning merrily, adding warmth and comfort to the room. Blankets and pillows were laid out in front of the fire and just the idea that in a few minutes they would be lying there making love sent butterflies somersaulting through her stomach.

'Oh my god, are we really going to do this?'

Dougie stroked her cheek.

'Only if you want to.' Then he whispered theatrically, 'Please say yes, please say yes, please say yes.'

She laughed again and leaned her forehead against his chest. He wrapped his arms around her and kissed her head. 'Oh Dougie, if we do this everything changes between us.'

'Everything has already changed between us, but in the best possible way.'

She looked up at him and knew he was right. She leaned up and kissed him and he cupped her face in his hands and gently kissed her back. She didn't make a move to take it any further, but neither did he, seemingly content to just kiss her. And it was wonderful, she had never felt so loved and so adored with a man before, but then Dougie was her best friend, it was never going to be anything but magical.

She pulled back slightly. 'I love you,' she whispered against his lips and he smiled as he kissed her again.

She slid his jacket off his shoulders and then went to work on his tie, cursing that the bloody thing seemed to be knotted up tighter than the locks on Fort Knox. When her fingers struggled to make any progress, Dougie took over, still kissing her while she started work on the buttons of his shirt. Finally the tie came off and she was able to finish undoing the buttons on the collar. She dragged his shirt over his shoulders and down his arms where they became stuck over his hands.

He gave a little moan of protest against her lips. 'Cufflinks,' Dougie muttered.

She stepped back and sighed with frustration. 'Dougie! Didn't you learn your lesson with the whole drawstring debacle?'

'I thought they were sexy,' he said as he struggled to get the cufflinks off. Finally he freed himself and showed her the cufflinks, little black studs with the letter *E* engraved in them. She smiled hugely when she saw them and leaned up to kiss him again.

He slid his arms round her back and unzipped her dress then stroked up her bare back and slipped the dress off her shoulders where it fell to the floor. His mouth was on her neck, trailing kisses over her shoulder as he slid her bra straps down her arms too. He unclipped it round the back and let that fall to the floor as well.

She moved her hands to the button on his trousers. He kissed her again, cupping her breasts and running his thumbs across her nipples. She gasped against his lips and she stood almost frozen to the spot as she enjoyed the wonderful sensations of Dougie touching her body before she remembered that she should be undressing him too. He brought his mouth back to her neck; his stubble grazing her skin was an incredible feeling. But it was all too much, too many feelings, too intense, too much of everything. And even though, with Dougie's hands on her, the very last thing she wanted to do was crack a joke, she knew she needed a little bit of light relief from what was about to come.

She unzipped his trousers, slowly. 'I get to see you naked,' she sang. 'I get to see you naked.'

She felt him smile against her skin. 'That's kind of a necessity if we're going to have sex. Well, it isn't but definitely certain bits have to be naked.'

She pushed his trousers off his hips and let them fall to the floor. He quickly stepped out of them. She left his tight black boxer briefs on, wanting to slow it down just a little bit. 'What if getting naked puts the other person off? Maybe we should blow out all these candles and do it in the dark.'

'I've already seen you naked baby, there's no possible way that you could put me off. Besides, staring at your beautiful body is part of the fun.'

She stepped back a little to appraise him. He was magnificent in every way. She moved back towards him, caressing her hands over his body as he stood there and watched her. Then suddenly he was kissing her again, gathering her close against him.

Without taking his lips from hers, he scooped her up into his arms. She let out a little squeal at the sudden movement and giggled against his lips as he carried her over to the blankets. He laid her down and then lay down next to her as he resumed his kissing, his hands roaming across her body in the gentlest of touches.

He suddenly moved back onto his knees and she wondered what he was doing. He eyed her with a mischievous smile as he moved his hands to her knickers. He looked like he was up to no good. He ran both hands slowly round the waistband and then to her surprise he suddenly ripped the knickers clean off her.

She gasped and then laughed. 'I can't believe you just did that.'

'You said you wanted me to rip your clothes off,' Dougie said.

'I didn't expect you to actually do it.'

'Hey, I have to give the people what they want.'

Eden reached out for his shorts. 'I'll tell you what I want.'

He caught her hands and pinned them above her head as he continued to kiss her and she got the feeling that he was trying to delay the big moment too. Would he pull back, would he change his mind? Surely he wouldn't go to all this trouble and then back out at the last minute? Keeping her wrists pinned over her head with one hand, he slid the other up her thigh. She moaned softly against his mouth when he touched her between her legs. His touch was exquisite and he captured her cries of pleasure against his lips as he quickly brought her over the edge.

She was breathless as he settled himself between her legs, the delicious friction of the cotton of his boxers moving against her most sensitive area sending quivers of pleasure through her body again.

He stared down at her with complete adoration in his eyes and the biggest smile on his face.

She slid her hands down his back and then into his shorts, squeezing his bum playfully. She tried to push the shorts down but his weight on top of her meant she couldn't reach past his thighs.

'Off, off, off, off,' Eden chanted and Dougie laughed.

He stood up and Eden leaned back on her elbows to watch. Dougie started singing the famous striptease music, 'The Stripper', as he started wiggling his bum and playing with the waistband of his shorts, pulling it down a little bit and then pulling it back up again. Eden laughed as he turned around and sexily lowered his shorts, bending over so she could see his bottom as if he really was a stripper. He had a marvellous bum.

'You're too good at this,' Eden said, laughing. 'Did you go to night classes to learn this as well?'

'These moves are all my own, baby.'

He grabbed a cushion and held it over his manhood and turned around, then kicked his boxers across the room. Eden laughed again but the laughter died on her lips when she saw Dougie's expression of horror.

She turned round to see what he was looking at and saw that his boxers had landed on top of one of the candles and had caught fire.

'Crap,' he said, dropping the cushion and running across the room. Eden scrabbled to her feet too as he grabbed the vase of roses and poured it over the flames, putting them out before it had a chance to get out of hand.

As they both stood there naked, staring at the smouldering remains of Dougie's shorts, and the water dripping down the walls, Eden couldn't help but laugh, giggling uncontrollably at the mess.

'Well, when you promised me a night of smoking hot sex, I didn't expect this,' she said.

'I'm so sorry,' Dougie laughed. 'Looks like I owe you some more roses too.'

He picked up his soggy boxers and shook out the water and then held them open to reveal a gaping hole right at the front. Eden laughed.

'Aww, these were my lucky pants,' he said.

'Well fortunately for you, you're still going to get lucky tonight.'

Dougie immediately dropped his shorts, his eyes lighting up as he gathered her against him. 'I haven't ruined my chances?'

'Dougie, the world could end, aliens could come down and take over the planet and I'd still be sleeping with you tonight. I've waited twelve years for this; nothing is going to stop me now.'

He grinned as he shuffled her back towards the blankets. 'Well let's get on with it then.'

'That's the most romantic thing that anybody has ever said to me.'

'I'm filled with romance, me.'

She reached for him, wrapping her hand around him, making him take a sharp intake of breath. 'Why don't you fill me up with some of your romance too?'

He smiled as he lowered her to the floor, lying on top of her and kissing her sweetly. He pulled away slightly to grab a condom, and her gaze was drawn down as he slid it on, her eyes widening as she suddenly realized how big he was.

'Stop staring at it like it might kill you,' Dougie said.

'It might, it's bloody big enough.'

Dougie laughed as he moved back over her. 'What every man dreams of hearing.'

A delicious thrill ran through her as he settled himself between her legs. They really were going to do this. She ran her hands over his back and shoulders and then up his neck to stroke his hair. He stared down at her, the humour suddenly fading from his eyes replaced by something much deeper. Love, affection, friendship, it was all there on his face.

He slid inside her, filling her, and she wrapped her legs around him. His breath was accelerated and she could feel him trembling slightly, with excitement or nerves, she didn't know which. He stared at her for the longest time, not moving, just taking her in.

'Best sex ever,' Dougie said.

'We've only just started.'

He shook his head. 'It doesn't matter; being with you was always going to be the best sexual experience of my life.'

She smiled and as he started to move against her, she knew he was right. It didn't matter whether the sex was good, bad or earth-shattering, it was going to be amazing because they belonged together and right here in his arms, with Dougie deep inside her, was definitely the best place in the world.

CHAPTER 19

The fire had almost died out completely, just a faint glow amongst the embers was the only thing that remained, but Dougie didn't have the energy to move to relight it. Most of the candles had gone out too, though some were still flickering brightly, competing with the twinkling fairy lights to brighten the room.

The room would most likely get a bit chilly now but he had never felt more content and happier in his life as he did right now, with Eden lying naked on the blankets in front of him, his chest to her back, his arms wrapped tightly round her.

He pulled a blanket over them both, making sure she was entirely covered apart from a tiny sliver of her shoulder which he wanted to leave open so he could kiss her. He laid his lips against her warm skin, breathing her in as his hand caressed over her silky stomach.

She hadn't really said a lot since they'd finished making love. He frowned with concern. In fact, he wasn't sure she'd said anything.

Straight after, when they were still trying to catch their breath, he'd asked her if she was OK and she'd nodded and then they'd kissed for the longest time. Eventually, when he realised he was probably crushing her with his weight he had rolled off her and she had rolled onto her side facing away from him. He had curled himself around her and they hadn't moved since.

Maybe she was asleep; his whole body felt so deliciously weary after they had made love that he'd understand if she felt the same.

He leaned up on his elbow and swept her hair back from her face so he could look at her. Her eyes were wide open as she stared at the dying embers in the fire and she had the biggest smile on her face, which was something of a relief.

'Are you OK?'

She nodded again.

'You're very quiet.'

'I just… wasn't expecting it to be like that.'

He swallowed. Had he taken it too far? 'In that it exceeded your expectations or didn't meet them?'

She rolled onto her back to look at him, stroking her hand through the stubble on his jaw as she smiled at him fondly. Was this the part where she told him the sex was nice? He wasn't sure his ego could take that.

'Both. It wasn't what I thought it would be and it far exceeded my expectations. I thought when I made love to you for the first time it would be beautiful, and it was, but it was so much more than that. I've never laughed during sex before, in fact I don't think I've ever laughed so much in my entire life as I did tonight. And it made it so much better than I thought it would be. It felt like… I wasn't just making love to the man I loved, I was making love to my best friend and there was something so wonderfully different about that.'

He smiled with relief. He knew exactly what she meant.

He hadn't expected it to turn out like it had either. He had planned for a night of pure romance, flowers, candles, fine food, and he had assumed that it would be beautiful and sweet too. But when they had begun to make love, Eden had started giggling about his pants catching fire and there'd been lots of silly fire puns after that in between the most heated of kisses. Then she'd started singing the 'Hokey Cokey' and he'd followed her instructions to the letter, pumping his hips in time with her words, 'in, out, in, out'. And when she sang 'shake it all about' and he'd obliged, she had laughed so hard she snorted, which made her laugh harder and did wonderful things to their bodies where they were joined. He'd been unable to stop laughing too and when she'd demanded that he do the 'Hokey Cokey' on her, neither of them had been able to stop giggling for several minutes. Then he'd shifted her legs higher so he could take her deeper and all humour had vanished for the next few minutes as they both found their incredible release, Eden clinging to him and shouting out his name. It had been without a doubt the most unexpected, tremendous, extraordinary sex he'd ever had.

'You are so silly and I love you so much for that. You didn't have to do any of this to woo me, I'm already well and truly wooed.'

He smiled and kissed her. 'Doesn't mean I'm going to stop doing nice things for you.'

'OK, but maybe next time we can have sex to "Agadoo" instead.'

He laughed. 'OK but I'm not using a real pineapple, that might hurt.'

'Agreed.'

She rolled back onto her side, facing away from him, and he snuggled into her again, sweeping her hair over her shoulder so he could kiss the back of her neck.

'It's almost midnight,' Eden said.

He looked over her shoulder and saw it was just a minute until the clock struck twelve.

'I promise you, I'm not going to turn into a pumpkin.'

'Or a gremlin?'

He laughed.

'Well I can't promise that.' He playfully bit on her shoulder and she giggled.

'You'd be Gizmo anyway if you did; you're too sweet to be anything else.'

He wasn't sure he liked being called sweet but if it made her happy then he'd go with it.

'So you're not going to disappear or run away again back to America?'

'Definitely not.' He kissed her shoulder.

'Even if the thing you came home for doesn't work out?'

He stalled in his kisses. She had clung onto that throwaway comment he had made on the beach the other morning about there being a bigger reason why he had come home. She was the main reason but she didn't know that. He hadn't meant to make it sound like he would go back to America if it didn't work out between them. In reality he had come home for many more reasons than just Eden. It had simply been cold feet over whether he had done the right thing by moving his whole life back to Hope Island and he was bound to have those fears.

'Nothing is going to take me away from you, you're way too important to me for that.'

'More important than the thing you came here for?'

He didn't want to say that she was one of the main reasons he had come back here for. That put way too much pressure on the relationship for her.

'You're the single most important thing in my life at the moment. I'm not going anywhere.'

The clock on the mantelpiece suddenly chimed midnight and he resumed his kisses on her shoulder and neck. The clock finished chiming.

'See, I'm still here,' Dougie said.

'In that case, you can make love to me again.'

He smiled against her skin. 'You're so demanding.'

'You'll find that being married to a princess is very demanding.'

His heart skittered at the mention of marriage. He had tried to be blasé about it over dinner to show her he was in this for the long haul but he was still fearful of it. He didn't want anything to ruin what they had and marriage had ruined his parents' relationship. But if that was what she wanted then he'd just have to man up and get on with it.

Although he was very happy to comply with her most recent demand.

He slid the hand that had been around her stomach down her outer thigh and gently back up as he continued kissing her neck. He ran his hands back down her leg and lifted her knee, hooking it over his own leg. When he slid his hand back up it was on the inside of her thigh and she moaned softly at his gentle touch. She arched against him, leaning into his hand, then she settled her head on her bent arm and he linked fingers with her. He stroked and caressed, nibbling little kisses along her neck. Her fingers tightened against his, her breathing becoming faster, and he had never been so turned on before giving pleasure to someone else. Watching her fall apart, crying out his name as he stroked her, it was an incredible feeling.

Breathless, she turned her head to face him and he kissed her hard, her hands stroking through the curls at the back of his head.

Blindly and without taking his mouth from hers, he reached behind him for a condom. He'd had the foresight to scatter them around. He quickly found one and tore his mouth from Eden's long enough only to rip open the foil packet with his teeth before he was kissing her again, and sliding the condom on.

He pushed inside her and she moaned against his lips. God, she felt so indescribably good.

She started rocking her hips against his, setting the pace, and it was slow, lazy, unhurried love-making. He felt like he could lie here all night like this; that just being connected to her in this way was enough.

He continued to kiss her for the longest time, holding her hand, stroking across her body with the other.

But as the feelings inside him started to tighten, like a coiled spring about to release, he felt her fingers tighten around his again, that tell-tale hitch of her breath that said she was nearing the edge too. God, they were so perfectly in sync.

He moved against her again, feeling the change in her body as much as he could feel it in his own, and as he captured the moans of pleasure from her on his lips they both hurtled over the edge together.

She pulled back slightly to stare at him, her hands still caressing the back of his neck as he tried to catch his breath.

He had no idea why it was so good with her but it was, it really bloody was.

She smiled at him as if she knew what he was thinking.

'You OK?' she asked.

He laughed and nodded. 'There is no way in the world I'm walking away from that.'

She grinned and turned away from him, closing her eyes. 'Good.'

He kissed her on the shoulder and then laid his head down on the pillow too. Their fingers were still linked and he wrapped his arm around her and closed his eyes.

This was where he belonged.

🌲🌲

Eden walked into Pots and Paints the next day and smiled to see that Clare already had everything in hand. The cakes had been made and the smell of warm mince pies filled the air. There were a few tables filled with parents and children painting mugs and plates with poster paints as with only three days until Christmas there would be no time to glaze them and put them in the kiln before the big day. Most of the tables were filled with the islanders who had just come in for a coffee or cake. Clare clearly had everything under control. She was such a godsend, and always worked her arse off for Eden. Whenever either one of them had a day off, the other always took the early morning shift the next day so they could make the most of another lie-in.

Although Eden hadn't had much of a lie-in that morning when Dougie had woke her up to make love to her again. Then they'd ended up having a shower together and he'd made love to her again. The memory of it was enough to make her smile even more. He couldn't keep his hands off her, which was fortunate as she couldn't get enough of him either.

He'd gone out for a run before she'd left the house and she knew he would be in here after. It was becoming a regular habit and she loved it.

Clare looked up at her and smiled but her smile grew even bigger as Eden walked round the counter towards her. She took her hat and coat off and hung it up and turned back to face Clare.

'Does your beautiful smile have anything to do with that rather gorgeous boyfriend of yours?' Clare asked.

Word had certainly got around the island quickly. Though they had hardly been discreet. And was Dougie her boyfriend? Regardless of what they were now, Dougie was the sole reason for her being so happy and she didn't care who knew it.

'Yes it does.'

'So you two are a thing now?'

'We're something,' Eden said, unable to stop herself from smiling, even if she couldn't pinpoint what that something was. 'He says he loves me.'

'Oh, Eden, I'm so happy for you. You two have finally got together after all this time. Everyone said that he came back here for you and I was so sure he had a thing for you for years and now it's really happened.' Clare flapped her hands around excitedly. 'And you love him right? Of course you do.'

'I really do, I don't even care who knows it any more, I love him,' she raised her voice. 'I love Dougie Harrison.'

'Well that's good to know,' Dougie said, and she spun around to see that the man himself had come in. It was clear he'd been out for a run; his red hair was slightly damp from the fog outside and the running top that he was wearing hugged his chest and his broad arms. It was hard not to remember spending the night wrapped in those arms. He was watching her with that glorious charming smile. And the wonderful thing was she didn't even feel embarrassed about Dougie having heard her because she was pretty sure he felt the same.

She walked back around the counter and leaned up and kissed him, just briefly. He smiled against her lips as he kissed her back.

'I thought I might get some lunch in here if that's OK? I've got a bit of work I need to get on with so I won't disturb you.'

'Of course you can stay, what would you like to eat?'

'I'll have a ham and mozzarella toastie please and a gingerbread latte and no arguments about me paying this time.'

'OK, coming right up.'

She slipped back behind the counter and Clare gave her a huge grin. Dougie settled himself at a nearby table and pulled his iPad from his bag.

'Oh I meant to say, the Pots and Paints bank account is looking a bit short this month, what with the kiln repairs we did last week and the new pottery wheel we had delivered,' Clare said.

'That's OK, would you mind transferring some money from my personal savings account to cover it?' Eden said as she busied herself doing Dougie's toastie. She had known Clare for so long she trusted her completely and would often get her to pay bills from the bank account or transfer money over from her personal account whenever it was needed.

'No problem, I'll do that now,' Clare said and disappeared into the little office in the corner.

Eden glanced over at Dougie, watching him as he pulled his glasses on and moved things around on his iPad. Why was it a man in glasses was so sexy? Or was it just Dougie?

'Holy crap!' Clare's voice rang out loud and clear from the office and Eden quickly rushed in there.

'What's wrong?' Eden said, seeing that Clare had the online banking screen up. Maybe the account for Pots and Paints was looking a lot lower than it should be.

'Did you win the lottery or something?' Clare said, her eyes wide in shock.

The shop had done particularly well in the last few months but Eden was always careful that after her and Clare's wages had been paid and any overheads and bills had been sorted, any profits were squirrelled away into savings to cover any repairs or new equipment she might need in the future. Maybe it was the savings account that was looking quite healthy – she had no idea what was in there but she knew it was probably several thousand.

'What do you mean?'

Eden moved closer and saw the large number on the balance. She blinked a few times as her eyes adjusted to so many zeros. It couldn't be right. She stared at it and her heart started to pound furiously.

Her balance on her personal account showed a figure of just over a million pounds.

CHAPTER 20

'No, it can't be,' Eden said, probably way too loud. 'Click into my account, let me see where this money came from.'

Clare followed her instructions with a shaky hand and clicked on the account to show all the credits and debits coming in and out and there it was. Exactly one million pounds deposited that morning. She looked at the details and saw that it was a counter credit, which meant it was paid in at a bank somewhere either via cash or cheque. Of course it wouldn't show any more detail than that.

Tears smarted her eyes because her second wish had just come true. But this one she didn't want, because if all of her wishes were coming true it meant that Dougie only loved her because of her wish.

No, this was ridiculous. This was just a simple mistake, that was all.

'Everything OK?' Dougie appeared in the doorway, looking worried.

'Is this to do with you?' Eden said.

'Is what to do with me?'

'This million pounds,' she gestured to the screen.

'What million pounds?'

'It seems Eden has a rich benefactor,' Clare said, unable to take her eyes off the huge amount on the screen.

'Someone put a million pounds in my account this morning, was it you?' Eden demanded, knowing that her voice was really shaky.

'Me?' Dougie was incredulous. 'I love you and everything but why would I give you a million pounds?'

'Because you're being all lovely and sweet and you want to do nice things for me.'

'Yes, but I wouldn't give you a million pounds, that's way too nice even for me.'

'This is you,' Eden insisted. 'There is no one else I know that could give me a million pounds so easily. This is some kind of Dougie joke. Take it back, I don't want it.'

Dougie laughed. 'It's not mine, honey. Why do you think it's mine?'

'Because of these silly wishes you made me do at Mistletoe Cove.'

He stared at her in shock for a moment. 'You wished for a million pounds? How would I know that? I didn't see what you wrote on that piece of paper. And then you put the wishes inside a sealed envelope and threw them into the blowhole. How could I possibly know what your wishes were?'

'If it's not you, how do you explain this?'

He shrugged. 'This is what you wanted; it's what you wished for. Your wishes are coming true.'

'I didn't want this, I don't want a million pounds, what the hell am I going to do with a million pounds? You need to take it back.' Eden knew her voice was getting high with anxiety but she couldn't do anything to stop it.

Dougie frowned. 'Why did you wish for something if you don't want it?'

'To prove to you that all this stuff about wishes at Mistletoe Cove was a load of rubbish. I thought it was all just another little Dougie joke; I thought if I asked for something ridiculous, it would prove that you were lying or joking about Mistletoe Cove when it didn't come true.'

Dougie's frown got deeper. 'You were supposed to wish for something that you really wanted. That's how it works. Were all your wishes silly wishes?'

'No, I asked for things that I never thought would happen!'

'Things you really didn't want?'

'I didn't want this, I don't need money. Pots and Paints is doing really well. This was just the first thing I thought of to prove to you the wishes wouldn't come true. I don't want a million pounds. Money doesn't buy you happiness. I change my mind about the wish; I'll go back to the blowhole and ask for a puppy instead.'

'If you don't want the money, I'll have it,' Clare said, only half joking.

'No love, this money isn't mine. If this isn't Dougie then there's been a mistake. My mum and dad used to work in a bank, I know that for every credit there has to be a debit. Money doesn't just magically appear in someone's account, it has to have been taken from someone else's account and put into mine and that someone is probably mightily pissed off by now. If it's a cheque then the bank can trace who wrote the cheque and who the payee was supposed to be and then they can take the money back. I need to go down to the bank now and sort this out. Clare, will you be OK to watch the shop for a few minutes?'

Clare nodded, still staring at the money in shock.

'I'll come with you,' Dougie said.

Eden grabbed her coat and pulled her hat on as Dougie gathered his things and joined her out on the street.

'Why not enjoy the money?' he said as he fell in at her side.

'I'll enjoy it when I can give it back,' she said.

'You wished for it, and your wish has come true. Don't question it, just have fun with it.'

'Wishes don't come true.'

'Well this one has. There must be something you'd want to spend the money on.'

'It's not my money,' Eden said.

'Say that it is, say that it's a genuine gift from the powers that be, the wishmakers, the fairies, your fairy godmother, someone has given you a gift, do with it what you want.'

'If it's mine to do with as I please, then I'll give it away,' Eden said desperately. She wanted no part of this. She didn't want to go anywhere near that money. The further she distanced herself from it, then she wouldn't have to face the possibility that Dougie didn't really love her at all. 'I bet Bella's homeless charity could benefit from a million pounds, I could give Clare a hefty Christmas bonus and she can take her kids and husband to Disney World in Florida. What about your gaming company? I could buy shares in your company or give you some money for new equipment. I could help the air ambulance or the seal sanctuary or pay Rome back for all the money he gave me to start my own business.'

'It's supposed to be a gift for you,' Dougie said, quietly.

'There were no rules with the wishes that said that I couldn't use the money as I see fit. I don't need a million pounds, Dougie. That's a ridiculous amount of money. How do I take back the wish?'

'Well if you really don't want the wish then you have to go back to the blowhole and ask for the wish not to come true or something like that. I don't think this will work with the money though – now it's in your account, you can't give it back. You might as well enjoy it.'

'If I find out you had anything to do with this, me and you are going to fall out.'

'Why do you think it's me?'

'Because you have the money. Rome said you got two and half million pounds from the sale of your apartment in New York.'

'Dollars. Not pounds. It's a lot less than that in pounds.'

'And it's still a lot more money than most people will ever see in a lifetime. And you worked bloody hard for that money; you should be the one enjoying it.'

'I am. I bought a house in one of my favourite places in the world next door to one of my favourite people in the world. That's a pretty spectacular way to spend my money.'

'I'm sure there are other things you can do with it, rather than giving half of it away to me.'

'It wasn't me. How would I know that you wished for a million pounds? Have you told anyone what you wished for?'

She thought back to her conversation with Bella and Freya. She had told them about her wish that Dougie loved her, but she hadn't told them about the other two wishes, other than that they were silly nothing wishes.

'No, no one knows.'

'Then how could this possibly have anything to do with me? I don't understand why you're not happier about this. Anyone else in the world who had been given a gift of a million pounds would be over the moon.'

Eden didn't break her stride as she hurried along the street to the bank. 'I told you before we went to Mistletoe Cove; I have everything I could possibly want. I'm very happy in my life, a million pounds isn't going to change that. I love my job, I love living here on Hope Island. Money isn't going to make me happier. In fact, it's making me bloody miserable right now.'

'Why is it making you miserable?'

'Because… because I don't want the legend of Mistletoe Cove to be true.'

'Why not?'

Eden shook her head, not prepared to voice her insanity.

'What's wrong in believing in magic and having hopes and dreams? Why not chase those dreams and make them come true once in a while?'

'Because I learned a long time ago that the belief in the tooth fairy and Santa are silly, dreams of living in a big castle and getting married to a prince are nearly impossible and actually completely overrated. I learned that my teenage hopes of travelling around the world and seeing every little corner of it are completely impractical and irresponsible when you have a business to run and bills to pay. I learned that I will never ride on the back of a magical unicorn or a flying dragon and that dreams never, ever come true.'

She frowned as she looked at Dougie, because while the rest of that was all correct, her dreams had come true the day that he said he loved her. That was everything she ever wanted. Maybe dreams did come true after all.

'I don't believe that dreams don't come true at all,' Dougie said. 'Everything I ever wanted has come true. I wanted to live in America, I wanted to have my own gaming company and—'

'I know, you wanted to meet Harrison Ford.'

'I wanted you. To be with you,' Dougie said.

She stopped to look at him and he drew her into his arms and kissed her on the forehead. 'Dreams come true for people every single day, big dreams, little dreams, ridiculous over-the-top dreams, sometimes people wait years and sometimes it happens in a matter of seconds. Some people have to work hard to make their dreams a reality and for some it happens without them even trying, which hardly seems fair. But they do come true. We have to have dreams to give us something to hope for. Don't ever give up on them.'

Hope bloomed in her heart. Dougie Harrison was holding her in his arms, kissing her and he'd told her he loved her. He was right. This was proof that dreams did come true. And nothing beat this feeling of seeing her dream become a reality. Maybe now her one dream had come true she needed some new ones. With a million pounds, the possibilities were endless. She shook her head. No, maybe she could believe in dreams again, maybe she would start making some of her dreams come true, but she couldn't believe that a million pounds had magically appeared in her account. That was a stretch too far.

'OK, so what if this million pounds arrived in cash in a big envelope that said, "To Eden Lancaster, with love from the fairies", on the outside?' Dougie said.

'Must be a bloody big envelope,' Eden said, pulling out of his arms and carrying on to the bank.

'Well I'm guessing that's why the fairies paid it straight into your account. The point being, you would have no way of sending the money back but you would know it was a gift. So what would you spend it on?'

'I don't know. There's these new pottery paints I've been thinking of buying for the café. They are kind of metallic and look amazing, they're quite expensive though, so I guess I would treat myself to them.'

Dougie groaned in frustration. 'Not something for the café, not something for anyone else, what would you buy for you?'

Eden thought about it for a moment. 'I don't know, some new shoes maybe, I don't really have any nice shoes, I live in my Converse. I'd love a pair of nice heels, something dressy. I saw a blue sparkly pair in the window of the shoe shop in town the other day and I did entertain trying them on. But when would I ever wear them? I suppose if I really did have a million pounds I'd buy them.'

Dougie sighed. 'OK, a nice pair of shoes, that's a start I suppose, maybe a dress and a handbag to go with it.'

Eden shrugged. 'I guess.'

Dougie shook his head. 'Why is it you're over the moon with something simple like a gift of a bunch of white roses, but a million pounds and you can't even crack a smile?'

'It's what the million pounds represents that I'm not happy about. The roses you gave me were so sweet and so unexpected and...' she had to swallow down the ache in her chest. She had to remember how lovely Dougie had been to her before they went to Mistletoe Cove. They'd spent two nights sleeping together, he'd bought her roses. Surely he wouldn't have done that if he hadn't had feelings for her too? Feelings that were there before she wished for them. 'Right now I'd take a hundred white roses over a million pounds any day.'

'OK, what about building a proper studio out the back of your shop to develop your workshops? This was something you were passionate about, so let's make this a reality. We can fit it out with a dozen pottery wheels and desks for the children to work at. You could use the money to hire another assistant to help in the shop so you can give more of your time to teaching children. You could use the money to go on a pottery wheel course to get proper instruction, something more than I or any YouTube video could teach you. You could buy all the resources, books and tools that you need and make your workshops the place to go to on the island. You could even teach adults too in the evenings.'

Eden hesitated because that was exactly her dream. When she had done her pottery course at college she had found it so therapeutic and calming. When she was working with clay she could focus only on that, on sculpting the clay into different shapes and pieces, on spending a long time smoothing out all the cracks and bumps to make the surface of the clay perfect. It helped to clear her mind and at a time when Dougie had just left to go to America leaving her heart in smithereens, she'd needed that time to focus on something else more than anything. She wanted to give that to the people of the island. The pottery painting café had achieved that in some small way, it was fun and a good draw for the tourists, but people would often get disappointed when their works of art never turned out as they wanted them to. But you could really lose yourself when working with clay and creating something simple, something that people could take their time to get right. It would be so rewarding. To be able to offer that to adults and children on a regular basis would be incredible.

Dougie mistook her silence for her refusal.

'What about a nice holiday, a trip of a lifetime, somewhere you've always wanted to go to? You've never been anywhere on holiday.'

'That's not true, I went to France once on a school trip and I've been to Scotland for a long weekend with Stephen. That was lovely.'

'Fantastic,' Dougie said, dryly. 'Now she's talking about her ex.'

'Scotland was lovely, not the ex,' Eden said, hoping to reassure him.

'You always said Stephen was perfect.'

'He was, but he wasn't you. I never loved him because I was always in love with you and the poor man couldn't compete.'

'Oh.' Dougie smiled at this.

She nudged him. 'Don't feel too happy about his misfortune.'

He tried and failed to straighten his smile but realising he had got distracted he snagged her arm and pulled her to a stop. 'We could go on holiday somewhere. With a million pounds, we could go anywhere in the world. We could go to Paris, Vienna, Rome.'

'I can't leave the shop for two or three weeks, that's not fair to Clare.'

'So you close the shop for a few weeks, give Clare some of the money so she can go on holiday too. You've worked so hard to set your pottery painting café up and make it a success and I know that any money that isn't spent on wages or bills gets put away for a rainy day, and that's a very sensible attitude to take, but don't you think you could treat yourself once in a while? You deserve a holiday.'

It was true that, apart from the odd day off here and there or the very occasional long weekend away, she'd never gone on holiday. Financially she was doing fine, she paid herself and Clare a decent wage, the shop had been bought outright several years before when Rome had received a huge cash settlement after the accidental death of his fiancée. He'd helped to pay for everything she needed to start her business and as such she only had consumables and electricity bills to pay every month. They didn't make a ton of money from their little pottery painting café, but they made enough to be comfortable. She'd never dreamed of closing down for two or three weeks and just jetting off to far-off destinations. All that lost income horrified her. And there always seemed to be something else that she had to pay out for: repairs on the kiln, a new fridge, even a new roof the winter before when a storm had ripped off several tiles and then caused a leak. She didn't dare take any of her hard-earned savings and fly off to some exotic location because what if she had to buy a new kiln or a new floor as the current one was looking a bit tired? But with a million pounds she could do all those things, she could buy a new floor, redecorate the whole café, buy a brand new top-of-the-range kiln, build a studio with all the tools and equipment to teach her workshops and still have enough left over to treat herself to a holiday of a lifetime, somewhere wonderful with just her and Dougie.

'I've always wanted to go to New Zealand,' Eden said, softly, picturing the mountains, the waterfalls and lakes, the Bay of Islands she had heard so much about, the glow-worms, the volcanoes, the wildlife, the colourful geothermal pools that she had seen on a documentary just the other night, the hot springs, the glaciers and even a trip to Hobbiton after falling in love with it in *Lord of the Rings*.

'We could do that, we could go. Once the kids go back to school in January, it would be quieter for you, we could go then. It would be warmer in January too as that's summer in New Zealand. We could spend a week or ten days on the North Island and do the same in the South,' Dougie said, excitedly. 'I've always wanted to go there too.'

She found herself smiling at the thought of touring this beautiful country with Dougie at her side. But then the smile fell off her face.

'I don't know why we're even having this conversation. The money isn't mine and when the bank realise their mistake, they'll be taking it back.'

She turned and walked in the direction of the bank and Dougie fell in at her side again. She pushed the door open on the bank and was relieved to see it was empty of customers. She walked up to the counter with Dougie at her side and recognised Cathy, one of her mum's friends. Her whole face lit up at seeing Dougie. Eden smirked as Cathy subtly fiddled with her hair – despite being old enough to be his mum, Dougie still made her giddy.

'Dougie, how lovely to see you again,' Cathy said. 'What can I do for you?'

Dougie deferred to Eden and Cathy seemed to notice her for the first time. 'Oh hello, Eden dear, how's your mum doing?'

'She's fine, definitely enjoying her retirement. Cathy, I had some money put into my account this morning and I think it was a mistake. I wonder if you could check to see where the money came from?'

'I can have a look, dear. Do you want to give me your bank card?'

Eden handed it over and Cathy set about bringing up her details. Her eyes widened. 'Oh, I see what you mean, that's a very nice little sum isn't it, how lovely.'

'Yes but I don't think it's mine,' Eden said, trying to keep the exasperation out of her voice.

'Well it's a counter credit, it was paid in via a banker's draft, which is a special bank cheque. There are no other details than that.' Cathy shrugged helplessly, passing Eden's card back over the counter.

'You must be able to trace where the money came from. Someone, somewhere, is missing a million pounds and when they find out, which I'm guessing will be soon, they will want it back. I'd rather that happens before I book my all-expenses-paid trip to New Zealand.'

Cathy shook her head. 'Of course there could be a mistake, but with that amount of money, I doubt it. A banker's draft would have to be checked thoroughly before the payee is written on it as the amount and payee are printed on the cheque on a printer. And for it to be paid into your account the cashier would have to check the name on the banker's draft matched the name on your account number before processing the credit.'

'Look, this has to be a mistake,' Eden said, urgently. 'Maybe it should have gone to a different Eden Lancaster.'

She knew she was clutching at straws but she couldn't accept that her wish had come true.

'It's possible I suppose, but I imagine there aren't that many Eden Lancasters in the world and whoever paid it into your account must have known your account number.'

'OK, but there must be a way we can trace this money. Then we can get in contact with the person and give it back to them.'

Cathy looked doubtful and then she looked at Dougie for a second as if Eden was mad. 'Well we could trace it, but it's a bit tricky you see as the banker's draft doesn't even have any details of the person who issued the cheque. It's a cheque that comes directly from the bank. We would have to get in contact with the bank and branch where the banker's draft was issued and it's not that easy to find those kind of details. And then we would have to ask them to provide details of who issued the banker's draft and which account the money came from. I can start an enquiry for you.'

Eden nodded. Finally she was going to get some answers. 'Yes, how long will that take?'

'Well with the Christmas holidays coming up, I think you're probably looking at four to six weeks.'

'Six weeks! Are you kidding?'

'It's not a straightforward request, it will take time for someone to look into it for you,' Cathy said.

'OK, fine, start an enquiry.'

Cathy leaned over the counter, conspiratorially. 'My advice dear, just start enjoying the money.'

'And what happens if I have to pay it back?'

'What happens if you don't?'

This was ridiculous. 'Can you please look into this for me and let me know as soon as you've found anything?'

Cathy nodded and Eden walked out back onto the street. She rounded on Dougie as soon as the door closed behind them. 'This is crazy, how can they not know where the money came from?'

'I know where the money came from.'

'Where?'

'Mistletoe Cove.'

'Urgh, you're impossible.' She started walking back towards the shop.

'Don't you think it's a bit too coincidental that just over twenty-four hours after you wished for a million pounds that you end up with a million pounds in your account? As Cathy said, it's very unlikely to be a mistake. There really can't be any other explanation for it.'

'So fairies wrote the banker's draft?' Eden said.

'Well I'm not exactly sure how these things work but yes, I guess so.'

'I didn't know fairies had bank accounts.'

'Of course they do, that gold sparkly fairy dust isn't cheap, you know.'

Despite the situation, Eden couldn't help but smile.

'We have gas, electricity, water bills; the fairies have fairy dust bills, which must be paid for by direct debit. The gold glittery fairy dust is obviously the most expensive. It makes sense to me that the banker's draft was taken from one of the fairies' accounts.'

'You're such an idiot,' Eden said, losing her anger a little over this whole ridiculous situation. She couldn't escape the thought that Dougie had given it to her, despite his refusal to admit it. He was too adamant about her spending it and why would he want her to spend it unless there was no chance of her having to pay it back? No one could believe in the power of wishes that strongly. But if it really wasn't him, then Dougie was right, it was way too coincidental. She didn't want to admit to herself that her wishes were coming true because she couldn't bear the thought that he was only in love with her because of her wish. But if she had got this money because of her wish, or because Dougie had given it to her, then maybe she should do what Bella and Freya had suggested about her first wish and just enjoy it.

'Look, why don't we book a holiday to New Zealand early next year?' Dougie said. 'And before you get all upset about the money not being yours and therefore you can't spend it, I am so confident that this money has come about because of your wishes in Mistletoe Cove that if I'm wrong, and you have to pay it back, I will give you any money we spend in New Zealand so you can pay back the million pounds in full and not be out of pocket. But I firmly believe that this money is a gift, so you should enjoy it, even if you only enjoy a tiny part of it for now. I'll even pay for my own ticket so you'd only be dipping into this million to pay for you.'

Could she really do that? Drop everything and go on holiday for a few weeks, spend a few thousand pounds on going on a trip of a lifetime, to somewhere she'd always wanted to go to?

'Life is for living, for wringing out every last drop of joy, not simply existing. I know you're happy in your job, you're happy here, but there's a whole world out there to enjoy. You work hard in your job; you deserve a break.'

God, she wanted to. Dougie was so brave, giving up his job to start his own gaming company, selling his home in America so he could move back to Hope Island. She wanted some of that bravery too. And with a million pounds in her account maybe it was time to throw caution to the wind and book a holiday. If she'd won the lottery she wouldn't think twice about doing something like that. Why couldn't she enjoy this money? If Dougie was prepared to cover her if she had to pay it back, there was no risk.

'We need to be back by the end of January for Bella's wedding,' Eden said.

Dougie grinned, sensing her wavering. 'I promise, we'll be back in plenty of time for the wedding.'

'And I'll pay for you, if that million pounds really is mine, then I can definitely afford it.'

'If that's a condition of you going, then fine, you can pay.' He inclined his head towards the travel agent's, obviously knowing that if she didn't go in there now, she'd change her mind.

A delicious thrill ran through her at the thought that she was really going to do it. Was this insane?

Dougie held out his hand for her and she found herself nodding. She linked her hand with his and he led her into the travel agent's. He pushed the door open and before it had even closed behind her, Dougie was talking to the shop assistant.

'We'd like to book a holiday to New Zealand please.'

CHAPTER 21

What the hell had she just done? January 2nd they were flying out to New Zealand, spending three weeks exploring the two islands, and she couldn't stop smiling about it. She had never been so ridiculously frivolous and impulsive before and she was loving this feeling.

It was Dougie that made her feel this way. She felt happier and more carefree than she had in a long time and maybe, just maybe, she was starting to believe in magic again. Not the magic of Mistletoe Cove but the magic of having her dreams come true. The magic of being in love, of having that love reciprocated. She had waited so long for Dougie and now she was with him, it felt like anything was possible.

She still wasn't entirely happy about her wishes from Mistletoe Cove coming true, if they were. It meant that Dougie only loved her because she wished for it, that his feelings for her weren't real, and that possibility broke her heart.

She looked up at him as he sipped from the celebratory hot chocolate he'd bought for them both. It had so much whipped cream on the top that it looked like a 99 ice cream. He lowered his cup and she smirked to see he had cream on his nose.

She reached up to wipe it off and he looked down at her with such affection that she couldn't believe that his feelings for her weren't real. As she wiped a tiny drop of cream from the corner of his mouth, he kissed her fingers.

She couldn't deny the way he felt about her. It was evident in the way that he made love to her, spoke to her and looked at her, and she had to believe this was real and not just because she had wished for it.

'What else are you going to spend the money on?' Dougie asked, taking her hand as they walked.

She smiled at him and shook her head. She had already told him in the travel agent's that she wasn't going to buy anything else until she knew for sure the money was hers. If that million pounds didn't belong to her then the trip to New Zealand had taken a very tiny percentage of that, so she didn't feel too bad at the moment. If she had to pay it back, she could afford it. She had been so good at saving her money over the years; it was time to enjoy some of it. Didn't mean she was going to go crazy though. Not yet anyway.

Dougie saw her expression and laughed. 'I know, I know, you're not going to spend any more just yet, which is far too sensible for my liking, but at least you can start to plan what you'll use the money for when the bank confirms the money came from the fairies.'

Eden laughed. 'If the bank contact me to say the money came from Fairies Incorporated, I will eat my own hat.'

'Fairy Gifts Limited more likely, so you're probably safe on the hat-eating side of things.'

'Good to know. And no, no more plans just yet. I'm going to give Clare some money so when I close Pots and Paints for three weeks she can go on a little holiday too. I was going to pay for her to go to Disney World with her family but I think I'll save that for later in the year when I know the money is definitely mine. Other than that, no more plans. I don't want to get my hopes up for all these wonderful things I could do with the money and then not be able to carry them out. Six weeks isn't too long to wait.'

'Well I guess it's down to me to make your dreams come true in the meantime.'

'You already did when you told me you loved me.'

'Ah no, you need to have bigger dreams than just me,' Dougie waved away her words. 'As my mum would always say, aim higher.'

She pulled him to a stop. 'Don't say that. You are all I've ever wanted.' She rested her hand on his heart. 'This was all I've ever wanted and you've given me that. Don't put yourself down because by doing that you're actually belittling my dreams and you wouldn't want to do that, would you?'

He smirked slightly. 'No, I wouldn't.'

'Good.'

'Doesn't mean I'm going to stop trying to make your dreams come true though. What else was on this list of yours?'

God, that list seemed so silly now, when all she'd wanted was Dougie and for him to genuinely love her.

'I just want you, forever.'

'You want to get married?'

She shook her head. 'I know the prospect of marriage scares you so we don't ever have to do that if you don't want to. We can stay exactly as we are.'

'But your dream is to get married.'

'My dream was always you.' He just didn't seem to get that.

He stared at her for a moment. 'Let's work on the rest of that list first before you decide if you want to be with me for the rest of your life. I have a plan for tonight actually, and if this isn't on your list, then it should be.'

She sighed. It was going to take a while to convince Dougie that he was enough for her, but she had a while. She loved him so she would be patient.

'I have some work to do so I'll see you tonight at home,' he said, bending his head and kissing her in a way that suggested they were going to be doing a lot more than kissing again that night.

He pulled back and then placed a kiss on her forehead before he turned and walked back towards her house.

She watched him go. She was having a hard time keeping up with all of Dougie's plans but as she was still reeling with excitement over the last plan he'd put into place she couldn't really mind.

She turned and made her way back to the café to tell Clare that she was giving her three weeks off in January. She was sure that would be a bit of welcome news.

🌲🌲

Dougie let himself back into Eden's house, just as his phone started to ring. He dug it out of his pocket and smiled when he saw that it was his dad, Brian, calling.

He dumped his bags and quickly answered the phone. 'Hey Dad, how's it going?'

'Good son, how's life on Hope Island?'

'It's great to be back.'

'I do miss the place.'

'You should come back and visit some time,' Dougie said as he flicked the Christmas tree lights on and watched them dance over the branches.

'Oh I will, and now that you're there I have even more reason to do so. Things are a bit busy at work at the moment but I'll definitely try to get over for the spring. How are you settling in to your new home?'

'I'm not in there yet, the carpets are being fitted after Christmas and then I can set about getting all of my furniture delivered. I'm staying with Eden for a couple of weeks until I can get that sorted.'

'How's it going with Eden? I know she was a big reason for you moving back to Hope Island. Are you two…?' Brian trailed off.

Dougie smiled. He had never really discussed his feelings for Eden with his dad, never really discussed them with anybody, but Brian knew. His dad had seen how close they were growing up and how much Dougie would talk about her every time he came back from Hope Island. It wouldn't have been hard for him to work out.

'Good, Dad, really good. We're actually seeing each other and, well, I think this is forever for me.'

There was silence for a moment and Dougie waited for some comment about forever being a long time or how marriage was a terrible idea. His dad had been dating a lovely lady called Gaby for the last six months and he was happier than Dougie had seen him in years. But that didn't mean that he had changed his mind about marriage or that he was looking for any kind of long-term relationship. Brian had been bitter and angry about relationships for too many years to count.

'Oh Dougie, I couldn't be happier for you.'

Dougie felt his eyebrows shoot up. 'You are?'

'Of course I am. You love her, don't you?'

'Yes I do. She means the world to me.'

'Love is something special and wonderful. If you love her then never let her go.'

Dougie sat down on the sofa and pushed his hair off his face. 'She wants to get married.'

'Already? What am I saying; that girl's been in love with you for almost her entire life.'

Dougie smiled that his dad knew that.

'I don't think marriage is on the cards just yet, but I know she wants it eventually.'

'And you don't?'

Dougie sighed. 'I want forever with her. But I didn't exactly have the greatest role models when it came to a wonderful marriage. Getting married ruined yours and mum's relationship.'

There was another silence from his dad, then Dougie heard him sit down, probably in his favourite battered old leather recliner judging by the tell-tale squeak. 'Is that what you think?'

'You were happy for years before you got married and afterwards you would argue constantly. I can't see how I would think anything else.'

His dad sighed. 'We were never happy, Dougie. Well, I guess we were at the beginning, in fact the first two or three years we were together it was pretty bloody great. And then, I guess we just became really complacent. We stopped making an effort. We'd go to work, we'd come home, we'd end up eating at different times because our work would mean we'd never get home at the same time and we'd both go to bed too exhausted to even talk let alone do anything else. We didn't argue, because I think one or both of us would have had to care to argue and we just didn't. We existed. I don't think we were unhappy but we definitely weren't happy either. We never got married because there was always something more important to spend our money on – even after you were born, marriage just didn't seem a priority. We worked fine, so why do anything to change that? But when you were thirteen, your mum had an affair.'

Dougie sat up straight. 'With somebody on the island?'

'Somebody from her work on St Mary's.'

'I had no idea,' Dougie said softly.

'We agreed not to tell you. I don't blame your mum at all. I neglected her, I know that. We hadn't made love for years; of course she was going to go somewhere else. It was a bit of a wake-up call for me. I didn't want to lose her. She promised that it wouldn't happen again and for some reason we both fought for our relationship, when there was nothing left to fight for. I thought maybe if I asked her to marry me it would show her that I did love her. So we got married. And it obviously didn't change anything. I tried to change, I made an effort, I plied her with gifts but nothing I did was ever good enough, I guess it was too little too late. I didn't trust her and your mum felt trapped and probably angry at me for all those wasted years. She'd had a taste of what it felt like to be adored and she resented me for never giving her that. All that anger, contempt, frustration and disappointment came out in arguments over the next few years. I think she continued to have her affair and, in an attempt to stop it and to inject some excitement into our lives, I moved us to America where she promptly left me. It wasn't marriage that killed our relationship; we'd managed that on our own years before.'

Dougie stood up and went to the window, staring out at the fairy lights that were strewn across the street. He didn't know what to say. For years, he had believed that marriage was the thing that had ruined his parents' relationship when that hadn't been the case at all.

'Would you ever get married again?' Dougie asked.

His dad gave a little chuckle. 'Well actually that's the reason I'm calling. Me and Gaby have got engaged.'

Dougie felt his mouth pop open. 'Wow, Dad, that's… That's fantastic. This is… I… This is so surprising. You seemed to be so anti-relationships for so long after Mum left. I never thought that you would ever find love, least of all get married again.'

'I love her and I want more than anything to make this work. I learned my lesson with your mum – I know that you have to make an effort and take the time to talk and listen, really listen. I know I need to make her feel special every single day and tell her that I love her. Maybe if I'd done all that with your mum we would have still been together, or maybe it never would have lasted between us. I know we never showed you what a loving relationship really looks like but if you want a good role model for marriage then you need look no further than Eden's parents.

They have been happily married for probably forty years and from what I saw when I lived there they were both completely and utterly in love with each other.'

Dougie smiled. 'They still are now, anyone can see that.'

'Exactly. Dougie, don't be afraid of marriage. If you both love each other then no bit of paper or a fancy white dress will ever take that away from you. If you truly do love Eden with everything you have and you want forever with her then ask her to marry you. I don't mean now, you've only been together for a few days, but maybe, a few months down the line, if you still love her as much as you do now, then ask her. I tell you, nothing will ever beat that feeling of seeing the woman you love crying with happiness because you ask her to marry you. If you can make her that happy, then why wouldn't you do it?'

Dougie didn't say anything for the longest time. He felt such a sense of relief all of a sudden. Why had he been so fearful of marriage? His dad was right, it was silly to be scared of a label or a marriage certificate. He knew what he had with Eden and was confident she felt the same way. And maybe it was a bit too soon to be rushing into that, but he wasn't scared of it any more.

'Thanks Dad.'

'Oh, I'm glad I could help.'

'So when's the wedding?'

'We're probably looking at late next year. I think Gaby wants a Christmas wedding.'

'Well let me know when and I'll come over and give you away.'

His dad laughed. 'Give Eden my love.'

'I will.'

Dougie said his goodbyes and hung up, feeling lighter than he had in years.

CHAPTER 22

Eden let herself into her house later that day and was surprised to see there was no sign of Dougie. The log fire was burning merrily in the grate, the fairy lights were twinkling on the tree and the scent of her 'Sparkling Snow' Yankee Candle drifted around her. Dougie had clearly done everything he could think of to welcome her home, except be there himself.

She called out to him and she heard him curse upstairs, heard several bangs like he was throwing stuff inside her wardrobes, and then a thunder of feet as he came running down the stairs.

He appeared in the lounge wearing only his tight black boxers which was the best welcome home Eden had ever received.

He looked flustered as he leaned against the door frame in what he clearly hoped was a nonchalant way, but he wasn't quite pulling it off.

'Well this is a lovely welcome,' Eden said, leaning up to give him a kiss and slipping her hands into the back of his shorts and giving his bum a friendly squeeze. 'And I'm going to ignore the fact that you're obviously up to something as you're always up to something.'

'I'm not up to anything,' Dougie said and she arched an eyebrow at him. 'OK, OK, I might have had a little accident upstairs and there might just be a very large stain underneath your bedroom rug.'

Eden laughed. 'You really are good at this wooing malarkey, aren't you?'

Dougie wrapped his arms around her and kissed her nose. 'Hey, I have my moments.'

'Are you like this with all the women that you date?'

'No, only with you.'

Eden smiled. 'Well it seems you have me at a disadvantage. Why don't I get out of these clothes and then we can have mad passionate sex? And for your information, welcoming me home with hot sex is probably the best way to greet me after a long day at work.'

'We're not having sex, well not until later, but this is much better. But yes, you definitely need to get your kit off.'

'You're so romantic,' Eden said, pressing a kiss against his chest in the hope that she could put sex back on the menu. 'I don't think I've ever been told to get my kit off before.'

'Less talking, more stripping,' Dougie said, unzipping her coat and flinging it over the back of the sofa. 'In fact, get naked and meet me upstairs in your bedroom.'

He placed a kiss on her forehead and turned and ran back up the stairs humming 'The Stripper' again.

'And we're definitely not having sex?' she called after him.

'Nope.'

She thought for a moment. 'Are we having a nudey party?'

He laughed. 'Something like that.'

She smiled and quickly slipped out of her clothes and followed him upstairs. She walked into her bedroom to see there were a few candles lighting the room but thankfully not as many as last time so no risk of fire again. She smiled at the way her practical brain worked. Instead of focussing on the romance that Dougie had tried to create she was thinking of fire hazards. She noticed her rug wasn't where it normally was by the side of her bed but at a very odd angle in the middle of the room, clearly covering up the stain. Gentle sea sounds were coming from her stereo and there was a wonderful sweet smell in the air. And there was Dougie standing by the bed, his eyes roaming over her appreciatively. God he made her feel so confident.

'So how does this nudey party work?'

'I'm going to give you a massage,' Dougie said.

She couldn't help but smile at that lovely gesture. 'You are?'

He nodded. 'I've looked it up and I know exactly what I'm doing.'

'Oh, a massage courtesy of Google, I feel in very safe hands,' she teased.

He grinned. 'Trust me.'

She walked up to him and kissed him. 'I do.'

'So lie face down on the bed and we can get started.'

'Do I get to massage you later?' Eden said, running her hands up his strong back.

'If you want to.'

'I definitely want to.'

He smiled at her. 'OK.'

She slipped out of his arms, tied her hair up in a loose bun and lay face down on the bed.

'So I have a clementine oil to use which I thought sounded a bit more festive than the normal lavender oil. If you're going to have a massage three days before Christmas it definitely needs to be a festive massage.'

'Do I get to eat mince pies while you massage me?'

He chuckled as he climbed onto the bed with her. 'No, the crumbs would get everywhere.'

'Fair point.'

She heard him pour the oil into his hands. The smell was divine and was definitely what she had smelled when she had walked into the room.

'Is the clementine oil what is underneath my rug?'

'Shhh,' Dougie said and she grinned because she guessed that it was.

He rubbed his warm hands over her shoulders and down her back to spread the oil around and then cheekily spread it over her bum too.

'You're such a pervert,' Eden said.

'Hey, a bum massage is very important if you spend a lot of time sitting down.'

'I spend all day on my feet.'

'That shows that your bum gets ignored. I'm here to put that right.'

'Well, thank goodness for that.'

He pressed his thumbs gently into her spine, as he moved his hands up her back and then spread his hands out to her shoulder blades. It was heaven and she couldn't help emitting a little moan.

He rubbed his hands round her neck, over her shoulders and then down her back, straight over her bum, his fingers trailing wonderfully over the apex of her thighs. She arched her bottom up slightly at his touch and he chuckled softly. Frustratingly he slid his hands down her thighs and to her feet, where he started massaging her toes. The feel of it sent an unexpected punch of desire straight to her stomach and she let out a noise that sounded almost animalistic.

'Is that good?' Dougie asked as he rubbed and stroked her toes.

'Ah, oh god, yes don't stop,' Eden muttered.

He spent an inordinate amount of time on each toe and the balls of her foot before swapping over and doing the other foot. By the time he started working his way up her thighs, she was in complete heaven. He skirted his fingers round her inner thigh but she was so blissfully relaxed that he could have done anything to her and she wouldn't have cared. He moved so he was straddling her bum, though he was clearly careful not to put any weight on her as he ran his hands up and down her back. More of the warm oil was poured onto her back and he gently rubbed it into her skin, stroking and caressing everywhere and occasionally putting slight pressure where he kneaded her muscles. Her mind cleared so she was aware only of his hands against her skin, his gentle touch. It was heavenly.

Eventually, when she was practically comatose, he pressed a kiss to the back of her head and gently climbed off her, lying down on his side next to her.

'How was that?' Dougie whispered.

'I can't move,' Eden murmured.

'I'll take it that it was good then.'

She reached out and placed her hand over his heart. He linked his fingers through hers and she smiled. This was perfection.

♣♣♣

Dougie watched Eden dozing next to him with the biggest smile on her face. He had kind of hoped the massage would lead to sex afterwards and when she had offered to massage him after he had massaged her, he loved the thought of her hands all over his body. He wasn't going to get any of those things now but he couldn't find it in him to care. If there was a utopia then this was it. The woman he loved lying naked in bed next to him with a smile on her face because of the way that he had taken care of her.

He looked down at her fingers entwined with his over his heart. He wanted this forever and he should have felt scared how quickly things were progressing for them but he didn't. He knew part of that was because he already knew her so well; she was his best friend. There were no nerves or second-guessing. This was what love felt like.

'I love you,' he whispered and her smile impossibly grew bigger.

He stroked his hand down her hair and then down her back. She was still a little oily. He thought about getting a wet towel and cleaning her up but he didn't want to disturb her. They could have a shower together shortly when she woke up properly. He liked the idea of that.

Her eyes fluttered open, that pretty denim blue gaze watching him with such affection.

'Hey beautiful,' Dougie said.

She shifted slightly so her cheek was resting on his shoulder. 'That was wonderful, thank you.'

'So I'm not doing too badly in the wooing?'

'You get a gold star in wooing,' Eden said.

'Good to know.'

'You know, having a massage was on my list too.'

'Two gold stars for me then.'

She looked up at him, her eyes narrowed slightly with suspicion. 'You're crossing off lots of things on my list actually.'

'Because I am the perfect boyfriend.'

'I don't need the perfect boyfriend, all I ever wanted was you. You don't have to try to impress me or win my heart. It's already yours.' Dougie stared at her and she sat up. 'I know you don't believe me but you and this is everything that I want and need.' She bit her lip as she thought for a moment. 'I have something I want to show you.'

She swung herself off the bed and padded across the room.

'Is the thing you wanted to show me you walking around stark naked? Because I can completely get on board with that,' Dougie said.

Eden laughed as she walked over to a black-flowered wooden chest and lifted the lid. She fished around inside for a moment, moving aside what looked like several photo albums, diaries, souvenirs and other memorabilia from her life until she found what she was looking for. She pulled out a tattered pink sparkly notebook and a deep blue diary and brought them back over to the bed and sat down next to him. She stroked her hand over the cover of the pink notebook, clearly undecided whether to show him or not.

'I think I was around seven years old when I realised I loved you and that love has changed over the years but it was always there. I was thirteen when I made this so please bear that in mind when you look at it. It's very embarrassing.'

She handed him the pink book and he held it in his hand, somehow feeling the weight of its importance. He opened it, the pages creaking and cracking – evidently they had not been opened for many years – and there on the first page was a photo of him and Eden stuck right in the middle of a big red heart. He smiled. The photo had clearly been taken when they were twelve or thirteen years old and they were both wearing Santa hats and laughing. He had his arm around her shoulders and she was looking at him with complete and utter adoration and love. He ran his fingers gently over the photo.

He turned over the page and there was another faded photo of the two of them when they were no more than four years old, holding hands as they played together in the sea. This page was decorated with pink sparkly heart stickers. On the next page, also covered in hearts, was a picture of Dougie giving Eden a piggyback in a race against Rome and Bella when they were around nine or ten. This page was also graffitied with words like 'Dougie and Eden forever' and 'True love always'.

He carried on flicking through. Every page was covered in hearts and words of love, surrounding photos of them in various stages of growing up, always together and side by side, always best friends. Most of the photos showed her staring at him with complete love in her eyes. He'd never seen how she felt when they were kids. He had always cared for her but his emotions hadn't turned to love until he was much older, or maybe he had never recognised them for what they were. But it was obvious that for her those feelings had always been there. While he looked through the photos, Eden flicked through her diary, obviously trying to find the right page she wanted to show him. He turned to the last page of the notebook and smiled when he saw that it was a photo of a bride and groom, clearly cut out from a magazine, with Dougie and Eden's heads over the top of the real heads.

'Gah,' Eden said, snatching it off him. 'I'd forgotten about that page. I was thirteen, don't judge me.'

'I'd never do that.'

'And if that wasn't embarrassing enough, this is my diary. I never kept a diary religiously or wrote in it every day, but I'd write my thoughts in here from time to time so this book spans a few years. This entry is from my fifteenth birthday.'

She handed it over to him and he smiled to see her writing filled with hearts instead of dots over the Js and Is. He started to read it

Today was my birthday and I had some cool presents but my favourite one was from Dougie. He'd made me a fairy necklace. It was the most beautiful thing I've ever seen. He had carved her out of wood, her wings were made from sea glass and her hair was made from copper wiring. I have never loved anything as much as this necklace. He said it was magical and that if I wished on it my wishes would come true. I must have wished on it a hundred times already. Always the same wish. I wish Dougie loved me too. I love him so much it actually hurts.

Dougie swallowed down the lump of emotion in his throat as he looked back at Eden.

'I still have that necklace,' Eden said, taking back the diary and flicking through to the next page she wanted to show him. 'Though the rope chain broke as I wore it so much and the clasp on top of her head broke too, so she spends her life sitting in my jewellery box.'

She handed him the next page. 'This was from the night we kissed on Mistletoe Cove when I was seventeen.'

> *I just kissed Dougie! Oh my god it was incredible, he is such a good kisser. We went to Mistletoe Cove and we were toasting marshmallows on the fire and then he just leaned over and kissed me. It was the best kiss I've ever had. I always hoped that he loved me and now it's clear that he does. I never knew what it meant to cry with happiness but tonight I did. I wonder if we'll get married soon. Maybe he might want to wait until I'm eighteen. I wonder how many children he wants. I'd like three. Oh god, I really hope they are red-headed babies with his beautiful curly hair.*

'My teenage self was getting a bit carried away after just one kiss, but at that age you never think rationally or sensibly. The point being that I have been in love with you for almost my entire life. I loved you when you were a scrawny, gangly, freckly little boy. I loved you when you were a geeky nerdy teenager obsessed with computer games. I loved you when you moved to New York and bought your own tiny apartment and were living on cheese toasties, or grilled cheese as you started to call it, as you were so completely broke and couldn't afford any food. I don't care about the gifts you give me or the nice things you do to try to woo me, though they're very much appreciated. I don't care how much money you have, all I've ever wanted was you for the rest of my life.'

Dougie had always thought that if he ever came back to Hope Island he would have to pull out all the stops to get her to fall in love with him and though she'd said that she had always been in love with him, it had never really sunk in until now. She really had been in love with him her entire life. He didn't need to prove himself to her any more. He felt like he had been given a wonderful gift.

For want of something to do, because he couldn't find the words to express what she had showed him, he turned the page. Although there was still a good quarter of the book left, it was evident that this was the last diary entry she'd ever written.

> *Dougie is moving to America. I am heartbroken. I literally feel that my heart has been shattered. How can it hurt so much? I trusted him. He's my best friend and I never thought he would ever hurt me but he has in the worst possible way. I don't know if I can ever forgive him. God, I can't stop crying. And the worst thing is I have to smile and be happy for him on the outside because this is what he wants. He wants to move to America more than he wants to be with me. Mum says if he didn't want to move to America with his parents, he could move in here with us but I'm not even going to suggest it to him. I've never seen him so happy. He's happy to be moving away from me. And that hurts more than anything. My dreams of getting married to him were just that, dreams, and they will never come true.*

Fuck. Shit. Fuck.

He had destroyed her. He was the reason she had given up on all her hopes and dreams. He had taken away her belief in magic and her carefree happiness. Dougie felt tears in his eyes.

'Oh god, don't read that one,' Eden said, taking the diary back off him. 'That's just the ramblings of an over-emotional teen.'

'I'm sorry,' Dougie said, the words getting stuck in his throat.

'Don't be, you were eighteen and you were living your dream, don't be sorry for that. And maybe we never would have lasted if you had stayed. We were both so young. Can you imagine if we got married and had children when we were eighteen? We weren't ready for that.' She laughed. 'You're barely ready for that now. We needed this time to realise what we really wanted from our lives, what was important, and the fact that you came back to Hope Island at a time when everything is going so well for you speaks volumes for me. This is where you chose to be now, here with me, and that's all I need.'

'I will never do anything to hurt you ever again,' Dougie said. 'I'm here for the long haul. This is forever for me.' He had never meant it as much as he did right then. He loved her and he was going to spend the rest of his life showing her how much. Even the prospect of marriage didn't scare him any more.

'As long as you don't turn into a pumpkin at midnight on Christmas Eve or suddenly decide you don't love me any more, I'm happy. I don't need anything else from you.'

He shook his head. 'Never going to happen.'

She was his future now and he knew that this was where he belonged.

He leaned over and kissed her.

🌲🌲🌲

Eden smiled against his lips as he kissed her, running his hands down her arms and then grazing his fingers down her back.

He rolled her back so he was on top of her kissing her with an urgency she'd never felt from him before. His hands were everywhere, stroking, caressing, holding her to him all at once as if scared to let her go.

She wrapped her arms and legs around him, holding him against her, cupping one hand round his neck, stroking his curls, trying to soothe him. But there was a desperation to him now, kissing her as if she was the air he needed to breathe.

He pulled back slightly, kissing her neck, her collarbone and then capturing her breast in his mouth.

'Oh god, Dougie,' Eden moaned at the sudden unexpected sensation of his tongue against her nipple.

He didn't say anything as he moved lower, kissing and stroking across her belly before he settled himself between her legs, kissing her most sensitive area. Her orgasm ripped through her so fast and so hard, it was almost a shock after the sleepy, near-comatose state she had been in a few minutes before.

He quickly kicked off his shorts, reaching for a condom from her bedside drawers and then he was in her and on her, kissing her hard as he moved against her. This frenzied need for her was such a turn-on that she quickly felt that delicious feeling coiling in her stomach, travelling lower. She felt her breath catch at the back of her throat and he pulled back ever so slightly to speak.

'I love you,' Dougie whispered against her lips and it was those words that sent her crashing over the edge.

CHAPTER 23

Eden woke early the next morning as the muted greys were just starting to light up the room. Dougie was wrapped around her back, one arm round her stomach, and there was a part of her that wanted to lie there in blissful ignorance for a while.

She hadn't slept well, that million pounds sitting in her account just didn't sit well with her. She knew she needed a walk on the beach to clear her head.

She disentangled herself from Dougie's arms and wrapped herself up in a ton of clothes before stepping out onto the street. It was cold outside and she was surprised to see a sparkling layer of frost on the ground; the Scilly Isles so rarely got frost or snow.

The world outside her little cosy haven was almost deserted, though there were a few people hurrying along the cold streets to get to their shops in preparation for the day ahead. She crunched over the frost and headed towards Buttercup Beach. She went down the steps onto the hard sand. She looked out on the pinky horizon for a moment but was distracted by a movement at the far end of the beach. As she looked that way she realised it was Rome out for an early morning run.

He waved at her as he spotted her too and she waited for him. He enveloped her in a big hug as he approached and she hugged him back, glad of his warmth and his company.

He held her at arm's length for a moment and obviously didn't like what he saw.

'You OK?'

'I'm fine.' She smiled to reassure him but he clearly wasn't convinced. He sat down and pointedly looked at the sand next to him so she sat down too.

'How's married life treating you?' Eden said, keen to avoid the inquisition that was bound to be coming.

'It's absolutely perfect. How's things with you and Dougie?'

She wasn't surprised he had heard, nothing stayed secret on Hope Island.

She let out a tiny sigh. 'Perfect.'

Rome looked at her with narrowed eyes. 'Why does it sound like you're not happy about that?'

'I'm not unhappy. It's just… It is perfect, too perfect, and that's what worries me.'

'I've never pretended to understand women, but perfection is surely a good thing?'

'I'm worried it's not real. He hasn't even been back a week and we've told each other we love each other and we've even talked about marriage. You know what Dougie is like, he's never had a serious relationship and always been so against marriage after his parents' relationship ended so badly, and now suddenly he's the perfect boyfriend… It feels so unbelievable.'

'Bella told me about the wishes at Mistletoe Cove,' Rome said.

'I know, it sounds crazy. Wishes don't come true but everything started happening between me and Dougie straight after I wished for him to love me and then did you hear about the million pounds on the jungle drums?'

Rome nodded. 'Yes, though I wasn't sure whether to believe it. People don't just have a million pounds magically appear in their accounts; I figured the jungle drums had got it wrong this time. Is it true?'

Eden nodded.

'Wow. That's a lot of money.'

'I know,' Eden said sadly.

Rome nodded knowingly at her understated reaction. If anyone understood how awkward it was to suddenly be the recipient of a large unwanted sum of money, it was Rome. He had received a huge amount of cash after his fiancée had died in a terrible rollercoaster accident. He'd had no idea what to do with it as he'd felt it was wrong for him to benefit from her death. He'd ended up giving most of it away to friends, family and charities.

'Hang on. You wished for a million pounds? That doesn't sound like you.'

'Not because I wanted it, just to prove to Dougie that all this nonsense about wishes coming true at Mistletoe Cove was a load of rubbish. I didn't think for one minute that it would come true and somehow it did. How utterly ridiculous is that? Money doesn't just magically appear in someone's bank account and I can't help thinking if that has come true, what if Dougie only loves me because of the wish too? And that's complete madness. But it's not just the wishes. I had this list of things that I thought I wanted in a romantic relationship, silly things like being carried to bed or watching the sunrise together, taking a bath with him or having a massage, and slowly one by one he's crossing all the things off my list too. There's no way that he would know what was on my list. He was fast asleep when I talked about it with Bella and Freya. So how could he possibly know these things unless…'

'Unless it was really magic?' Rome said incredulously. 'You're right, it is complete madness. If Dougie says that he loves you, then he loves you. There is no magic at work here. Why do you think that he could only love you if he was under some spell?'

'It's not that, it's not that I think I'm unlovable or anything, but if Dougie genuinely loves me and the wishes are all just nonsense, then how do you explain the million pounds?'

'That's Dougie, the man is loaded even though he doesn't like to admit it. Who else could hand over that much cash so easily? Well Isaac probably could but I find that even more unlikely. This is Dougie, he's up to something.'

'Exactly, that's what I thought, but he flat out denies it and he couldn't possibly know that I wished for a million pounds, no one knew that. The wishes were in a sealed envelope and I threw them into the blowhole.'

Rome clearly thought about this for a moment.

'And if it is Dougie playing some joke, what part am I playing in all of this? Am I the punchline?' Eden said.

'Dougie wouldn't do that to you.'

'I know he wouldn't, but I can't help wondering if he's doing all this just to be nice. He's up to something. I've never seen Dougie like this before.'

'I admit, he is acting a little bit funny,' Rome said. 'But love does strange things to a man.'

Eden stared out over the inky sea and they sat in silence for a while.

'What is all this really about?' Rome asked, gently. 'You and I both know wishes don't come true, not in magical circumstances anyway. So what are you really worried about?'

She didn't answer at first then she leaned her head against his shoulder. He put his arm around her.

'I'm scared of losing him all over again.'

'You don't trust him?' Rome said.

'He already broke my heart once and it really hurt. It destroyed me and there's been no one serious for me ever since. Even with Stephen, I couldn't fall in love again. Maybe that was because I was still in love with Dougie or maybe it was because I was too scared to fall in love again. I keep telling myself to enjoy this time with him and to not worry about the "what ifs" but if he walks away again after all of this, if this turns out not to be real at all, it would be so much worse than last time and I don't think I could ever get over that again.'

Rome sighed. 'Firstly, you're a Lancaster; you're a strong, independent woman. There is no man in the world that can take that from you. There are no guarantees in love and if it ends in a few months or a few years down the line, it will hurt, but I promise you, you will get over it.'

Eden winced a bit, knowing he was talking about how he'd felt when his fiancée died and how eventually he had found love again with Freya. It seemed silly to talk about not getting over a break-up when Rome had had to get over the death of someone he loved.

'Secondly, if this turns out to be some big joke, I will kick Dougie's ass and he knows that. But you know Dougie, you might not be able to trust him with your heart yet but you know he would never do anything like that to you.'

'That's true.'

'And thirdly, when I said love does crazy things to a man, it's true. I would have done anything for Freya when we first got together, anything to put a smile on her face. I sold the flat above my shop to her for a pound just to make her happy. You would not believe the paperwork involved in doing that, and it was almost a waste of time because she moved in with me a few days later, but I don't regret it for one second as it made her so happy. I took her on safari when the whole issue of snakes and man-eating spiders scares the crap out of me but I did it anyway because I love her. As far as I can tell, Dougie is crazy in love with you so just enjoy the ride. We all make mistakes and he was eighteen when he broke your heart and moved away. Eventually you're going to have to forgive him for that and learn to trust him again otherwise you'll never be able to move on with your life. And if you can't, that's not fair on him either. Your relationship will only work if you can trust each other and with him trying to prove himself to you, which is what it looks like he's doing, it seems like he's scared of losing you as much as you're scared of losing him.'

Eden looked up at him. 'That's pretty good advice.'

'Occasionally I have some pearls of wisdom to share. Let go of your past and enjoy what you have now. Worry about tomorrow, tomorrow.'

'And I shall get that printed on a t-shirt.'

He laughed and kissed her on the head. 'On that note, I'll leave you to your walk before I come out with any more clichés. I'll see you tonight at Rosa's.'

She nodded and he got up and ran off the beach and up the steps towards the park.

Eden looked back out at the horizon and then stood up herself. She dusted herself down and headed back home to the man she loved.

Rome was right and if this relationship was going to work she had to trust Dougie again. She had to trust that this thing between them was real and forget about this nonsense about the magic of Mistletoe Cove.

🌲🌲🌲

Eden looked at her watch and frowned slightly. She and Dougie were supposed to be at Rosa's for seven to meet Bella, Isaac, Rome and Freya for their weekly dinner and it was already five past.

He had been there when she had got home from work, welcoming her with a big hug and a kiss. No sex, sadly, but she was sure he would make up for that later, and then he'd rushed out saying he'd be back soon. That had been an hour ago.

He was up to something, and she chastised herself for thinking that, but as he had left with a big mischievous grin on his face she hardly thought she was wrong.

She knelt down by the Christmas tree and looked at the presents he'd left for her. It was Christmas Eve tomorrow and she couldn't wait to wake up in his arms on Christmas morning, maybe make love before they came downstairs to open their presents. Just the peace and quiet of the two of them before the noise and chaos of Christmas lunch with her wonderful family.

She ran her hand over the biggest present, which had appeared the day before. It was a box but she knew she wouldn't be able to guess what was inside it. The next present was soft and misshapen and she ran her fingers over the bumps trying to feel what it was. Some parts of it were hard and lumpy and there was something a bit crunchy in there too.

She reached for the small square one that had appeared only that day. Just as she picked it up the door flew open and Dougie was standing there, blowing on his hands. He saw what she was doing and he put his hands on his hips.

'Hey, you're not peeking at your presents, are you?'

'No, I was just… rearranging them to make room for all the hundreds of presents I've bought you.'

He laughed. 'Come on, we're going to be late.'

'And whose fault is that?' Eden said, replacing the square box and standing up. She grabbed her bag and coat and pulled her hat on and was just doing up her buttons when she stepped out onto the street and froze.

There standing on the street in front of her, stamping his feet, was a unicorn. Well OK, it wasn't, it was Saint Nicholas, the white shire horse from the Christmas market, only without his sleigh and with a long pink sparkly horn strapped to his head.

Dougie closed the door behind her and stepped up by her side. 'You said that you knew you would never get to ride on the back of a magical unicorn so I thought I would try to fix that for you.'

Her heart swelled with love for him. 'You are so silly.'

The man who had been the driver of the sleigh ride was standing by Saint Nicholas' head, holding the reins. He smiled at Eden.

'Come on then, we don't want to be late,' Dougie said, holding his hands out so he could give Eden a leg-up. She stepped into his hand and braced herself on his shoulder as he pushed her up into the saddle. Once she was settled Dougie climbed up behind her.

'God, we're so high up,' Eden said as she gathered the reins. She had ridden a horse before but not very often.

'Don't worry. I won't let you fall,' Dougie murmured in her ear and she smiled.

The man started leading them down the street towards Rosa's as Dougie wrapped his arms around Eden, holding her against him.

'I'm working on the flying dragon, but that might take a while,' Dougie said and she laughed.

'You're making all my dreams come true.'

'I'm working on it.'

People stopped and stared as they clip-clopped slowly down the darkened street. Some of them laughed and pointed, others took pictures.

'You'd think they'd never seen a unicorn before,' Dougie said as he smiled and waved at the small crowd.

They arrived outside Rosa's restaurant and Saint Nicholas came to a stop. Dougie slid down from the back of the horse and held out his hands to help Eden down too.

She swung her leg over and slid down into his arms, wrapping her arms around his neck and giving him a brief kiss on the lips before he lowered her to the floor.

'Thank you.'

'My pleasure.'

He took her hand and they both called their thanks to Saint Nicholas' owner before they made their way inside.

Bella, Rome and Freya were already waiting for them, though there was no sign of Isaac. They had clearly seen how they had arrived as Bella and Freya were leaning over the back of the booth watching them and Rome was standing up too. They were staring at them with a mixture of shock and happiness.

Dougie sat down and pulled her into the booth next to him. 'Yes, we are seeing each other, yes, I am sleeping with your sister and it's fanbloodytastic and yes we love each other,' he said. 'Any other questions?'

Eden blushed at the quick rundown of their relationship and decided to change the subject in case there were lots of questions.

'Where's Isaac?'

'Oh, he's just finishing up on a telephone conference call, he'll be down shortly,' Bella said.

Eden watched her carefully. Though Bella was smiling, it didn't quite meet her eyes.

'Is everything OK?'

'Yes, fine,' Bella said, her voice high with anxiety.

Everyone looked at her with concern. She wasn't fooling anyone.

'And the wedding plans, are they going OK?' Eden asked gently.

To her surprise, Bella suddenly burst into tears.

Eden's heart dropped. All the plans for a wedding Bella didn't actually want had clearly taken their toll. Eden had seen this coming and she should have done something to stop it before now.

'Hey, what's wrong?' Freya asked as Eden leaned across the table to hold Bella's hand and Rome put an arm around her.

'This bloody wedding, I hate it. The five-star hotel with its giant ballroom and crystal chandeliers, the seven-tier wedding cake, the chocolate fountain, the two-thousand-pound flower arrangements, the photographer, the videographer, the band, the DJ for when the band is having a break, the five-course meal, the finest champagne, I don't want any of this stuff,' Bella cried. 'The way I'm feeling at the moment…' Eden looked up as Isaac walked through the door '…I don't want to get married at all.'

Isaac's face fell as he clearly heard what Bella said, though Bella had no idea that he had just come in behind her. Only Eden had seen him.

Crap.

Isaac stood there frozen in shock for a moment while Eden tried to get Bella's attention to let her know he was there. But before she could, Isaac turned and walked out.

Shit.

Eden quickly scrabbled out of her seat as she heard Freya encourage Bella to tell Isaac how she felt. Dougie looked up at her sudden departure and then glanced over at the door and obviously saw Isaac too as his eyes widened in panic. Eden ran after Isaac, catching up with him just a few metres away from the café.

'Isaac, wait,' Eden said, wishing she hadn't just taken her coat off as he turned to face her; it was freezing outside. 'She didn't mean it.'

'She sounded pretty serious,' Isaac said, his voice choked.

'It's not you, she loves you more than anything. I know you had your rough patches at the very beginning but I promise you this is not that. It's the wedding she's getting upset about, not being married to you.'

He looked at her in confusion and then took his coat off and wrapped it round her. 'Why would she be upset about the wedding? She's the one planning it all. I know I've taken my eye off the ball with this wedding but I've given her everything she wants.'

'She doesn't want the big affair. She's doing all that because she thinks that's what you want. If I know Bella, she'd be happy with a tiny little wedding in the park or on the beach, just you, her, a few witnesses and maybe a nice meal afterwards and a bit of dancing. She doesn't need the glitz or the glamour and for someone who has spent her entire life on Hope Island, that's where she wants to get married, not some fancy hotel in London.'

He frowned. 'Then why the hell didn't she say something?'

'She wanted to make you happy.'

'I'd be happy with whatever she is happy with. I just want to be married to her and I don't care whether we do that in a registry office here on Hope Island or on a beach in Mauritius, I just want her to be my wife.'

'Will you come back in and talk to her? Maybe we can straighten this out,' Eden said.

Isaac hesitated and looked away. Panic ripped through Eden; there was no way she was letting him walk away from this.

'Please, come in and talk to her.' She would ask nicely now but if she had to drag him back inside she would.

'She should have told me how she felt,' Isaac said. 'How can we ever have a proper relationship if she won't be honest with me? We don't stand a chance of making this marriage work if we can't talk to each other.'

'Can I ask you something, do you want this big fancy wedding?'

'No, I wanted to get married here, just a few friends, something small but—'

'And did you tell Bella that?'

Isaac sighed, seeing her point. 'I just wanted to make her happy.'

'That's all she wanted too, it's not the worst crime in the world. This is all so new to you both, it hasn't even been a year since you two met. You will both make mistakes in this relationship and you will learn from them but the important thing is that loving each other means seeing past each other's mistakes and forgiving them. You say she should have talked to you, here's your chance to talk to her. It works both ways.'

Isaac nodded and Eden sighed with relief. He followed her back in just as Bella was coming out to look for them.

Bella threw herself into Isaac's arms as soon as she saw him. 'I'm sorry, I didn't mean I didn't want to get married to you. I really want that, I just…'

Isaac held her tight. 'What *did* you mean? Eden says it's the wedding that's upsetting you; want to tell me what this is all about?'

Bella led him back to the booth and he sat down next to her. Eden took her seat again next to Dougie who squeezed her hand.

Bella took a deep breath. 'I know you want this big wedding in London, but… I don't want that. I know I'm being ungrateful and that you've spent thousands on this big party but…' a sob caught in her throat. 'That's not how I want to celebrate our special day. I've been going along with all of this because I knew it made you happy and I just kept telling myself that it didn't matter how I got married, just as long as we *were* married. But it does matter, this is supposed to be the best day of my life and I don't want to get married that way.'

'Hang on, I don't want the big party either, I was only doing all that for you.'

Bella stared at him incredulously. 'You didn't want it? But Claudia said…'

Isaac's face darkened at the mention of his PA. 'What did Claudia say?'

'It doesn't matter,' Bella said, quietly. 'She was just trying to do the best thing for you.'

'It does matter, what did she say?'

'When we announced our engagement, she came in to see me and said that she knew we had talked about getting married at

Christmas but that the end of January was the best time for you in your diary, as selling off your companies in London was still going to take several weeks. She had already taken the liberty of contacting the Kensington Tower Hotel in London, one of your favourite hotels, who were able to accommodate us. She already had all these menu choices and florists we could use and recommended a band and then she produced this huge guest list of people that I would need to invite and I didn't know any of them.'

Isaac shook his head. 'She had no right to interfere like that. I told her that you might need some help organising the wedding but I didn't expect this. Christ, my wedding is not a big PR stunt. It's about marrying the woman I love. She came to me and said you wanted the Kensington Tower Hotel, which had a capacity of five hundred people, and asked if I was happy for her to take care of the guest list. I thought how ridiculous it would be if it was just us six in a room that big, so I just went along with it assuming if you had chosen a location that big then you obviously wanted a big grand party to fill it. Why did you agree to the Kensington Tower Hotel if you didn't want to get married there?'

'I tried to tell her. When I told her I wanted to get married to you here she said that would make you look silly and it would be expected that you would get married in London. She said that you had attended several clients' and business associates' weddings over the years and they would expect to get an invite to your wedding too. I didn't want you to look silly in front of your colleagues so I just decided I would go along with it all to make you happy.'

Isaac looked gutted. 'She told you it would look silly? How can marrying you in my home look silly? Besides, I don't care what anyone thinks of me. I'd get married in a clown suit with oversized purple shoes if that's what you wanted. This day is about us promising to love each other for the rest of our lives, not what anyone else wants or thinks.'

'And then your mum gave me this long list of relatives that I needed to invite and everything just got so much bigger than I ever wanted but I thought this was what you wanted too,' Bella said.

Isaac groaned. 'I just went along with all this because I thought you wanted some big extravagant wedding. Christ, this is all my fault. I've been so busy trying to tie up my connections with my companies in London so I could give all my time to you here and to working with Dougie on Fairy Gifts after Christmas that I completely took my eye off the ball when it came to our wedding.'

Eden cocked her head at the mention of Fairy Gifts; she had heard that name before –although now was definitely not the time to focus on that.

Isaac took Bella's hand. 'The wedding wasn't turning out how I imagined it would, so I just decided to let you have full rein in whatever you wanted to do. But nothing is more important to me than you and our wedding day. We really need to talk to each other more. Bella, what is it that you want?'

'It doesn't matter, I'm just being silly. We can't cancel the wedding now, hundreds of people are coming, we've already paid out thousands of pounds and I refuse to let you lose all of that. Your mum arrives tomorrow and she has all these big ideas for the wedding too and I don't want to let her down.'

Isaac sighed. 'Our wedding day is about us, me and you, not Claudia, not my work colleagues, not my mum or any of my distant relatives I haven't seen for years. I don't want this wedding and you don't want this wedding so I'll be damned if I'm going to let our special day be dictated to us. We can always continue with the big party in London anyway so we don't have to cancel the whole thing, but we can get married our way first. What do you want for our wedding day?'

Bella stared at him, a slow smile forming on her face. 'What do you want?'

'You saying I do.'

She smiled. 'That part is guaranteed, how did you imagine the day itself?'

'I actually thought we could use our house. We are always at our happiest when we are there, just the two of us and our crazy dogs. It makes sense that we would celebrate our life together under our roof. Invite these guys, your parents, my mum, maybe a few others.'

'I thought that too. When you first proposed on Blueberry Bay, I imagined that we would get married there, on New Year's Eve, just before midnight so we could start the new year as Mr and Mrs Scott. Then we'd go back to our house and dance and drink and eat nibbles. No speeches, no staged photos, nothing fancy. Just me and you under the stars declaring that we would love each other forever.'

He smiled at her. 'I really like the sound of that. I know we only have just over a week until New Year's Eve but do you think we could arrange our wedding for then? I'm off work now until the new year so I can take care of a lot of what we need.'

'Really?' Bella said, her smile widening.

'I want that more than anything,' Isaac said. 'I'll handle Claudia and my mum.'

'Then I can handle the rest.'

Eden smiled at them as the discussion continued about how they were going to pull it off in such a short amount of time. If only they'd talked about it before now, they could have prevented all of this from happening. Communication was such an important part of a relationship and as she looked up at Dougie she knew she needed to talk to him about her fears of losing him and her concerns about the validity of their relationship. Isaac was right: if they were going to work then she had to be honest with him.

CHAPTER 24

The conversation had moved on from Bella and Isaac's wedding as Dougie finished off the last piece of pizza.

He was glad that everything was sorted out for them – he loved seeing Bella with a smile on her face – but if he was honest he was finding it hard to concentrate on any of the conversation that evening.

'Are you OK?' Eden asked softly as the waitress cleared their plates away. 'You've been very quiet all night.'

He nodded. He knew he had hardly said a word because there was only one thing on his mind and he could barely breathe with the nerves and excitement of it all.

'Well, since we are all here,' Rome said. 'And it's a night for sharing and happy news, now you two have decided to actually talk about the wedding you both want, Freya and I have something we'd like to share as well.'

Dougie looked up and focussed on his best friend as Rome pulled a photo out of his wallet and placed it on the table, with his hand over the top.

'We went for our scan yesterday and we thought you'd like to see our little bean.'

Eden and Bella immediately got excited, squealing and cooing before they had even seen the photo. They both pored over it and ooohed and ahhed at the tiny grainy image.

'Wait, is that…?' Eden pointed at the photo.

Freya grinned. 'Yes it is, we're having a little boy.'

The noise was deafening as both Eden and Bella squealed so loudly that everyone in the restaurant looked over at them. Dougie smiled and congratulated Rome and Freya as Eden passed him the photo so he could see for himself.

He stared at it, stunned with how clear the image was. He could see the tiny fingers, the dark patch in the head which was probably the brain, and the little white dot in the middle of the chest that was probably the baby's heart, and sure enough the tell-tale sign that Freya was carrying a little boy. He couldn't take his eyes off the photo. The tiny little lips and nose, the little fat belly. Suddenly this baby felt more real than it had before. They were going to have a son and Dougie couldn't have been happier for them... or more envious.

He suddenly felt that the last twelve years had been such a waste. He had focussed on his career, on building his life in America, when really he belonged here. If he'd come back years ago or never left in the first place, this was the life he would have had with Eden. Getting married and having babies, and yes they could still have that life, but in many ways he was starting from square one all over again, trying to gain her trust, trying to prove to her he was in this for the long haul. Maybe it was time to skip forward a few steps. He wanted forever with Eden and maybe it was time to prove that.

🌲🌲🌲

Eden was lying with her head in Dougie's lap as they watched the end of *It's a Wonderful Life*. The fire was crackling in the fireplace, the fairy lights were chasing each other around the tree and Dougie was gently stroking her hair. This was bliss.

The film came to an end and Dougie switched off the DVD and the news came on instead. She was about to launch into how important it was for Dougie to see his worth, just as George had finally done in the film, but what was on the news caught her attention.

She sat up and listened.

'*Meteorologists are warning of a large snowstorm due to hit Cornwall on Christmas Eve night, with snowfall expecting to reach up to thirty centimetres and reaching as far west as the Scilly Isles. Experts thought at first the snowstorm would pass straight by the south-west of England but that's no longer the case. It will hit the Scilly Isles just before midnight on Christmas Eve and then travel east covering most of Cornwall and Devon over Christmas Day. It looks set to be a White Christmas, folks, and snow unlike anything we have seen in these parts for around seventy years.*'

'Oh my god, that's amazing,' Dougie said, next to her. 'We've never had a white Christmas here, have we? Not a proper one like that? Thirty centimetres, wow that's nearly a foot.'

Eden couldn't breathe. The last of her wishes was coming true. The million pounds she could possibly put down to Dougie but there was no way he could have anything to do with this.

No, this was just a coincidence, nothing more. Three coincidences that just so happened after she had wished for them. It didn't mean anything. She abruptly grabbed the remote control and turned the telly off.

Dougie looked at her in surprise.

'I'm going to bed.'

She quickly got to her feet and Dougie got up too. 'Well I'd better make sure that you get there safely,' he said mischievously.

She went upstairs and got undressed and into bed, not ready to face the possibility that what she and Dougie had was not real. Dougie got undressed too and joined her in bed, immediately pulling her into his arms and kissing her. He rolled so he was half on top of her, and he pulled back slightly, stroking her hair from her face as he looked down at her. She could feel how ready he was to make love to her and she wanted that too, to feel that connection between them and to know how real it was.

'It was wonderful to see Rome and Freya's baby tonight,' Dougie said.

'Yes, I'm so happy for them.'

He kissed her sweetly as he settled himself more between her legs.

'I can't wait to see you carrying my baby,' he said softly.

Her heart leapt and definitely not in a good way. 'What?'

He moved his hips against her in what he clearly thought was a playful way. 'I want to have a child with you. Lots of children in fact.'

Panic hit her hard in the chest and she quickly pushed him off her and scrabbled out of bed.

'What is going on with you?' Her voice was high with sudden anxiety.

He sat up, clearly stunned.

'What's wrong?'

'Where has all this come from? Apart from that one kiss in Mistletoe Cove twelve years ago, you've never shown any sign of having any feelings for me. And now you come back here, tell me you love me, want to be with me forever and that you want to make a baby.'

'I didn't mean tonight, well... unless you want to.'

Her eyes bulged. 'Of course I don't want to.' She tried to ignore the hurt in his eyes. 'This is all so new and everything is happening so fast. You haven't even been back here a week yet and now you're talking about babies. We have no idea if this thing between us is going to last.'

'Well that's what I wanted to talk to you about tonight.' Dougie got out of bed and picked up his jeans, pulling out a small black box from the pocket. Her heart thundered in her chest. 'I was going to ask you tonight at Rosa's but with Bella and Isaac having a meltdown over their wedding and Rome and Freya sharing their baby news, it didn't seem like the right time. But I want you to know that this is forever for me. I love you and I know I've never acted on it before but I do. I want to spend the rest of my life making you as happy as you make me.' He got down on one knee and opened the box towards her. 'Will you marry me?'

She stared at him in shock and horror, her hands going to her face in such a way it probably made her look like 'The Scream' by Edvard Munch. He was kneeling on the floor of her bedroom, stark naked, asking her to marry him. It was the stuff of her wildest dreams and fantasies all rolled into one.

'You don't believe in marriage,' she stammered.

'I do now.'

'This isn't you,' she murmured.

'What?' He stood up.

She looked over at the clock on the wall and saw that it was just past half past eleven. Suddenly she knew what she had to do.

She started throwing her clothes back on, piling on the layers as Dougie stood there with the ring box in shock.

'What are you doing?'

'I need to go back to Mistletoe Cove.'

'Now?'

'Yes, before midnight.'

'You have another wish?'

'I need to put something right.'

Dougie was silent for a moment before he started throwing his clothes on too. 'I'll come with you.'

'No, I'm fine, stay here.'

Dougie ignored her as he carried on getting dressed.

She ran downstairs and had pulled on her coat and hat and grabbed a piece of paper and a pen and stuffed them in her pocket by the time Dougie appeared in the lounge, tugging on his boots.

She grabbed a torch and stepped out onto the street. He picked up his head torch and followed her, closing the door behind him.

'Are you OK?'

'I will be,' Eden said, hurrying down the street and cutting into the park. Dougie fell into step beside her.

None of this made any sense. His feelings for her coming out of the blue, all the things on her list he was systematically making come true for her: massages, cooking a candlelit dinner for her, making love to her in front of the fire just like she had imagined. If he was going for the title of perfect boyfriend he was ticking every box. Although she had laughed and joked with him since they'd been together, just as she had always done, she hadn't been able to escape the feeling that something wasn't right from the very beginning. He was acting differently and, while at first she had thought he was up to something, now she couldn't escape the fear that something else was going on here. And with her other two wishes coming true too, it was suddenly very hard to try to ignore and pass off as merely a coincidence. Something else was going on. She was going to go back to Mistletoe Cove and put this right. She would wish that Dougie didn't love her any more. It broke her heart to ask for that when she had wanted him to love her all her life. But she had to do this. It was crazy to think that Dougie was under some magic spell and that was the only reason he loved her but three big coincidences were a bit too much to ignore. If she did this and he still loved her then at least she would know once and for all that this was real and she could stop doubting everything. And if doing this broke the spell and he didn't love her any more… She swallowed down the pain in her chest… Well, at least she could start getting over him before they walked down the aisle and had lots of babies.

'What's going on?' Dougie said as they climbed over the hill towards Mistletoe Cove.

'I just have to do this. I can't live in fear for the rest of my life.'

'Something's upset you, tell me what it is?' Dougie said.

She found the opening to the cave and slid down into it, landing on the big rock just under the entrance that they had pushed there as kids so they could get in and out easily. Dougie lowered himself into the hole too.

She quickly picked her way through the cave, using her torch to light her way until she came to the entrance. There was no fire on the beach now, no lit fairy lights to make it romantic and welcoming.

She quickly scrambled down onto the beach and then climbed up to the blowhole. Dougie was right behind her.

'Eden, what are you doing?' he called over the roar of the sea.

She ignored him as she got to the top and checked her watch. It was just a few minutes until midnight. She pulled her paper and pen out of her pocket.

I wish Dougie didn't love me any more, she wrote, swallowing down the sob in her throat at having to write that.

She quickly folded the piece of paper so Dougie wouldn't see as he stood there in the moonlight watching her with concern.

She moved to the edge of the blowhole.

'What are you wishing for?'

'It doesn't matter,' Eden said, checking her watch.

As it struck midnight and far off in the town she heard the clock chime, she threw the piece of paper into the hole. To her dismay, Dougie was quicker, snatching the paper from the air and opening it so he could read it. She reached over to grab it back before he saw the words but it was too late. She watched his face fall.

'You don't want me to love you any more? After everything I've done for you, you don't want me?'

She grabbed the paper back and before the last chime of midnight, she threw it into the blowhole.

He stared at her and if she had taken a picture of her face when Dougie had said he was moving to America, it probably would have looked exactly how he was looking right now. He was devastated and her heart broke in two because of it.

Had she got this all wrong? If the wishes were just a load of nonsense then she had hurt Dougie for no reason.

The blowhole suddenly erupted spraying water up into the air and soaking them. She shook water out of her hat, wiping her face and realised that Dougie was already climbing down the rock face.

She quickly climbed after him but by the time she had reached the bottom he was already climbing the steep steps back up to the cave entrance.

'Dougie, wait!'

He didn't.

She climbed up the steps after him; she needed to explain but there was no sign of him in the cave. She scrambled up onto the big rock and hauled herself out into the field but there was no sign of Dougie anywhere, no tell-tale pinprick of light to show he was walking back home.

She called for him, casting her torch around everywhere she could, but he had gone.

CHAPTER 25

Eden lifted her head as the door of Pots and Paints swung open, hoping it was Dougie but it wasn't, it was Rome.

When she had arrived home the night before, there had been no sign of him and he had taken all his clothes and bags and just disappeared. She had waited up all night in case he came back, called his phone countless times and then wandered round the island trying to find him before turning up at the ferry docks at five that morning just in case he was going to get the first ferry off the island. There had been no sign of him and she was not only getting increasingly desperate to see him, but increasingly worried too.

She had finally come into work feeling exhausted from complete lack of sleep, hoping that he might turn up there to talk to her but it was approaching lunch time and there was no sign. It was Christmas Eve and though the pottery café was half empty, she knew a lot of families liked to come to her café the day before Christmas as part of their traditions, where they would all paint something to reflect their year or as gifts to each other. Although she had been tempted not to bother opening up and instead to continue looking for Dougie, she didn't want to let anyone down. Clare was coming in for a few hours at lunch time to help just in case it got a bit busy and then at two o'clock the café was closing and wouldn't reopen until the end of January after she had come back from New Zealand –something that probably wouldn't happen now.

It was Christmas Day tomorrow and her dreams of spending Christmas with the man she loved had disappeared as quickly as the man himself.

Bella, Isaac and Freya were sitting at the table with her as Rome approached and sat down.

'OK, I've asked all round the island and though he hasn't been seen by anyone today, rumour has it he turned up at the Royal Oak Hotel late last night. I went to see him but the receptionist said she wasn't allowed to give out information about guests staying there, especially ones that had left explicit instructions that said they didn't want anyone to know where they were.'

'Typical Dougie,' Isaac said.

'Oh god, I need to talk to him,' Eden said, though she had no idea what she would say.

'You still haven't told us what happened,' Bella said.

'I broke his heart.' She sighed. None of this made any sense. 'My third wish that I made at Mistletoe Cove was that we would have a white Christmas. Did you all hear the news about the impending snowstorm?'

They nodded. It had been all over the island that morning. Everyone was very excited.

'I saw that on the news last night and the next thing Dougie was talking about having a baby and then he proposed and I just freaked out. I went back to Mistletoe Cove and wished that he didn't love me any more and he saw my wish.'

Eden put her hands over her eyes, trying to block out the image of his face when she had broken his heart in two.

'He proposed?' Bella said, quietly.

'I don't understand,' Isaac said. 'You love him, why didn't you say yes when he asked you to marry him?'

Obviously he knew some of her situation from Bella but probably not all of it.

'Because I stupidly convinced myself that his love for me wasn't real. Everything was happening so fast and he was behaving like the perfect boyfriend, he was crossing off everything on my list of what I thought should be part of a romantic relationship, things he couldn't possibly know because he was asleep when I told Bella and Freya. I just kept on thinking it was all too perfect. And marriage. Dougie has never been interested in marriage after his parents split in a really bad way. He even said when he first came home that he had no interest in getting married and then last night he whips out this massive diamond ring and I always hoped he would get there eventually, maybe a few years down the line he might propose to me, but not after six days. It just didn't feel like this was the Dougie I knew and loved. It felt wrong and I got scared,' Eden gabbled.

They all fell quiet until the door was pushed open again. Eden looked up and saw Clare walk in with a big grin on her face. The grin fell off when she saw them all sitting around the table, looking worried.

'What's happened?'

Eden gave her a rundown of the wishes at Mistletoe Cove and bullet-pointed what had happened over the last week, Clare looking more and more anxious as she went on.

When Eden had finally finished, Clare spoke. 'Oh no, I think some of this is my fault.'

That was the last thing Eden expected her to say. 'How is it your fault?'

Just then the phone in the shop rang and Clare rushed to answer it, no doubt so she wouldn't have to explain herself.

After a moment she called out to Eden. 'It's for you, it's the bank.'

Eden got up and went to take the call.

'Hello?'

'Hello Eden, this is Julie, from the bank. We are just packing up for the day, ready to close for Christmas, and I saw you had made an enquiry about the million pounds that was paid into your account. Well I was here when it happened. The funds for the banker's draft came from a company called Fairy Gifts Limited.'

'What?' It couldn't possibly be true. Then a memory jolted her stomach. When she had joked that the money would come from Fairies Incorporated, Dougie had said it was more likely to come from Fairy Gifts. That was also the name Isaac had mentioned when he was talking about the company that he was starting with Dougie.

'Yes. It's owned by Dougie,' Julie went on. 'I was here when he came in and asked for the banker's draft to be made up and then, as soon as he had it, he paid it into your account.'

Eden stared out at the cold grey street outside, not really seeing it. 'Just to clarify, Dougie Harrison gave me a million pounds.'

'Yes, I presumed you would know what it was relating to, that you were getting involved in his company now that the two of you were together. I didn't realise—'

'Thank you, Julie,' Eden said, robotically.

'Well OK, I'm sorry if that wasn't the news you wanted to hear. Merry Christmas.'

'Merry Christmas.'

She hung up and walked back around the counter to her family and friends.

'That was the bank,' Eden gestured over her shoulder, emotion and confusion swirling in her stomach. 'They said it was Dougie who gave me the million pounds.'

'Well I thought that,' Rome said.

'But how did he know that was my wish?' Eden said. 'No one knew.'

'That's what I was going to tell you before the phone call,' Clare said, taking a deep breath. 'Dougie asked me to tell you some story about my gran and wishes coming true at Mistletoe Cove. I asked him why and he told me it was a surprise for you. I didn't think it would be this or that you would wish for him to love you and that would lead to so much stress and doubt on your part. I just thought he was going to do something nice. I'm so sorry.'

She looked distraught about her part in this but Eden couldn't find it in her to be angry with Clare.

'Did he tell Rosa to do the same?'

Clare nodded.

'So this was all just a joke for him all along.' Anger punched her in the gut. 'I need to talk to him. Clare, can you watch the shop for me?'

Clare nodded. 'Go, I'll be fine.'

'If I'm not back at two, will you be OK to close up?'

'Yes of course.'

Eden pulled her coat on and made to walk out but Rome snagged her arm. 'He loves you, you know that. And maybe he went over the top in an attempt to show you, but he does love you, don't screw this up.'

Eden didn't know anything other than that her fear that she had been the punchline in some big joke had come true.

She walked out of the café, needing some answers, and quickly made her way down towards the Royal Oak. She walked up to the reception desk, recognising Milly, the young daughter of the mayor. She was probably only seventeen, which would hopefully make this easier.

Eden smiled sweetly at her, even though inside she wasn't feeling sweet at all.

'Hi Milly, I need to see Dougie, can you tell me which room he's in?'

'I can't give out room information, I'm afraid, and Mr Harrison has said that he doesn't want to be disturbed by anyone,' Milly answered professionally, smiling back just as sweetly.

Anger with Dougie bubbled over inside her and she leaned across the counter. Something in her face made Milly step back.

'I really need to speak to Dougie and I will go and knock on every single bedroom door in your entire hotel if I need to, disturbing all of your guests, but I am not leaving here until—'

'Rose Suite, top floor,' Milly said, looking suddenly like she was fearful for her life.

Eden returned her smile to her face. 'Thank you.'

She marched to the lifts and jabbed the button for the top floor. The corridor was deserted when she arrived, apart from one member of housekeeping who was busy cleaning one of the rooms. Eden didn't recognise her but she knew the hotel took on seasonal staff from the other islands as there were quite a few tourists staying on the island over Christmas. Eden found the door for Rose Suite and hammered her fist against it. There was no answer, and no sound from the other side. She knocked again; still no answer.

The housekeeper looked over at her in confusion. 'Is there a problem, miss?

Eden fixed her with her best smile again. 'Yes, I've left my key inside my room and I think my husband is in the shower.'

The housekeeper smiled. 'No problem, I can let you in.'

She walked up to the door and pressed the key card against the lock. The light flashed green and Eden turned the handle, thanking the lady as she let herself into the room.

She was faced with a big lounge room first, with views over Mistletoe Cove in the distance but no sign of Dougie. His bags were there, but he hadn't unpacked. He didn't look like he planned on staying. TV sounds were coming from the bedroom so she walked in there to see him propped up against the pillows, watching some cheesy Christmas movie, looking like he hadn't slept either. His eyes snapped to hers as soon as she walked in but he didn't move, didn't say a word. There was no affection, no sign of any love at all.

'Security is lax round here,' Dougie eventually said, grabbing the remote control and turning the TV off.

'You gave me the million pounds,' Eden said, not sure why she was leading with that when there was so much more to say, but she had to get to the bottom of it once and for all.

He stared at her for a while, clearly deciding whether to admit it or not. Then he shrugged. 'Yes I did.'

He got up and rummaged in his bag, pulling out a familiar envelope that sparkled with gold glitter in the light from the window. He threw it on the bed in front of her.

'You never threw your wishes into the blowhole, I had two envelopes in my pocket, you threw an envelope with a blank piece of paper in there and I kept your wishes so I could see what you wished for.'

She picked up the envelope and pulled out the piece of paper from inside. Sure enough, her handwriting, her wishes, stared back at her, not showing any signs of water damage at all. Emotion clawed at her throat.

'And what about my list? What my perfect relationship would look like. How did you know about that?' Eden asked.

'I wasn't really asleep when you were talking to Bella and Freya. I was dozing but I heard everything you said.'

Anger flared up inside her. 'So all this, telling me you love me, giving me the money, crossing off everything on my list, it was all just some stupid joke?'

It was his turn to get angry now. 'Is that what you really think? What kind of arsehole do you think I am?'

'I don't know, you took me to bed, made love to me and lied to me. What was it, a pity shag? You knew that I loved you and thought that you would have sex with me to make up for the fact that you didn't return the feelings?'

Dougie stared at her in horror. 'I loved you; I did all this because I loved you.'

Somewhere in the back of her mind, she registered the word 'loved', not 'love'.

'I came back here for you,' Dougie said. 'Yes, getting to see Rome and Bella was a tiny part of it, as was working with Isaac on our new gaming company, but you were the main reason I sold everything I had and moved back here. I wanted to be with you, even if we could only be friends. I loved you so much I didn't want to be away from you any more. I did everything I could to make you happy, but it wasn't enough. You say you love me but you don't really, do you? Maybe you were in love with me twelve years ago, or in love with the idea of being with me, but you're not in love with me now. The massage, the candlelight dinner, making love to you in front of the fire, the ride on the unicorn, I gave you a million pounds for Christ's sake. I did everything you wanted and it still wasn't enough. And instead of just talking to me, telling me that you didn't actually love me any more, you went all the way to Mistletoe Cove to wish that I didn't love you,' Dougie choked out.

'Wait, that wasn't what happened,' Eden said.

'Then please, enlighten me.'

She hesitated, knowing that what she was going to say made her sound crazy, especially now she knew the truth about the wishes.

'I started to believe that these wishes were real and I know how insane that sounds, there is no such thing as magic, but with Clare telling me how her gran's wishes came true and then Rosa as well, and you were so adamant that it was all real... I knew there was no way you could have known about the million pounds and you lied to me and said it wasn't anything to do with you. And deep down, I knew you were lying. I knew you were up to something and it just made me start doubting everything. And then with the news of the snowstorm and all the things on my list you were crossing off, do you know what, it scared me, it scared the crap out of me, because if those wishes were coming true, then it meant that you only loved me because you were under some spell. And the rational part of my brain said it was crazy to think that, I knew magic didn't exist, but I couldn't escape the fear that none of this was real. You came back here and three days after you arrived you were telling me you loved me when you had never showed any sign of having feelings for me before. Not even a week after you told me you didn't want to get married you were proposing and telling me you wanted to make a baby. Everything was too perfect and I kept thinking of that old adage of "If it seems too good to be true then it probably is." It was all happening so fast. We hadn't even gone out on one date and there you were offering me a ring and telling me you wanted forever. And I got scared that you were only doing it because of the wishes. I wanted you to love me because of me, not because of some stupid wish I made. So yes, I decided to try to undo the wish and part of it was just trying to prove to myself that everything you said was real so I could put these fears away once and for all. And it *was* real, you loved me all along?'

He swallowed. 'Yes.'

Relief, frustration and guilt washed over her. She wanted to shake him and kiss him and cry with happiness and anger all at the same time.

'Damn it Dougie, if you loved me, why not just go about it like a normal person instead of all this nonsense with the wishes?'

'I wanted you to believe in magic again. I had no idea what your wishes were going to be when I came up with this idea, but I wanted to make them come true for you. When I told you that I loved you, I hadn't even seen your wishes then, that came from the heart, not because of something you wrote on a piece of paper. I hadn't even planned on telling you then. I just wanted to kiss you and then ask you out. I planned on doing it all properly, taking it slow, but our kiss in Mistletoe Cove was something else, I know you felt that too. And then you quite rightly wanted to know why I had kissed you and then we spent the night in bed together and you wanted to make love straight away and god, I couldn't say no to that. Yes it was happening fast but I had never been so happy before. It felt right. But even if I hadn't done these stupid wishes, I wouldn't have done anything differently in our relationship. I probably wouldn't have given you a million pounds, and I wouldn't have wasted time and money trying to get a snow machine here for your last wish, but I would have still tried to cross off everything on your list. I wanted to make you happy. But I don't regret the wishes. Your hopes and dreams were such a big part of who you were when you were younger and you lost that. I wanted to bring that back for you.'

Tears filled her eyes at this beautiful gesture from him but she still felt unjustifiably angry at him; if it hadn't been for the wishes she wouldn't have started doubting his feelings for her.

'Yes, my hopes and dreams died the day you left for America. I loved you so much and you kissed me and you left. You broke my heart because going to America was more important to you than I was.' She wasn't sure why she was bringing that up now after all this time, but she'd never had an opportunity to tell him how she felt before and suddenly it seemed important to tell him how much he had hurt her all those years ago, that her fear had come from being hurt again. Not just her craziness over believing in the wishes.

'And that's a decision I've regretted every day since then.'

'Yet it still took you twelve years to change your mind.'

'I had no idea I had anything to come back here for. Do I need to remind you that you never told me how you felt either? But that's what the crux of all this fear was, wasn't it? It was that you didn't trust me.'

What Rome had said the day before came back to haunt her, because he'd said the same thing.

'You know what, I didn't. I was working on it but I didn't need gifts of money or flowers or jewellery to make me trust you, I just needed time.'

'If you really loved me, you would trust me,' Dougie said.

'Don't give me that. I love you so much and I was desperate for you to see your worth, to see that I didn't need all those treats and gifts, I just wanted you. But the truth is, you didn't trust me either. Just like your dad was so desperate to keep your mum and he plied her with gifts to make her stay, that's what you were doing with me. You didn't trust that I loved you enough. How would it have worked if we had got married, you'd give me gifts every day to try to make sure I never left you? You didn't trust in my love either.'

Silence fell on them as they stared at each other. They both had a fear of the past repeating itself, of losing each other, but it was this fear that had made them lose each other in the first place. There had to be a way back from this.

'What happens now?' Eden asked.

'Well you've made it clear that you don't want to get married or have children so I'm not entirely sure where that leaves us.'

'Of course I want that with you, just… not a week after we got together. I still love you,' Eden said, the words choking her.

'Even though you think I'm an arsehole who lied to you to get you into bed?'

'I don't think you're an arsehole but yes I still love you, even though you think I'm shallow and materialistic and the only way I could possibly love you is you giving me a million pounds.'

Dougie looked away angrily.

Outside the grey clouds looked dark and threatening but it was nothing compared to the atmosphere in the room.

It was quite clear that he wasn't going to say anything else so she turned and walked away. She opened the door and stormed out, pressing the button for the lift, half hoping he would come after her but he didn't. The lift arrived and she got in. She pressed the button and the lift whisked her down to reception and away from the man she loved.

She felt sick.

Dougie had done all these wonderful things for her and she had thrown them all back in his face. Her fear of getting hurt by the only man she had ever loved had made her hold herself back.

The lift doors opened and she walked out onto the street. The icy cold wind blew around her, shocking her out of her numb state.

There was no way she was going to let it end like this. She loved him, and yes they would have their teething problems and fears to get over, but if they loved each other then they would get through this.

She turned and marched back into the hotel and straight to the lift. She pressed the button but it seemed to be taking ages to get down, seemingly stopping at every floor. Not wanting to wait she took the stairs instead, running up them as fast as she could go. She finally got to the top and rushed down the hall to his room, banging her fist on the door again. Again there was no answer. There was no sign of the housekeeper either.

Eden ran round the corner to see if she could find her and luckily she was at the far end of the next corridor. She ran towards her and the housekeeper looked confused and surprised to see her again.

'I'm so sorry, I've done it again. My husband wasn't in before and now I've left my key and my bag in there,' Eden said.

The housekeeper rolled her eyes but agreed to help her anyway. Eden had to grit her teeth to stop herself from telling the woman to hurry up as they walked back up the corridor together. Finally Eden was let back into Dougie's room and she marched straight through to the bedroom again, but this time it was empty. She quickly moved into the bathroom but that was deserted too. Even his bags were gone.

'Dougie!' she called as she moved back into the lounge, wondering if there were any other rooms to this suite, but the place was completely empty. He had gone.

CHAPTER 26

Eden stamped her feet, and blew into her hands as she watched the last ferry get ready to leave the docks. She hadn't known what to do or where Dougie had gone but she couldn't risk him leaving the island without talking to him first so, after leaving the hotel, Eden had come straight down to the docks to wait in case he had showed up there.

She couldn't believe how spectacularly she had screwed this up. This past week, it had been everything she had ever dreamed of and so much more. Dougie had been so lovely and she had rewarded that kindness with doubt and suspicion. She had let fear of losing it push away the only man she had ever loved. And now she had lost it anyway.

She had no idea if Dougie would forgive her but she knew she wasn't ready to walk away from this. There were no guarantees in life or in love but she couldn't let fear hold her back any more.

She just had to find the man and make him listen to her.

She looked up at the dark early evening sky, with the promise of snow hanging in the air. But as the clouds rolled across, for a brief moment she saw a star shining down on the island. She closed her eyes and made one last desperate wish, that tomorrow, Christmas morning, she would somehow be waking up wrapped in Dougie's arms.

She watched the ferry leave and turned to head back towards town. She took the road that would lead her back to her house, hoping that he would be there waiting for her but somehow knowing he wouldn't be. She needed to get warm before she froze to death and then she'd spend the rest of the night looking for him if need be.

She walked back through the streets where Christmas decorations twinkled and families were gathered around enjoying the festivities and the thought of going back to her empty home made her heart break all over again. She passed her shop, all in darkness, and then turned down the little side street that would take her home. She passed Clare's house, which was all lit up, and she could hear the sounds of laughter coming from inside.

Suddenly the door flew open and Clare came barrelling out.

'Eden Lancaster, you are a pain in the arse. Where have you been?'

Eden stopped, stunned by this attack from her friend.

'Down at the docks, why?'

'Damn it, I didn't think to look there. Why were you there? OK, never mind. We've been looking everywhere for you, we called but you'd left your phone in the shop.'

'What's wrong, what's happened?'

'Dougie's been looking for you, he says if you want to talk, to meet him at Mistletoe Cove, but that was hours ago, I don't know if he's still there.'

Her heart soared.

'Here take this.' Clare handed her a torch.

She leaned forward and gave Clare a big hug and kissed her cheek.

'Get off, save that for your man,' Clare laughed.

Eden turned and ran towards the park and the path that would take her to Mistletoe Cove, the torch lighting her way over the hills. Surely, if he wanted to meet her at Mistletoe Cove, he wanted to sort this out. If he really wanted to call it off, he could do that at her house.

She came to the cave and quickly lowered herself into it. She could already see that the entrance to the other side of the cave was lit up with flickering lights from the beach.

She reached the cave mouth and looked down at the fire roaring on the beach, the fairy lights still hanging from the trees and the man she loved sitting next to the flames, with his head in his hands.

Suddenly he looked at his watch and she watched his shoulders droop. He stood up, picked up what looked like a remote and turned the lights off, then started kicking sand over the fire to put it out. He didn't think she was coming.

'Wait!'

His head snapped round to look at her and she quickly climbed down the steps to get to the beach. He ran straight up to her, placing his hands on her shoulders. He looked so relieved and happy.

'You're here. I didn't think you were coming.'

'I just got the message. I came back into the hotel just after I'd left but you had already checked out, we must have passed each other. Then I got scared you were going to leave so I've been waiting down the docks all afternoon so I could stop you.'

He look pained at this. 'I'm never leaving you again, you have my word on that. I know it might take you a while to trust me and I understand that—'

'I trust you. I do. God, you gave up your whole life in America to be with me, I don't need a bigger sign than that to prove you're in this for the long haul. I love you and I'm so sorry I doubted you.'

'Don't be. With hindsight the wish list was a terrible idea.'

'No it wasn't, it was the sweetest, loveliest idea and incredibly romantic. I just wanted this so badly, I've always wanted it, that I couldn't let myself believe that it was finally happening.'

'I know everything was moving too quick. I saw Freya and Rome get engaged a week after they got together and get married a month later and they're so ridiculously happy and now with their son on the way too, I just wanted what they have. But it's different for us.'

'It is, we've been best friends all our lives and now everything has changed. We've seen each other naked and there's no going back after that.'

He laughed.

She reached up to stroke his face. 'We both have baggage but if you're willing, we can help each other unpack.'

He swallowed. 'I'd like that very much.'

She leaned up to kiss him and he cupped her face in his hands and kissed her briefly before enveloping her in his arms.

She wrapped her arms around him and hugged him tightly against her before she leaned back to look at him.

'You made my dreams come true the night you said you love me, but I never want to stand in the way of your dreams. If moving back to Hope Island doesn't work out for you, personally or professionally, and you wanted to move back to America, I would come with you.'

He stared at her in shock for a moment. 'But you love it here.'

'I love you more and, as a wise man once said, there's a whole world out there to explore. I want to explore it with you.'

He smiled and bent his head and kissed her again before stepping back.

'I actually brought you here to ask you an important question. Eden Lancaster, I love you and I want this to work more than anything. So I will take this as slow as you need or want it to be. So let's start at square one.' He took her hand and dropped to one knee. 'Will you go out with me?'

She laughed and nodded and he pulled a wrapped small box from his coat pocket and she recognised it as the square box she had seen the day before under the tree.

'I had to unwrap this and add to it, since I put it under the tree, and then I wrapped it back up again, but I want you to have this tonight.'

She took the box from him and unwrapped it. She stuffed the paper in her pocket and opened the black box. Inside was the fairy he had given her on her fifteenth birthday, except it was reattached to a gold chain. It had been so long since she had looked at it, it was like looking at it for the first time all over again.

'I fixed it and… I added a little extra.'

She realised that around the neck of the fairy, like a tiny necklace, was her diamond engagement ring, glittering in the light of the fire.

Her eyes snapped back to Dougie's.

'The offer of marriage is a long-standing one, it's not going away just because you haven't yet said yes. So you can wear this fairy around your neck as a sort of promise to each other that we're halfway there and when you feel ready, if that's next week or ten years from now, you can put the ring on. I'll do the big proposal if you want to as well – I don't think me standing there stark naked in your bedroom while you looked petrified is something we want to tell our kids. So, when I see the ring on your finger, I'll know you're ready to be asked properly. I'll bring you back here and do this again or hire a hot air balloon and fly over our home so you won't miss out on your fairy-tale proposal.'

She smiled and slipped the chain around her neck, fingering the fairy and the ring. 'I really like that idea. And I promise, you won't have too long to wait.'

He stood up and kissed her again. He was hers now, and she was never going to let him go. God, the sensation of his lips against hers was like a drug she never wanted to escape from. The taste of his tongue, the feel of his warm fingers round her neck, cupping the back of her head, stroking across her face, the feel of his strong body. This was where she belonged.

He lifted her, gathering her against him, and carried her over to the fire, laying her down with him on top of her. The kiss continued, getting more urgent and needful, and his hands shifted to unzip her coat. She stopped him and laughed.

'I love you, but you're still not undressing me here.'

'Damn it!' he said and she knew that he'd only done it to make her laugh. Movement in the sky above Dougie caught her eye and she glanced up and gasped.

'Dougie, look.'

He rolled onto one side to look up and then smiled and rolled onto his back, taking her hand as they watched the fat white fluffy snowflakes dance and swirl in the air above them.

'God, it's so beautiful,' Eden said, watching thousands of snowflakes fill the sky.

'It is.'

'And you definitely didn't have anything to do with this?'

He laughed. 'No, this one is definitely down to the fairies.'

'Well maybe there is magic in the world after all.' She rolled over so she could rest her head on Dougie's chest but still watch the snowflakes dance. He wrapped an arm round her shoulders and kissed her head.

'Merry Christmas, Dougie.'

'Best Christmas ever.'

She smiled and, as she looked at the dark sky, she was sure just for a second that snow wasn't the only thing filling the air, there seemed to be a sprinkle of gold glittery fairy dust too.

EPILOGUE

Eden walked along the pathway that led through the trees to the secluded Blueberry Bay. Candles in storm lanterns lit the way and up ahead she could see more lights from the beach. It was a perfect New Year's Eve night. Not a cloud was in the sky and thousands of stars twinkled down on the wedding proceedings.

By her side, holding her hand, was the man she loved with everything she had. She looked up at Dougie, looking so sexy in his suit and tie. It was impossible to love this man any more than she did.

The last week had been the happiest of her life. Now she knew the truth about the wishes every fear had faded away. She knew Dougie loved her completely and was never going to leave her. No one would ever go to that much trouble to make her happy and make her dreams come true without being in love.

And because he clearly trusted in their love now, he seemed so much more relaxed too. He had still spent the week adorning her with love and attention, crossing off everything else that was on her list and surprising her with several utterly romantic things he said were on his own list, but he'd said it wasn't to try to keep her, it was simply because he wanted to make her happy and she believed him. She hadn't stopped smiling all week, so much so her face was almost aching because of it.

She had insisted on giving the million pounds back but Dougie had been adamant that she keep it and use it to make her dreams come true. They had reached a compromise that they would put it in a joint account and make both their dreams come true. Although Eden didn't plan on spending any more of it anytime soon, the trip to New Zealand was going to cost enough and she was going to pay some of that back into their joint account from her own savings. But despite her conviction not to spend any more of the million, Dougie had already used some of it to start the ball rolling on building her studio out the back of her pottery painting café, getting plans drawn up and permission from the council. He'd also put an order in for twelve pottery wheels and helped find a course to teach her properly how to use one after her private lesson with him had ended up with them both covered in clay, naked and sweaty – which was fine with her but not exactly the sort of lesson she could actually learn anything from. And while she was excited about her dreams becoming a reality, she was determined that they would soon be spending some of the money on making his dreams come true too.

They came to the section of the path where a little sandy clearing was lit up with lights and she knew that was where she had to wait for Bella. She stopped and pulled Dougie into it with her. Up ahead, she could see the moon covering the inky blue waters with its silvery blanket, more lanterns flickering with golden candles interspersed with flowers to make the aisle. She could see her mum and Isaac's mum sitting on the white chairs chatting away like they were best friends. Rome and Freya were busily putting the last-minute touches to their stained glass garlands that were draped across the backs of the chairs and over the archway at the far end of the beach where Isaac was patiently waiting with the registrar. It all looked beautiful in its simplicity. There were no other guests. A few others were joining them back at the house for the after party, but Bella and Isaac just wanted close friends and family there for the wedding.

She knew she had a few minutes as Bella was still putting the finishing touches to a gift she wanted to give Isaac after the wedding. It was time to give Dougie her gift.

She shivered a little as she looked back up at Dougie, an overwhelming love for him surging through her.

'Are you cold?' Dougie asked, rubbing her arms.

'Not really, these cloaks are surprisingly warm.' Eden stroked the white fur of the cloak that Bella had given her to go with the pearl bridesmaid dresses she and Freya were wearing. 'My hands are cold though.'

She was unable to stop herself from biting her lip, her heart thundering against her chest as he took the small posy of flowers from her and placed them down and then took her hands in his and blew gently on them.

'You look so beautiful tonight,' Dougie murmured, placing little kisses on her fingers, not taking his eyes off hers for a second. She loved it when he stared at her like this – as if she was the single most important person in the world for him. But right now, she needed him to look somewhere else.

But as his lips trailed over the fingers of her left hand he stopped and looked down at the engagement ring she was wearing on her wedding finger. He stared at it and then his eyes snapped back to hers.

'Douglas Harrison, I love you so much and I was crazy to ever doubt the love you have for me. You are my best friend, my home, my heart, you are all my dreams come true.' She dropped to one knee and his eyes widened in shock and surprise. 'Will you marry me?'

He dropped to his knees in front of her. 'Wait, this is my job. I'm supposed to ask you. I had something beautifully romantic lined up.'

'You have showed me enough romance in the last few weeks to last a lifetime. You've given me everything, let me give you this.'

He smiled and kissed her hard, pulling her against him, and she kissed him back, giggling against his lips as she wrapped her arms around his neck.

'Is that a yes?' she said, in between his kisses.

'Hell yes, it's a yes.'

She smiled against his mouth as he continued to kiss her.

Someone clearing their throat broke them from their kiss and she looked up to see Bella on the arm of Finn, and Freya who had returned from the beach to walk Bella up the aisle.

'I take it he said yes?' Bella said, smiling hugely. Eden had told Bella her plans to propose to Dougie, thinking that she might do it on their trip to New Zealand, but Bella had insisted she do it that night, saying it would be the greatest wedding gift of all to know both of her siblings were happy before she walked down the aisle.

Eden nodded, wiping away her tears. 'Yes he did.'

Dougie stood up and helped Eden to her feet too, and Freya, Finn and Bella all gave them both big hugs, clearly as excited as Eden was.

Eventually the excitement died down and Dougie kissed her on the cheek. 'I better go and do my best man duties, but I'll see you in a minute.'

Eden smiled and watched him go then turned back to Bella and Freya who both squealed excitedly for her again.

'Thank you for letting me do this tonight,' Eden said, squeezing Bella's hand.

'Don't be silly, I'm so happy for the two of you.'

Finn nodded his approval. 'Of course in my day it's normally the man who does the asking but things have changed quite a bit since then and as long as you're happy then we're happy.'

Freya and Eden took their positions behind Bella as music drifted out towards them from the beach.

Finn turned round to talk to her again. 'Have you given any thought to when you'll get married yet?'

'Not yet, Dad, but I certainly wouldn't pack away your best suit just yet.'

Finn smiled and turned back to face the beach before turning back. 'And children?'

Bella and Freya giggled and Eden smiled. 'Soon, I promise.'

Satisfied with this, Finn started leading Bella down towards the beach and as she stepped out onto the sand, Isaac turned and the look he gave Bella was the one of the happiest man in the world, which was surpassed only slightly by the huge happy expression on Dougie's face as Eden walked up the aisle towards him.

As Finn handed Bella over to Isaac and Isaac kissed her on the cheek, Eden glanced over at Dougie and knew that every wish she had ever made had finally come true.

A LETTER FROM HOLLY

Thank you so much for reading *Christmas at Mistletoe Cove*, I had so much fun creating this story and I hope you enjoyed reading it as much as I enjoyed writing it.

One of the best parts of writing comes from seeing the reaction from readers. Did it make you smile or laugh, did it make you cry, hopefully happy tears? Did you fall in love with Eden and Dougie as much as I did? Did you like the beautiful Hope Island at Christmas time? If you enjoyed the story, I would absolutely love it if you could leave a short review. Getting feedback from readers is amazing and it also helps to persuade other readers to pick up one of my books for the first time.

www.bookouture.com/holly-martin

To keep up to date with the latest news on my new releases, just click on the link below to sign up for a newsletter. I promise to only contact you when I have a new book out and I'll never share your email with anyone else.

If you haven't read the first two books in the Hope Island series yet, then you can find them here, I'm sure you'll love Bella and Freya's stories too.

Thank you for reading and I hope you all have a wonderful, cosy Christmas.

Love Holly x

ACKNOWLEDGEMENTS

To my family, my mom, my biggest fan, who reads every word I have written a hundred times over and loves it every single time, my dad, my brother Lee and my sister-in-law Julie, for your support, love, encouragement and endless excitement for my stories.

For my twinnie, the gorgeous Aven Ellis for just being my wonderful friend, for your endless support, for cheering me on, for reading my stories and telling me what works and what doesn't and for keeping me entertained with wonderful stories and pictures of hot men. I love you dearly.

To my friends Gareth, Mandie, Angie, Jac, Verity and Jodie who listen to me talk about my books endlessly and get excited about it every single time.

For Sharon Sant for just being there always and your wonderful friendship.

To my wonderful agent Madeleine Milburn and Hayley Steed for just been amazing and fighting my corner and for your unending patience with my constant questions.

To my lovely editor Natasha Harding for being so supportive and being a pleasure to work with. My structural editor Celine Kelly for helping to make this book so much better, my copy editor Rhian for doing such a good job at spotting any issues or typos and Loma for giving it a final read through. Thank you to Kim Nash for the tireless promoting, tweeting and general cheerleading. Thank you to all the other wonderful people at

Bookouture; Oliver Rhodes, the editing team and the wonderful designers who created this absolutely gorgeous cover.

To the CASG, the best writing group in the world, you wonderful talented supportive bunch of authors, I feel very blessed to know you all, you guys are the very best.

To the wonderful Bookouture authors for all your encouragement and support.

To all the wonderful bloggers for your tweets, retweets, facebook posts, tireless promotions, support, encouragement and endless enthusiasm. You guys are amazing and I couldn't do this journey without you.

To Tracey Gatland who patiently answered all my questions about life in the Scilly Isles.

To the lovely Clare Crissell who won a character named after her in the CLIC Sargent charity auction after paying a huge and generous sum. I hope you like your namesake.

To anyone who has read my book and taken the time to tell me you've enjoyed it or wrote a review, thank you so much.

Thank you, I love you all.

CPSIA information can be obtained
at www.ICGtesting.com
Printed in the USA
BVHW071737100119
537524BV00021B/1619/P